Cover the Mirrors

FAYE L. BOOTH

Cover the Mirrors

MACMILLAN NEW WRITING

First published 2007 by Macmillan New Writing
an imprint of Pan Macmillan Ltd
Pan Macmillan, 20 New Wharf Road, London N1 9RR
Basingstoke and Oxford
Associated companies throughout the world
www.panmacmillan.com

ISBN 978-0-230-52966-3

1 3 5 7 9 8 6 4 2

A CIP catalogue record for this book is available from
the British Library.

Typeset by Intype Libra Ltd
Printed and bound in Great Britain by
MPG Books Ltd, Bodmin, Cornwall

To Debbie,
who has endured more of my
first-novel musings, test-runs and angst
than anyone should ever have to.

Thy soul shall find itself alone
'Mid dark thoughts of the grey tomb-stone;
Not one, of all the crowd, shall pry
Into thine hour of secrecy.

– Edgar Allan Poe, 'Spirits Of The Dead' (1829)

Ghost: the outward and visible sign of an inward fear.

– Ambrose Bierce, *The Devil's Dictionary* (1906)

Cover the Mirrors

Chris, — little bro

Thanks for coming.

If my hair looks crap, fear not, I don't blame you. (Much.)

[illegible]

Prologue

Molly was fifteen when she began working with the dead. Well, that's what she always told people. It was worth it for the looks on their faces alone: their eyes would run over her good gowns and soft skin and she knew they were trying to imagine this young lady growing up amid corpses. But that wasn't quite how it worked.

Her Aunt Florrie taught her everything she knew, and it was these skills that brought the moneyed classes of Preston to their house in the evenings. As they stepped into the séance room and the door was closed behind them, a velvety darkness descended: only the faint light of two tiny candles prevented them from knocking into the vast table and bruising their mortal bodies.

The spirit medium – the best in the North, some said – seemed almost to glide to her place at the table. In the warm candlelight, Molly's red curls shone like fired copper and the little flames danced in her green eyes. Her skin seemed to glow, as if phosphorescent spirits flocked to her from the moment she set foot in the room.

Once Molly had blown out the candles and the sitters had joined hands, the dead would begin to make their presence known. Bells would ring; fruit and flowers would fall from the heavens, as fresh as if they had been bought that morning; furniture and ornaments would move as if they had lives of their own. Sometimes sitters would even feel the gentle caresses of spirit hands against their faces, reaching through the veil that divides the living and the dead.

Molly was someone very special; her clients had no doubt of that. A fresh-faced young woman, barely more than a girl, who had grown up steeped in death, yet radiated verve and spirit and life. Communing with the dead seemed to energize Molly and brighten the sparkle in her eyes.

After a séance, the sitters would gather on the landing, bubbling over with delicious dread at the thought of the ghosts they had just communed with: proof, no less, of life beyond death. The ladies (who knew Molly's business as they knew that of everyone else in Preston) would marvel over such a talent in one so young, and say that it must have been wonderful for her to grow up with her aunt's gift, to have been blessed with the ability to feel the presence of her departed mother. Molly would look at them – the sentimental tilt of their heads, the softened, sympathetic eyes – and know precisely what they wanted to hear. Florrie had taught her niece well and Molly knew that the most important thing about their profession was how to give paying customers what they wanted. Nodding her head slowly, and smiling her gentle, wise smile, Molly would tell them: 'Yes. It was as if we had never lost her.'

Part One

1 Spring 1856

Molly Pinner stood, a little precariously, on a padded footstool in the parlour of her aunt's new house in Ribblesdale Place, while the dressmaker and her assistant bustled about her, wrapping tape measures around her body. Their fingers dug into her skin through the thin, creamy cotton of the new chemise and petticoat that Florrie had arranged to be delivered the previous week. The two women coiled their tapes round the fifteen-year-old's body again and again, until she was on the verge of wresting herself free. But Molly wanted her new clothes too badly for that, and so she busied herself with studying the lace of her chemise, an intricate weave of China roses, full-blooming and in bud, flowing down her shoulder and across the top of her newly swelled breast. Digging her fingernails into her palms, she willed herself to absorb the pattern of the lace.

'You're done, Molly. You can get down now.'

Gretchen Houldsworth was an old friend of Aunt Florrie's, and Molly supposed that she probably didn't usually address her clients by their Christian names. Still, to revert to formality now would make everyone feel peculiar.

The dressmaker turned Molly around with a light touch

on her hips, and as she faced her, Molly could see the recognition in her eyes; recognition she had become accustomed to seeing in the faces of Florrie's oldest friends. Gretchen would have known Lizzie Pinner, and Molly had been told often enough that the resemblance between her dead mother and herself was quite uncanny. True, Florrie always said that Molly was a little fuller in her cheekbones, and her strong nose was nothing like Lizzie's tiny, upturned one. But the coppery-red hair, the eyes which could look the picture of divine innocence one minute and as confrontational as a moggy cat's the next, the pale complexion (even if Molly's was peppered with a few freckles) . . . Molly knew she'd never be mistaken for anyone else's daughter by those who had known Lizzie.

Nobody had ever told Molly anything about her father: what he had looked like, what he had done for a living, where he had gone. Until she was almost eight, it had scarcely even occurred to her that she must have had a father. Florrie was the only family she had ever known, and that suited Molly perfectly well.

She watched as Gretchen's daughter and apprentice, Caroline, fished a package wrapped in tissue paper from her mother's bag. Molly knew what this was going to be. A few weeks ago Gretchen had measured her for her first corset. By her own admission, Gretchen had neither the experience nor the equipment for corsetry, but she was more than capable of measuring her clients and passing the order on to a corsetière she knew in Southport.

Gretchen and Caroline worked with quick fingers, hooking the corset together up the front of Molly's body. As Gretchen's discreet, experienced hands quickly tucked

Molly's small breasts behind the stiff boning before fastening the last few hooks, she shot the smallest look at her young client. Molly, trying not to look startled at this unexpected handling, dipped her the tiniest of nods: she now knew how to do this for herself, and at what stage in the fitting.

Molly ordered her face not to flush, and set her jaw as Gretchen and Caroline began to lace her. She felt the pressure wrap around her back and across her ribs, pushing against her stomach and up across her chest, until it was done and she was free of the tugging around her body.

She looked across into the mirror and smiled. Clad only in flimsy white underclothes, with the corset shaping her body into a ripple of curves, Molly was grateful once again for the Queen's need to be entertained. Since Her Majesty's penchant for spiritualism had become common knowledge, everyone with money to spare – and an interest in the latest fashions – seemed to have acquired an insatiable appetite for tilting tables, spirit boards and 'materialization cabinets'. As people from all around the North flocked to Aunt Florrie's door, she and Molly had been able to move out of the rickety little terrace in Ashgate Lane and into the new house in Ribblesdale Place, just around the corner from Winckley Square, the wealthiest part of Preston. Here, Molly and her aunt had a drawing room and a dining room as well as three rooms for servants in the attic. Best of all, they now had a separate séance room; no more cramming sitters into the parlour. It was a long way from their life in Ashgate Lane.

And, of course, there were the clothes. Florrie had decided that as Molly was fast approaching womanhood (indeed, she had been bleeding for almost a year now) she should have clothes befitting her age. After all, they could afford them now. Naturally, Florrie couldn't resist a whole new wardrobe for herself, either.

'Well, we don't want the clients thinking that the spirits save all their favours for them, now do we?' Florrie had said with a wink. 'That'd just make me a skivvy to them in the hereafter, wouldn't it?'

Florrie always spoke like that of the spirit world – at least, behind closed doors she did. When one of Florrie's regular customers had come bustling up to them as they were browsing the shops one Saturday, Molly had done her best not to laugh at her aunt's transformation into a queen of mystery, all slow nods of the head and unfinished sentences. To tell the truth, Molly wasn't entirely sure why Florrie needed to put such an act on in the first place. Surely her talents were enough to keep the clients coming.

And the people who attended Florrie's séances were *clients* these days, of course; never *punters*, as they once were. This money lark was taking some getting used to; not that Molly was complaining. Now Caroline was lifting a china-blue gown with tiny pearl buttons down the back from a box lined with tissue paper.

'Just sober enough for the day, but pretty enough to see and be seen in, wouldn't you say, Molly?' Gretchen smiled.

A tap at the parlour door made everyone start and turn around. Katy, the maid-of-all-work (another new acquisition, and a somewhat nervous and mouse-like one), took half a step into the room.

'Miss Tranter asked if you would join her in the drawing room after your fitting, Miss Molly.'

Molly dipped her head in a little nod and Katy backed silently from the room. Molly wasn't sure if it was that Katy was irritating, or just that she wasn't used to having a servant about the place, but she always had to resist the urge to take the girl and shake her.

Molly's new house dress rustled as she made her way up the stairs to the drawing room. Gretchen and Caroline had had to dash off to another fitting, but promised to bring Florrie's new shawl next time they came. Molly concentrated on feeling for each step with her toes through the thin soles of her house slippers, and tried to avoid tripping on her new layers of petticoats. As she pushed the drawing-room door open, she saw her aunt peering through the window on the other side of the room. Molly smiled.

'Now, now, Florrie – think of your complexion!' Nobody had been too concerned about the pallor of Florrie's and Molly's complexions back in Ashgate Lane, but it seemed that delicately subdued skin tone was another luxury they could now afford. For her part, Molly was rather relieved. She didn't find the idea of a sun-burnished skin to go with her red hair appealing, particularly if it meant more freckles. Of course, these days they could afford to buy lemons just for Molly's skin.

Aunt Florrie laughed. Her laugh was still the laugh Molly had grown up with: not the repressed little titters of the wealthier ladies who attended the séances these days, but a hearty cackle, and hearing it always gave Molly a feeling of security that felt like having warm bathwater poured down her back. Florrie never changed – at least not outside the séance room. She could deliver any pretence for her paying customers, but it stopped when she recited the closing prayer and escorted the clients to the door (or, nowadays, had Katy do it).

'I think I'm as weatherworn as I'm going to get, don't you?' Florrie grinned. In truth, she looked a great deal less aged than most of the women with whom she had spent her youth; that was what came of an indoor trade. Grey was beginning to speckle her light-brown hair and lines had recently begun to trace their way around her eyes, but Florrie could not truly be called weatherworn. Molly laughed.

'Come and look at the new calling cards.' Florrie had business cards already, but she had not needed calling cards until now. Indeed, before, she had worked nearly every day and had had no time in which to make calls, or to receive them. But now that she conducted séances only three days a week, instead of six, Florrie had decided that she wanted time to call on friends, even if most of her girlhood friends were still working practically every day.

'Not that I plan on getting too cosy with the moneyed lot,' she said with a smirk. 'Wouldn't do much for my air of mystery, would it?'

Molly laughed and stepped closer to look at her aunt's new cards. Florrie snapped the little silver box open and held it out to her niece, who picked out the top card to read it.

'"Miss Florence Tranter. Ribblesdale Place, Preston. *At home to visitors every week on Wednesdays*"?'

Florrie arched an eyebrow, but smiled, before returning her attention to the cards in Molly's hands.

'Yes, I have an official "at home" day now – who'd have

thought?' Molly replaced the card in its case and took a seat on one of the freshly dusted drawing-room chairs. She was hardly likely to complain about their newly acquired wealth, but so much still felt peculiar. Underneath her coiled hair, the back of her neck prickled a little, and she swallowed hard.

'Aunt Florrie?'

'Hmm?' Florrie was polishing a fingerprint off the silver card case with her handkerchief.

'What about Jenny? All this . . . it's strange enough for *us*.' Molly's best friend for as long as either of them could remember, Jenny had been raised by her father, Peter King, the local ironmonger and a foul-tempered soul with a weakness for the drink. Molly and Jenny had grown up just a couple of doors apart in Ashgate Lane. They had gone to the local charity school together, but since leaving their lives had been very different. Jenny had taken a job in one of the local mills – Hamilton Cotton – pounding yards of new cotton cloth in tubs of bleach, six days a week. Molly couldn't help but wonder how Jenny would take to being let into the new house by Katy and escorted to the drawing room. When Molly had lived in Ashgate Lane, Jenny simply used to turn up and tap on the parlour window.

Florrie tutted sympathetically, inclining her head slightly.

'Molly, you've known Jenny for fourteen years. She's not going to turn from you now; none of my friends have from me, have they?'

That wasn't what Molly was afraid of.

'I don't mean that. I just mean . . . she won't be used to all this: the drawing room, the doorbell, Katy . . .'

'And we are?' Florrie laughed. 'Look, tell her she can just show up at the back door, like she used to.'

Molly smiled.

'Now, the other thing I called you up here to talk about: I think it's time that you started working with me.'

Molly look startled. 'But . . . but . . . I don't have your gift, Aunt Florrie. What can I do?'

Florrie fell into peals of laughter and tiny tears squeezed from her scrunched eyelids.

'The gift ain't so difficult to come by. Don't worry, I'll show you everything. Lessons can start tomorrow. We'll do a run-through before the evening, then you can help me with the real thing. I won't make you do anything too hard just yet.'

Wondering how she would become a vessel for the spirit world by tomorrow afternoon, Molly nibbled at a fingernail before catching herself doing it and pulling her hand away from her mouth.

'Oh – and I've taken Eddie Rathbone on to help around the place. Some of the work's just too heavy for a little thing like Katy.'

Molly, snapping out of her reverie, looked confused. 'I thought he worked at the butcher's?' She couldn't recall ever having met Eddie, but she knew of him, as she knew of almost everyone else who had lived nearby while she was growing up.

'He did, until they caught him with a handful of black pudding in his pocket. And his mother was a friend of mine, God rest her. She was expecting her pa to be watching over him, making sure he's always got employment. Going was easier on her, thinking that.'

'Why ever would she think that?' Before she finished her sentence, Molly had a feeling she knew exactly why.

'I told her.'

The following morning, as Molly walked past the séance room on her way downstairs for breakfast, she paused and looked inside. She had done this many times before, both at Ashgate Lane and the new house, but today was different. The room, its polished floorboards chilly underfoot, was dominated by a large round table surrounded by chairs. The only other piece of furniture was a cherrywood cabinet standing against the wall. Closing her eyes, Molly tried to listen for the whispers of the spirits, her skin prickling as she imagined them touching her. But, as usual, nothing happened.

When they lived in the two-up, two-down, Molly had burrowed into her blankets while the muffled sounds of the séance drifted up from the parlour below. Late into the night she would hear voices, most often Florrie's, becoming hazier as she sank into sleep, and the hollow knockings and rattlings said to indicate the presence of spirits, but she herself never saw or felt a thing. It had never occurred to her to fear the strange sounds: it was all she had ever known. Sometimes she would lie there wondering if her mother was among the spirits floating around Florrie's circle, but the only face she could conjure when she tried to picture Lizzie was Florrie's – maybe with a small difference: a longer nose or a more pointed jaw.

Molly's stomach growled, despite the sickness that rolled

inside her at the thought of a room filled with invisible eyes, hands and mouths. She left the séance room and made her way down to the dining room.

After breakfast, Molly and Florrie went up to the séance room to begin the lesson. Florrie stepped into the room behind her niece and closed the door. Molly blinked in the dim light, until the room became less fuzzy. The only illumination came from the two tapers Florrie had just lit; heavy black curtains banished any trace of sunlight.

'Well, that's the table, as you can see. Little to remark upon there. That's the cabinet –' here Florrie opened the door to reveal a space that looked surprisingly shallow to Molly's eyes '– but you won't be working with that just yet. I'll start you off upstairs; there's something new I've been wanting to try.'

'Upstairs?' Molly was perplexed. The next floor housed only their bedchambers. Florrie smiled and pointed up to the ceiling above the table. She took one of the candlesticks from the tabletop and held it up to the high ceiling where a trapdoor, painted blue like the rest of the room, was just visible.

'I'm not going through there, am I?'

'Not unless you fall.' Florrie smiled, placing a hand on Molly's shoulder and opening the door. 'Come on.'

Florrie's bedchamber had been freshly tidied by Katy while they had been eating breakfast downstairs. Florrie strode across the room and knelt down beside the green rug. Molly knelt beside her, smoothing her new dress over her knees to avoid wrinkles. Suppressing a cough, Florrie rolled the edge of the rug back to reveal the other side of the trapdoor.

'I got the idea from one of my mediums' papers,' she was saying. 'Eddie made it for me when he came by the other day, so it's not the best but it does the job. Now, what you do is, you hook your finger in here –' Florrie slipped a finger into a hole at the edge of the trapdoor '– and lift the door away. But you don't just fling it off, of course. It'll make a noise and give the game away. Just slowly and carefully take the piece of wood out.' Florrie gently lifted the flap free of the hatch and lowered it down on to the floor beside her.

'What do you mean, give the game away?' Molly asked the question but she was starting to think she knew the answer.

'I mean the clients would think it frightfully rude if they knew that I was allowing my niece to chuck fruit and flowers at them from above. They're a bit more forgiving of such behaviour from the World Beyond.'

Florrie looked into Molly's eyes. She might not have counted spirit guides and the departed among her friends, but she was a good reader of people, and she knew her niece. Molly was a bright girl, very quick-witted, and she would do well in the business. She was fresh from school and would have sat through endless sermons on God's opinion of liars and cheats, but Florrie hadn't raised Molly to be pious. Like most residents of Ashgate Lane, they had hardly set foot in a church in recent years (though Florrie knew that questions would eventually be asked by their new, more observant neighbours).

'Look, Mol. Do you remember when we went to the

theatre the other week?' (Another new luxury, and one they both thought they could get used to.)

'Yes.' Molly's green eyes met Florrie's.

'Well, all those actors and actresses were playing a part, weren't they? Putting on a show. Sometimes people want to get out of their own lives for a while, so they go to the theatre and they watch somebody else pretending for a couple of hours: people falling in love, or killing each other – that type of thing.'

'And so?' Molly asked.

'We're not so very different. They come to us and we give them a show: spirits touching them, or moving around the room, or sending them gifts from above. None of them has ever asked if it's real. They want to keep seeing what they want to see; same way nobody ever asks why a man who's just been run through in a play isn't bleeding all over the stage. You understand?'

Molly's eyes were glittering, and a smile was beginning to tug at the corners of her mouth. Florrie suspected that her niece would enjoy the work of a spirit medium.

As the morning passed, Molly learned the order of a séance, when to open and close the hatch ('Don't keep flapping it about, you'll end up creating a draught or something,' Florrie admonished her), and what to drop down on to the séance table below, and when. Today, Florrie had bought some fresh spring crocuses and a couple of apples ('Be careful how you drop those, bruised fruit don't look very celestial'). Now that Molly understood that her aunt's talent was no nebulous, otherworldly gift, but merely the ability to spin the right illusions at the right times, and that it was this that had given them their new lifestyle, she found herself warming to 'spiritualism'. She might not have been able to hear the voices of angels, but she knew how to smile like one.

Eddie Rathbone arrived later that day, looking somewhat awkward as Katy showed him through to the parlour where Molly and Aunt Florrie were sharing a pot of tea.

Florrie asked him to take a seat. A tall, rangy youth with a tangle of blackish hair that seemed to be forever falling into his dark eyes, Eddie looked at the chair as if it might bite him, and Molly wondered how he would have coped if he had been brought through to the drawing room instead.

'Eddie, this is my niece, Molly,' Florrie was saying. Eddie looked up at Molly from under his thick eyebrows. He mumbled a polite greeting and Molly noticed a flush darkening his weathered skin. Florrie started to outline his duties, and Molly excused herself and made her way out of the room. As she turned in the doorway, she noticed Eddie's eyes flit furtively across to her before he cleared his throat and nodded earnestly at Florrie's words.

'So, what's he like?'

Molly had gone up to the mill to meet Jenny as she left work that evening. They wound their way through the streets, the spring sun making it seem earlier than it was. Molly had brought her parasol but she felt uncomfortable about using it.

'I've not spoken to him. He only arrived this afternoon.'

Jenny laughed and pulled her sleeves down a little. She

had always been taller than Molly, but she had shot up so much recently that she had outgrown all her clothes, and her thin wrists and ankles were often on display. Moreover, she had a scar on the back of her right hand – the result of an accident at the mill when she had first started working there – that she was a little self-conscious about.

'You can get *some* impression of him without speaking to him, though, can't you? What's he look like?'

Molly gave in to the aching in her cheeks from trying to control her smile. 'He's nice.' Embarrassed, she was about to balance her assessment with a mention of his grimy hands with their blackened fingernails, or his unruly mop of hair, when she noticed the splashes on Jenny's apron where the bleach had sloshed out of the vat. Jenny was looking at her expectantly. 'Nice,' Molly repeated.

The following morning, Molly bumped into Eddie on the stairs as he was carrying a coal scuttle up to Florrie's bedchamber. Despite the warming weather, Florrie was still feeling the cold, particularly in the mornings and evenings, when she would often sit by the fire with a shawl wrapped about herself, breathing huskily into the heat of the flames.

'Ah . . . good morning, miss. Just taking the coal up to your aunt.'

Molly smiled and looked away before she could blush. They stood, pressed against each other on the narrow stairway, and Molly willed her knees not to start trembling. Determined not to look coy, she met Eddie's black-eyed gaze and was somewhat startled to see the tautness of his jaw as he clenched his teeth.

'Eddie? Is that you?' Florrie's voice came from behind the door. Molly and Eddie leaped like cats on a fence and barged past each other, Eddie towards Florrie's chamber, Molly away from it. Molly did not allow herself to look back as she slid into her own room, closed the door and stood with her back to it. Glancing down, she noticed the streak of coal dust across her belly.

2

For the next few weeks, it seemed as though Molly and Eddie could not be in the same place together for even a moment without somebody else walking in. Katy appeared to have a gift for suddenly needing to be wherever they were, to dust or polish the furniture. One morning, Molly had followed Eddie to the kitchen, where she planned to affect a pretence of needing to talk to Katy. Of course, Katy emerged from the dining room with the dirty breakfast plates moments later and Molly had pretended that she had come to ask her to plump the pillows on the beds, before making a hasty retreat, clenching her teeth in irritation with herself.

In quieter moments, though, Molly battled with a growing sense of shame. Her apprenticeship as a 'spirit medium' and her interest in Eddie Rathbone (both of which were progressing painfully slowly) had been preoccupying her to the point where she was not giving as much thought to her aunt's increasing weakness as she might have otherwise.

Florrie still went about her daily business: making and receiving formal calls, in between inviting old friends for a pot of tea in the parlour and conducting her séances on Monday, Tuesday and Thursday. Her voice was still strong enough for Molly to hear it from upstairs and know when the room below had been sufficiently darkened to allow her to open the trapdoor and shower the 'spirit gifts' down on to the assembled circle.

But when Molly forced herself to think of it, she knew that Florrie was not as she once was. Her fingers felt cold when Molly took her hand, despite the warmth in the air as summer approached; and her lips often had a bluish tinge to them in the morning. She had developed a damp, clinging cough that needed little provocation: going outside or coming in, sitting by the fire, talking too long, all caused Florrie to shake violently under tensed shoulders as she tried to suppress the choking cough that rattled through her body.

But no matter how much Molly chastised herself for paying so much attention to one of her aunt's servants and so little to Florrie herself, she always found her concern about Florrie's state of health lapsing into delicious reveries in which she could feel the roughness of Eddie's stubble against her face, and the weight of his body pressing down upon her.

It had also occurred to Molly that she hadn't seen Jenny since they had walked home together from the mill almost a week ago. The two girls certainly looked different now: Molly with her slim frame laced into well-cut gowns; Jenny shapeless and gaunt in brown smocks and grubby working pinnies. It wasn't that Molly was ashamed of her friend, more that she was ashamed of herself for being the one to have acquired the things they had both wished for as young girls. And now that she was apprenticed to Aunt Florrie, while Jenny was bleaching cloth in the mill, Molly couldn't imagine they would ever share the same world again. On the afternoon before her sixteenth birthday, as she pulled the petals from some blossom surreptitiously cut by Eddie from the public gardens on the Square for tonight's séance, Molly knew she would never join Jenny in the mill. She would not go back to her former life.

That evening, Molly sat in darkness beside the trapdoor on a cushion borrowed from Aunt Florrie's bed, trying not to make a sound as she listened to the circle assemble below: the soft murmurings of the clients as they found their way into the room, the scraping of chairs as they took their seats around the table. As the sounds subsided, Florrie's voice drifted up through the ceiling, welcoming the sitters before beginning the standard prayer of blessing.

'In the name of the Father, and of the Son, and of the Holy Spirit, Amen.'

Molly counted silently in her head. Seven, eight, nine, ten. The candles in the room below would have been extinguished and the circle plunged into darkness, the best conditions for spirit apparitions. Softly, Molly hooked her finger into the hole in the trapdoor and lifted the wooden door free. From here, she could observe the séance in its entirety – or hear it at least. She listened to the whisperings and creakings and ran her fingers through the bowl of blossom beside her, inhaling the sweet scent of the petals.

Suddenly, a shadow fell beside her, making her jump and clap a hand to her mouth. She had not noticed the faint glow of the landing gas lights that had stolen into the room. Looking up, she saw Eddie standing beside her.

'How did you get in here?' Molly mouthed, not daring so

much as to whisper so near to the open trapdoor. Eddie shut the door slowly, silently, and lowered himself to the floor while Molly cringed for fear of creaking boards. He leaned towards her until his breath rustled the tendrils of hair falling from her clip. She felt her skin flush and was glad of the darkness, which somehow made everything less real and more permissible.

'Well, be quiet!' she hissed. 'You could ruin everything – what on earth did you let the light in for?' She could just make out the shape of Eddie's hands as he held them up in a gesture of surrender before settling down beside her. The minutes ticked by interminably. Florrie's measured tones rang out through the gloom while the sitters struggled to suppress their whispers and gasps, and the spirit world's appointed blossom-showerer tried to breathe silently while her skin prickled all down her body. Finally, Molly heard the séance coming to an end, and slipped her fingers back into the bowl.

'. . . we ask that the spirits who have been present with us here tonight offer us a token before they depart . . .'

Now was the time. Molly was gathering a handful of the blossom – delicately, so as not to crush the petals – when she felt the roughened skin of Eddie's fingers wrapping around her own, encasing her hand in his. She turned to look at him, trying to understand what was happening, but his face was blank and emotionless in the shadows. Slowly, Eddie lifted Molly's hand over the opening and scattered the blossoms with her, fluttering their fingers together to send a sweet-smelling shower down upon the table below, handful after handful, until Molly felt a laugh bubbling up in her throat.

As the last of the blossom floated down, Molly felt her

face turn towards Eddie's, as if guided by invisible fingers. She felt light and dizzy, her body free from her control. From far away she heard the quiet sound of wood on wood as Eddie closed the trapdoor. Then his lips found hers and he lifted a hand to her face. She felt a couple of remaining blossom petals that had stuck to his fingertips pressing against her cheek. His tongue pushed inside her mouth, coiling around hers as she met his kiss with equal force. Only when they heard Florrie's clients emerging from the séance room and heading down the stairs to the hall did they jolt apart, both flushed and breathing heavily. They sat side by side in the dark, flustered and wondering if the sitters had left the house and if it was safe to leave the room. Molly's hair – now rapidly tumbling out of its clip – fell across her face and she could smell the sweet, floral scent of the blossom mingled with the soot on Eddie's hands.

In the middle of the night, Molly awoke with a gasp from a dream of herself and Eddie tangled together; lips, tongues, arms and legs twisting around and pulling their bodies closer together. Her heart was pounding; a torrent of blood rushing in her ears. Her body arched towards the empty space above her, and she could feel a strange throbbing that started between her thighs and pulsed throughout her body. Her blankets had been pushed off and were crumpled up around her feet. Molly was accustomed enough to her dreams waking her in the early hours: as a child, she had often woken in a panic from nightmares of her birth, vague dreams of which she could only ever remember the metallic smell of blood and an unearthly screaming that she had always assumed to be her mother's death cry.

But as she had grown older, Molly would sometimes wake from her nightmares with an unbearable tearing pain low in her body, and it was from there that the sensation for which she had no name was now emanating. As the night air cooled the sweat dappling her body, she caught her breath and swallowed hard.

The morning of Molly's sixteenth birthday brought with it a sharp, clear light and a crisp breeze from the Square gardens, tangy with the scent of flowers and freshly cut grass. Once Katy had laced her into her corset, Molly selected her china-blue gown from her wardrobe, for the first time since Gretchen Houldsworth had delivered it. As Katy's nimble fingers chased down her back, fastening the pearl buttons, Molly entertained herself by imagining gold lockets, ivory cameos and sapphire rings sprinkled like sugar over the picture she saw in the mirror. She had woken early, before Katy had come in with her cup of tea, with feverishly guilty memories of last night's dream. Her thin nightgown no longer clung to her body, the strange, musky scent of her excitement no longer hung in the air, and Molly fell back on to her pillow with relief that nobody knew of her dream. Now she watched as Katy fastened a pair of pearl earrings to her lobes to match the pearls down the back of her dress, but behind the impassive mask gazing contentedly out of the mirror, Molly's thoughts were racing. She didn't feel she could stop what had been started last night with Eddie Rathbone.

*

Downstairs, Florrie greeted her niece with the rib-cracking embrace and kiss that had marked the beginning of every one of Molly's birthdays that she could remember. Her aunt was still looking pale, her skin mottled with spidery blue lines, but she seemed as pleased as ever to see Molly grow another year older. Beside Molly's plate were two parcels wrapped in tissue paper, which she first tried to open in a ladylike manner, before giving in and simply tearing the paper off. The first gift was a dainty fan of creamy lace, which fluttered delicately as Molly waved it in front of her face. The second was a gold brooch – Molly's first piece of real gold – set with a painting of a tiny white rosebud. Molly flung her arms around her aunt.

'They're perfect!'

'I'm glad. Come on now, let's see how this suits you.'

Eddie was outside tending the window boxes when Molly stepped out with a basket hanging from her arm. She had planned to collect some flowers to brighten up her aunt's bed-chamber, for she had noticed that Florrie was spending more and more time there, usually sitting in the padded armchair by the fire. Eddie looked up from watering the anemones and his eyes sparkled mischievously before he collected himself, glancing swiftly at the windows to ensure they were not being watched. Molly ran across to him, the thin soles of her slippers damp from last night's rain, and pressed a kiss on to his cheek. It was as much as she dared do and she savoured the warm smell of him and the feel of his skin on her lips. Stealing another quick glance around, Eddie slid his arm around her waist.

'I believe birthday greetings are in order,' he murmured in her ear. Molly smiled, feeling a blush spreading across her cheeks.

'I came to get some flowers – I thought I'd put them in a vase for Aunt Florrie's room. What's looking nice at the moment?'

'Ah, just wait a minute. Here, I got you these.' Releasing her, Eddie bent down to where his overcoat lay creased on the ground. Resting on the coat was a bunch of tulips, which Eddie laid in Molly's arms. The blooms were a milky white, streaked with a deep pink as if by an artist's paintbrush.

'They're beautiful,' Molly whispered, 'but how did you afford them?' Instantly, she cursed herself, convinced that Eddie would fly into a rage and stalk away. With a barely perceptible flinch, he cleared his throat.

'Your aunt's had me doing some extra work. I bought them from the florist this morning when I picked up the flowers for the séance tonight.'

The séance. A perfect opportunity to snatch some time alone again, Molly pondered. It was her birthday, after all.

When Molly walked into her aunt's bedchamber, she had a basket full of assorted spring flowers on one arm and Eddie's bouquet of tulips tucked under the other. Florrie was sitting in her chair by the fire with a shawl around her shoulders and a blanket on her lap, reading a novel. She looked up as Molly arranged the flowers in a vase, and spotted the tulips.

'I see someone has an admirer,' she teased. Molly blushed and dropped a marigold.

'Eddie gave them to me this morning. They're just for my birthday.'

'Not if he knows what he's doing they're not. See that book with the red binding on the shelf over there? Pass it to me.'

Molly picked up the thick tome and handed it to her aunt. *The Language of Courtship: Flowers and Their Symbolic Meaning*. Florrie flicked through the pages before coming to a stop and resting her fingertip below the line she had been looking for.

'See now?'

Molly blinked.

Tulip, Variegated: Beautiful Eyes, the book declared.

'Like I said, I think our Eddie's going a little soft on you.'

Florrie smiled, but it was an awkward smile, as if she were about to be the bearer of bad news. Molly felt a spark of nervousness ignite in the pit of her stomach and she instinctively turned her inquiring gaze upon her aunt, despite her burning cheeks. Florrie took a deep, rattling breath.

'Mol, I know you're getting to that age. And Eddie's a handsome young lad – I can see why you might be charmed by him.' At this, Molly let out a little squeak of protest. Florrie held up a hand. 'I know you like him, Molly. You wouldn't be looking so flustered now if you didn't. But the point of it is . . . don't lose everything you're working for just to satisfy a little infatuation. I'm not going to live for ever; that must be clear to you by now.'

Molly's face fell. Her aunt was about to confirm her worst fears – that her recent ill health was more than merely the last traces of a winter chill.

'I'm sorry, Mol.' Florrie sighed, reaching out to tuck an escaped copper curl behind her niece's ear. 'I know it's your birthday. I just want to remind you that the spiritualism business will be yours when I'm gone, and the reason it will go to you is that I don't have a husband who owned me and everything of mine before the ink was even dry on the marriage certificate. I can leave it to you because it's mine to leave, d'you understand?'

Molly nodded. Florrie closed the book and handed it back to Molly.

'And then there's all the other things that go with marriage. D'you remember Mrs Baker, back in Ashgate Lane?'

Molly paused, thinking, before nodding. The Bakers – all fourteen of them – had lived a couple of doors down from Florrie and Molly, and Molly couldn't remember there being a time when Mrs Baker wasn't heavy with child or carrying a baby in her arms. Mrs Baker had died of childbed fever in the end, after a wrenching labour that went on all night and kept the entire street awake with all the screaming. Molly shuddered, and Florrie reached over and patted her hand comfortingly.

'It's easy for a girl your age to see marriage as a romantic adventure and forget the rest, but just try to remember that it's not an easy life for a woman. Think before you get yourself into anything. Do you want to own or be owned?'

Molly nodded again. Her aunt's warning had spooked her. It wasn't just the thought of losing Florrie and then her legacy on top of that; she hadn't been thinking of marriage to Eddie. Was one kiss really such a commitment?

'Cheer up, Mol.' Florrie's voice shook her from her

thoughts. 'Go downstairs now and ask Katy to make us some lunch. I'll be down in a minute.' Molly smiled and turned to put *The Language of Courtship* back on the shelf. But while her back was turned she couldn't resist flicking through to check the meaning of the brooch Florrie had given her that morning. Finding the correct entry, she quickly scanned it.

Rose, White (In Bud): A Heart Ignorant of Love.

Later that day, Molly walked over to the mill to meet Jenny. She arrived early and stood on the other side of the street and watched a couple of sparrows drinking from a puddle that had formed between two cobblestones. She leaned against the wall behind her and whistled softly to herself. The huge red-brick face of the mill blocked out most of the sky in front of her and cast a shadow over the entire street. Grubby black stains were forming on the brickwork and a grey pall had settled over the tiny windows, preventing Molly from seeing if Jenny was behind one of them. They could have been looking at the same pane of glass and never known it. The mill chimney was belching out smoke and Molly coughed a little before digging a handkerchief out of her reticule and covering her nose and mouth.

A wagon rolled past, drawn by a hulking dray horse with white-feathered feet. The sparrows scattered and the carter, idly gazing around as he drove, started when he spotted Molly leaning against the wall, and stared at her. Molly quickly drew herself up straight, dusted off her dress and fixed her gaze on her feet until the cart rolled past. She had to remember that she now looked out of place in many of her old haunts. She had often come here after work to wait for

Jenny in the past (before Florrie's business had started bringing in good money, Molly had taken in piecework at home, sewing curtains and hemming tablecloths), and neither she nor anyone else had seemed to think anything of it. But now the street looked very dark and lonely in the shadow of the mill and Molly found that boredom was no longer her reason for wishing Jenny would come out.

Back at the house, the two girls clattered up the stairs to Molly's bedchamber. She and Jenny stood at her bedroom window, staring down at Eddie filling the coal scuttle outside. As he turned to go back into the house, the girls ducked behind the curtain.

'Not half bad, is he?' Molly grinned, collapsing on her back on the bed.

'No, he ain't,' Jenny agreed, flopping down beside her, 'but I think mine's nicer.'

'Have you still got something going with Joe Hallett, then?'

The corners of Jenny's mouth curled up into a mischievous smile. 'Yes. Actually, I was going to tell you something . . .'

'Oh aye?'

'Well,' Jenny smiled shyly, 'a couple of nights ago, we . . .'

'Did it?!' Molly squeaked.

'Yes. Over in Moor Park, standing up against an oak tree!' The girls squealed with scandalized laughter.

'Did it hurt?' Molly asked.

'Not exactly. It was more awkward, like he was trying to get in but couldn't fit.' Jenny paused before they burst out laughing again.

Molly thought back to her dream of Eddie the previous night and hoped that her face was too pink from laughing for her blushes to show. 'Isn't it strange, though – letting him muck about . . . you know . . . down there?'

Jenny considered this for a moment. 'Not really. It feels like it should, and you think it will, but something just happens inside you –' here she raised an eyebrow as a smirk danced on Molly's lips '– and it just becomes the thing you want more than anything. Like nothing's ever enough.'

3

Some days later, Molly was sitting in the parlour with Florrie. It was a Friday afternoon, that blessed day when they had neither a séance to prepare for nor calls to receive. Aunt Florrie now tired so easily that she had stopped making house calls.

'It's not as if I shall be missed,' she pointed out to Molly. 'It seems that in order to really make friends with the quality, you mustn't have a visible means of financial support.' The effort of putting on a mockingly well-to-do voice set Florrie off coughing again, and she drew a deep breath before continuing. 'I just hope spiritualism ain't going out of fashion; I ordered a new carpet for the drawing room recently and it's not paid off yet.'

Molly laughed. 'Never mind; your old friends still come to visit, and I'm sure the quality will keep coming to you for your mediumship skills. How many of them have asked you to speak to their dead relatives on their behalf, off the clock?'

'A fair few.' Florrie smirked. 'I'm always astounded by how little these people said to each other when everybody was still alive.' She picked up a periodical from the coffee table, one of the many spiritualist papers she had delivered to the house, and grimaced.

'What is it?' Molly asked.

Florrie swallowed a gulp of tea and held up the paper. 'More investigations in London. It's a bad business; I hope to God it don't start up here.'

'Investigations?'

'For fraud.' Florrie met Molly's eye and her expression was grim. 'Since spiritualism took off so well, there's quite a few who want to expose us for charlatans, which ain't such an appealing thought, given that's exactly what we are.' She exhaled thoughtfully. 'It's our livelihood though, ain't it?'

'Well,' Molly reasoned, 'if trouble comes, can't we just start up in a different line of business?'

'It's not just that though, is it?' Florrie's eyes flitted to the closed parlour door. 'They don't just wag their finger at you and send you on your way. See here.'

She handed the periodical over to Molly, who scanned the page quickly. 'Fraud Investigations Continue Apace', the headline trumpeted:

> The talents of one Miss Euphemia Holdroyd have been called into question, and Miss Holdroyd is presently being subjected to a series of tests in order to defend her good name and the nature of her abilities.

'They search you, you know,' Florrie said grimly. 'They strip you and poke around in all the layers of your clothing, trying to find how you do it. I think it's just an excuse, myself; this Euphemia Holdroyd will be young and pretty, you mark my words. They're far more interested in stripping off that sort than my kind.'

Molly looked open-mouthed at Florrie, who drew a laboriously deep breath.

'That's not the worst of it though, Molly; I wish it was. You get put away for the sort of thing we do, if they catch you at it. Seven years, you can get. Seven years picking apart old rope and sewing boat sails together. And the Lancaster Assizes aren't the most forgiving in the country.'

Panic had spread across Molly's face but she knew it was no use pleading with her aunt to stop talking about it. It wasn't in Florrie's nature to pretend that such a major threat simply wasn't there. Molly had always known that Florrie had no great fondness for peelers; even as a child she had learned a certain dread of lawmen from her, but she had never really understood why, until now.

'Then what if they do come here? What if they look upstairs in your room and find the trapdoor in the floor?'

'Then you tell them that you've not long since known about it; it's true enough, isn't it? Half a lie – it always works better. You've just found out about it, but you don't know what it does. That's the lying part. As for me, I'll tell them that it was there when we moved in, and I thought it was such a danger that I've been meaning to have it boarded up, and that's why I haven't had Eddie put a proper bolt on it. 'Course, I haven't had him do that 'cause noise would be a dead giveaway, but there's enough truth in it that you can lie with a straight face. Half a lie, Molly. Remember that.'

Her aunt reached across and took the paper out of Molly's hand, then gently took hold of her fingertips.

'For what it's worth, we have one of the better systems, I think. You just have to watch your back, Molly, and I mean all the time. Every moment you're in the séance room, or if you're ever asked to talk about it, *think* before you do or say anything. And don't look nervous, that's the worst thing you can do. Smile as if you have no doubt that you are the personal confidante of the spirit world, understand?'

'Yes,' Molly said, her voice shaking only slightly.

'Again.' Florrie raised an eyebrow.

'Yes,' Molly said firmly.

Florrie went to bed early that evening, but an hour or so after she retired she asked Katy to send her niece up. When Molly entered her aunt's bedchamber, Florrie was sitting up in bed, bolstered by several feather pillows. She was heaving under the last throes of one of her coughing fits, and Molly waited for it to pass. Once she had composed herself, Florrie patted the bed beside her for Molly to sit down.

'I think it's time you took the séances by yourself, Mol.'

Fear twisted Molly's stomach. 'Why? You're not going anywhere, Aunt Florrie, don't be silly.'

Florrie took Molly's hand in her own and squeezed it. Her fingers felt cold and bony.

'I'm not being silly. I know something's gone wrong in me, and it ain't going to get put right. I asked Eddie to call on Dr Hartley the physician this afternoon. He'll be coming round tomorrow.'

Tears stung behind Molly's eyes. 'If the physician's coming then he can do something. Write you a prescription, maybe.'

'Mol, I'm not daft and neither are you. You've seen me sick before, but was it ever like this? I can feel it, Mol. It's like something heavy is sitting on my chest and pressing all my breath out. When I breathe, it catches and I cough like a mad thing. I know I'm dying, and you know it, too. Dr Hartley is just coming to give me an idea of how long it's going to be and how to make it easier on myself.'

Molly held her breath and forced back a sob, but she felt one hot tear run down her face.

'So you need to take a few séances by yourself now. If you find you need to ask me anything afterwards, you can.' Florrie brushed the tear from her niece's face. 'I'll speak to Eddie on Monday; ask him to take you through what you'll need to do that night.'

Molly looked up, startled. 'Eddie?'

Florrie nodded. 'He's been working in there with me. Between the two of you, you've probably overheard all of it.' Florrie's eyelids were fluttering now, her breath coming slowly. She looked tired. 'Go and get some sleep,' she murmured.

As Molly turned to leave the room, Florrie leaned back on to her pillows. Molly dimmed the light as she went out, leaving the room bathed in the faint, greenish glow of the gas lamp.

On Monday morning, Molly and Eddie met in the parlour after breakfast. She watched him as he sat opposite her on the moss-green sofa, twisting his roughened fingers together.

'I'm sorry about your aunt—' he began.

'Please, Eddie. Don't. I can't think about that right now;

it's bad enough to see her so . . .' Her voice faltered and she let herself trail off. She would not cry in front of him.

Upstairs in the séance room, Eddie showed Molly the cherry-wood cabinet.

'This is the part I've been helping your aunt with,' he explained. 'The materializations.'

'*Materializations?*'

Eddie grinned. 'Meet the spirit guide of the great medium, Miss Florence Tranter,' he said, flinging his arms out in a theatrical gesture of introduction.

Molly giggled. 'What on earth are you babbling about, Eddie?'

'Your aunt's clients like to actually see a spirit, feel its touch, that sort of thing. This is the cabinet she goes into to bring forth her guide,' he said grandly. 'The back here's false, see.' Eddie reached into the cabinet, hooked the tip of his finger into what looked like a knot hole and pulled. The back of the cabinet opened like a door, revealing a deeper space behind it. 'That hides me away while you get in the front part, here. As far as the punters are concerned, the cabinet was empty when you got in, because they can't see me behind here.' He knocked on the false back of the cabinet, making a hollow, echoing sound.

'So, once we're both in the cabinet?' Molly asked.

'You start humming.'

'I start humming?'

'Yes.' Eddie grinned. 'Miss Florence always hums to call her spirit guide. Or to disguise any sound I make squeezing out from behind the false back, perhaps.' He ducked into the cabinet and pulled the false back closed behind him. His voice drifted through, muffled by the wood. 'Now you.'

Molly followed him into the cabinet and shut the door, plunging them into darkness.

'Don't forget to hum,' Eddie's disembodied voice said.

Molly started to hum. She felt light and dreamy closed in the darkened cabinet with only the sound of her voice. Behind her, the false back slid noiselessly towards her, and Eddie squeezed out from behind it. He closed the back of the cabinet and Molly's face was pushed against the thin cotton of his shirt. She could smell his skin and feel the beat of his heart pulsing against her forehead. Then, startled by the sound of Katy's footsteps on the landing outside, Molly pulled herself from Eddie's grip and he backed away and opened the cabinet door. Molly followed him out into the room.

'And that's what your aunt asked me to show you,' Eddie said, raising an eyebrow.

Molly smiled and headed for the door before turning. 'Eddie? Why exactly do the sitters believe that you are Florrie's spirit guide? You don't look all that ghostly to me.'

'Ah.' Eddie held up a finger and reached deep into the back of the cabinet. In his hand was a large piece of gauzy muslin which he threw over his head, veiling himself from top to toe in wispy translucence.

Molly laughed and headed up to Florrie's bedchamber to take tea with her aunt.

Dr Hartley arrived promptly at ten the following morning. Molly disliked him on sight. A small, skinny man with a sallow face and lines under his eyes, he was shown up to Florrie's room by Katy, while Molly sat in the parlour with her fingers wrapped around a cup of chocolate, listening to his footsteps echoing up the two flights of stairs and across the landings. Then the creak of Florrie's bedchamber door, and Molly could hear no more.

She sat, absentmindedly sipping the milky chocolate, until she heard footsteps on the landing again, whereupon she drained her cup and raced past Dr Hartley and up the stairs. She burst into Florrie's room, where her aunt was sitting up in bed as she had been last night. Her lips had their now familiar bluish tinge but otherwise her appearance was no different to how she'd looked for the past week. Molly wondered why she had expected Florrie to look worse after the physician's visit, but put such thoughts aside and sat beside her aunt on the bed.

'And so?' she asked.

Florrie reached over to her niece and wiped a smudge of chocolate from the top of her lip. 'He says it's my heart, Mol. I haven't got long.'

She looked at Molly, the pallor of the girl's face showing up the smattering of freckles, her eyes glittering with tears that Florrie knew she was trying not to shed. Lizzie had been the same when she felt trapped and afraid. Florrie took her niece's hand in hers, and was struck by how warm and soft her skin felt. She had hardly noticed it before.

'But you knew that anyway, didn't you?' she said. 'I told you last night that you're going to have to take over this place.'

Molly's lip trembled. 'But can't the physician do anything? If he's so clever, why can't he do something about—'

'About my heart?' her aunt interrupted. 'Come on, Mol. What can he do? If I were twenty years younger I'd still be a lost cause.'

Molly leaned forward and rested her head on her aunt's blankets. 'What will I do without you?' She could hear a crack in her voice now, and as she looked up into Florrie's face she was acutely aware of how much older her aunt seemed to have grown in the past few weeks. The whites of her eyes were discoloured, like dirty washing, and more and more grey was creeping into her hair. Florrie was dying, Molly realized, and a hard lump rose in her throat.

'Come on now,' she forced herself to say. 'How am I to take over the business? You'll be popping up over my shoulder every two minutes, telling me where I've gone wrong!' She was rewarded with a smile from Florrie. She didn't want to add to her aunt's fears, and she knew that Florrie was far more afraid than she let on. The ferocious sermons of Sunday school seemed to come back to people as they were dying, and although Florrie would never admit it, Molly knew that a part of her would be fearful of judgement in the afterlife.

'None of the family has ever spoken in my ear since they passed, not in all the time I've been doing this.' Florrie smiled wearily. 'But who's to know what will happen when I die?' Her eyes seemed to look past her niece – but at what Molly was not sure.

'Still,' Florrie continued, 'just in case, perhaps we should think of a sign between us. You know . . . if I *can* contact you.'

Molly tried not to look too startled. This was the first time, outside of the séance room, that her aunt had suggested that there might actually be a way for the living and the dead to speak to one another. She cleared her throat. 'Then what shall it be?'

'Something you'd know me by. How about my violet perfume?' Florrie asked, gesturing towards the blue pot on her dressing table that held the scent she had worn for as long as Molly could remember. Molly nodded, the determined set of her jaw belying her heartache, and Florrie sighed gently.

'What?' Molly whispered. 'What is it?'

Florrie rested her palm on her chest, easing her way through a difficult breath. 'You're the image of your mother.'

Molly smiled awkwardly. So many people had told her that, but to Molly, who had never met Lizzie, it meant nothing.

'I did my best for you,' Florrie was saying, reaching out and squeezing Molly's hand with her weak fingers. 'I only hope I did right.'

'Of course you did,' Molly replied, her voice thick with unshed tears. 'You're everything to me, you know that.'

'You're everything to me, too,' Florrie said lovingly. 'You have been ever since you were born. You were a long time coming, I remember that; Lizzie had a hard labour and we weren't sure if either of you would survive. Then when you were born, you were so small, but you were always a fighter. You got that from your mother.'

Molly was about to point out that it was Florrie's determination and focus that had set an example for her, but as she looked at her aunt now, ailing and breathless, propped up against her pillows, she stopped herself. 'Did she live long after I was born?' she asked.

Florrie paused, her eyes misty with remembrance. 'Not long; she was gone soon after. She was in no state to spend any time with you before she went, but she asked me to take care of you, and of course I did. I felt like you were my own child; it'd never have occurred to me *not* to raise you when Lizzie was gone. I never saw myself as the mothering type, but you were different. I can't imagine what I'd have done with my life if I hadn't got you.'

Molly found herself broken under a new wave of tears. 'What am I going to do without you?' she whispered.

Florrie stroked Molly's red curls. 'Make me proud,' she whispered back. 'Whether I can see you or not. You'll only have two months of mourning, then you'll show the world what you're made of.'

'Two months?' Molly protested. 'Is that all?'

'Unless my memory's getting as bad as my heart, I believe two months is all, for an aunt.'

'But you're not like most aunts. You've always been my . . . my mother.'

'I'm not having you spending another four months cooped up in the house for me; not when you don't need to,' Florrie replied.

'Well then, I'm wearing crape,' Molly insisted, a smirk playing at the corners of her mouth at this macabre bartering – fitting, somehow, for a spirit medium and her apprentice.

Aunt Florrie rolled her eyes. 'Done!' She laughed, before another coughing fit besieged her.

*

On the night of her first séance, Molly stood in the séance room. The room had been tidied and dusted and the furniture polished. The cherrywood cabinet stood with both its inner and outer doors open so that Eddie could get inside and close the false back. Florrie's old copy of *The Book of Common Prayer* lay on the table in the place that would now be Molly's. An assortment of spring flowers sat upstairs by the trapdoor, in a vase of water to prevent them from wilting. Florrie had offered Jenny threepence to take over Molly's old job with the trapdoor, and she had promised to come over straight from work. Everything was ready.

Katy let the sitters in at eight o'clock. Instructed by her aunt, Molly stayed out of the way in Florrie's bedchamber while they were escorted up to the séance room.

'Gives an air of mystery if you just appear from somewhere,' Florrie had said.

Beside the trapdoor, Jenny was tearing the petals off the flowers. She looked across at her friend and gave her a reassuring smile. Molly was nervous enough about her first séance, and her heart fluttered like a frightened bird every time her aunt drew a rattling breath. Florrie had tried to stay awake for her niece until she went down to start the séance, but her eyelids kept flickering as she sank into an exhausted sleep. She was snoring lightly.

Listening at the door, Molly heard Katy's feet on the stairs. She looked at Jenny. 'When I finish the closing prayer, yes?' Jenny nodded and Molly set off downstairs to the séance room.

The assembled sitters gasped and exclaimed at the sight

of Florence Tranter's young niece. Trying not to let her eyes flit too obviously, she checked that everything was as it should be: the cabinet door closed (with Eddie hidden inside) and the low light of the candles veiling the trapdoor above in shadow. The lady sitters were in a flurry of questions and platitudes: had Molly taken over from Florence now? And how was the dear lady? And how pretty Molly was! And how wonderful that she had inherited her aunt's gift! And so on it went.

Finally, Molly raised her hands, silencing the wealthy clients as firmly as she thought she could get away with. 'If you please, ladies, in this room we must focus on our task this evening.' That worked, and Molly wondered how far the influence of her powerful, occult charade extended. She took up her position at the table and opened the prayer book. The corner was still folded down on the correct page from Florrie's last séance. Molly would use it until she had learned the words by heart.

'Heavenly Father . . .' As she spoke, Molly could sense the expectation in the room as the sitters bowed their heads. The two delicate flames danced on top of the candles, battling valiantly against the darkness. 'In the name of the Father, and of the Son, and of the Holy Spirit, Amen.' Molly closed the book and laid it down on the table.

'Please join hands.' She blew the candles out.

4 Summer 1856

May melted into June, and in the early days of July the sun streamed through the windowpanes of the house in Ribblesdale Place. Florrie was spending almost all her time in bed now, except for occasional trips across the landing to Molly's bedchamber to borrow novels, an activity that Dr Hartley had expressly forbidden on a number of occasions. For their part, Molly and the servants tried to keep Florrie in bed. Molly would visit her two or three times a day to ensure she had everything she wanted, but every so often Florrie seemed to find some reason to creep down the landing. Molly wondered if her aunt was just proving to herself that she could, at a pinch, still do such things. But death was advancing on her like a winter fog, claiming first her fingers and toes with its chill stiffness, then crawling up her limbs to take her heart. And yet for all her talk of being resigned to her fate, Florrie looked as if she planned to challenge death itself.

Molly now took all the séances – Mondays, Tuesdays and Thursdays – and was quickly getting used to the routine, as well as perfecting her enigmatic medium's voice and the most effective things to say. One evening a nectarine, dropped through the trapdoor by Jenny, had landed on the séance table with such force that it had split, its soft flesh oozing juice on to the wooden tabletop, but once the candles had been relit, the sitters seemed all the more enthralled at the sight of such vigorous spirit activity.

Molly also took calls on Wednesdays; most of them, she felt, prompted by the visitors' fascination with this new, youthful spirit medium. On one such Wednesday, Molly sat in the drawing room taking tea with a regular client, Marianne Meadowcroft, listening with one ear to Marianne's gossiping while snatching discreet glances out of the window to where Eddie was digging fresh compost into the window boxes, which had burst forth in a cascade of colour and perfume as the weather had grown warmer. Eddie stood up from the chrysanthemums, swatting away a bluebottle.

'. . . but listen to me going on now,' Marianne was saying, after what seemed like an hour but could only have been fifteen minutes (she had been talking about hatboxes), 'when you have so many troubles of your own, poor dear! How is darling Florence?'

Molly wished Marianne would continue with her selfish ramblings. She looked across at her guest: she was blonde, round-faced and cherubically pretty, barely five years older than Molly herself but a young lady all the same, born into one of the local quality families.

'Not so well,' she replied. Marianne pursed her rosebud mouth, adopting an expression of concern as she waited for Molly to continue. But Molly did not elaborate and Marianne suddenly had to dash off to another call.

*

After looking in on Florrie, who had not woken from the hazy sleep that had followed the dose of chloral Dr Hartley's apprentice had delivered that morning, Molly stole downstairs to find Eddie. She found him at the kitchen door, kicking the mud off his boots on the wall outside. Katy was upstairs clearing the drawing room after Marianne's visit, so Eddie hooked an arm firmly around Molly's waist and pulled her in to him. Molly silently thanked Gretchen Houldsworth once again for her cinched figure; her head span as she tasted Eddie's lips on hers and her legs trembled deliciously.

'Has Florrie woken yet?' Eddie asked. Florrie had long ago put paid to the notion of him calling her Miss Tranter, or even Miss Florence. It hadn't felt right, she had said, to have her friend's son address her as if she were a lady born and bred.

Molly felt a chilly guilt freeze her bones. Why had she checked on Florrie before coming down to find Eddie? Out of concern for her, or just so that she could fall into Eddie's arms with a clear conscience?

'No, she's sleeping soundly,' she replied, hoping that her face wasn't a mask of guilt.

Eddie nodded. 'Hmm.' Then he curled a finger under Molly's chin and eased her face up towards his.

Molly let herself drown in a swirling pool of shame and lust as Eddie held her to him, kissing her deeply. She felt as if her whole body would melt.

That evening, Molly sat in the parlour after dining informally on cucumber sandwiches and Katy's jam sponge cake. She flicked idly through the latest periodicals from the spiritualist societies, fanning herself in a vain battle against the heat of the evening sun as it hung low in the west. She was reading about the wax casts some mediums were making of their materialized spirit guides, and wondering if Eddie would be receptive to the idea of plunging his hands into a bowl of warm wax, when she heard the doorbell. Molly absentmindedly brushed cake crumbs from her skirt while Katy scuttled down the hall to answer it. When Jenny burst into the parlour moments later, Molly was not surprised. Katy had long since given up trying to announce Molly's friend.

Jenny seemed agitated. She had clearly come straight from the cotton mill; her hands were twisting her bleach-stained apron.

'I'm in trouble, Mol.' Her voice was shaking. Molly poured her friend a cup of tea from the pot and added four spoons of sugar. Jenny took it, her shaking hands causing the cup to rattle on the saucer.

Molly glanced over Jenny's shoulder to check that Katy had gone. 'Whatever is the matter, Jenny? You look dreadful.'

Jenny bit her lip – and not for the first time today, Molly guessed, looking at the cracked and sore skin.

'I've been like this all day at work. I dropped a whole bolt of cloth on the floor after getting it out of the bleach and Mrs Pullen hit me with her cane 'cause it got all grubby and we had to start again.' Jenny lowered her voice. 'Mol, I'm expecting Joe's baby.'

Molly gasped. 'Never! Are you certain?'

'As certain as I can be. I've missed my time twice, and it

ain't shown up this month either. What am I going to do, Mol?'

Molly shifted over to the sofa to sit beside her friend. She put an arm around Jenny, and felt her thin shoulders shaking like branches in a storm.

'Have you told Joe?'

'Not yet. I didn't want to say anything until I was certain myself. I've missed my time for three months now; not much doubting that. My pa's going to be furious. I just don't know what to do.' Jenny sipped her tea, and the golden-brown liquid danced in the cup as she held it in her shaking fingers.

'Well, perhaps you should talk to Joe first. If he speaks to a vicar now and they post the banns, you can get married in three weeks if nobody objects, and if there's a wedding on the way, your pa might not be as angry.'

Jenny sighed. 'I know, I know. There are enough hurried marriages around here, after all.' She looked at Molly, suddenly aware of what she had said. 'Well . . . not around *here*. You know what I mean. Sorry.'

Molly squirmed. 'It's fine, Jenny. I knew what you meant.' Any one of her neighbours would have been horrified to hear news like Jenny's, but in Molly's mind such things were still more of an awkward inconvenience. Perhaps this was why people like Marianne Meadowcroft filled their time with aimless chatter about clothes and the relative merits of various teas. They had nothing more important to discuss – or, if they did, they refused to talk about it.

Jenny left soon after, in order to drop in on Joe before she was expected home to cook and clean. Molly stood at the parlour window, watching the sun staining the sky a strawberry pink as it sank behind the rooftops, and hoping that the light would hold out just a little longer to allow Jenny time to make the visit she needed to make. Molly ran her hands down her body, over the soft curves of her breasts and her tight-laced belly. She tried to imagine her friend as an expectant mother, the vast swelling pushing out from under her ribcage, stretching her out of shape. Molly shuddered at the thought of a screaming baby's head forcing its way out from between her legs. Apart from in her dreams, she'd only ever felt a strange pulse there, a rushing heat when Eddie kissed her or held her body against his, or slid her a sly smile when he came in to feed the fire in Florrie's room when Molly sat with her aunt in the afternoons. The very idea of forcing a baby out of her straining body was more than she could bear. And yet it was not sufficient to quell her desire for Eddie. She wanted to feel his body on top of hers, her legs pushed apart by his weight; his bare skin against hers. She picked up her fan again, cooling her flushed face as she shifted in her chair.

The following morning, Molly stirred at the sound of her bedchamber door closing. She lifted her face from the pillow to see Katy with her morning cup of tea.

'Good morning, miss,' Katy said. 'Did you sleep well?'

Molly struggled with the tangle of blankets clinging to her body. 'Yes, thank you, Katy.' She watched as the maid bustled around the room, setting the tray down on the bedside table and laying out Molly's undergarments. Sometimes Molly forgot that she and Katy were the same age. She realized that she knew nothing about the girl, and that she no longer imagined herself in the role of every sixteen-year-old girl she met, as she used to. It no longer occurred to her that she could just as easily have been the girl selling flowers at the train station or sweeping the floor at the bakery – or, for that matter, the girl she had seen from the window of the cab when she and Florrie had been returning from the theatre one night. As they had wound through the darkness of the smaller streets, Molly had spotted the thin young woman leaning against the sole lamp post lighting the corner of the crossroads. She had a black bruise around one eye, and scabs on her lips. Molly could not see herself in that girl's place now, any more than she could see herself in Katy's.

Getting out of bed and reaching to the bedside table for her tea, she tried a smile as Katy turned to her with a pair of dresses on her arm.

'The cream or the blue, miss?' she asked.

'The blue,' Molly said. 'Katy?'

'Yes, Miss Molly?'

'We're about the same age, aren't we? Sixteen?'

Katy started lacing Molly into her corset. 'Yes, miss. I turned sixteen a few weeks after you did.'

'Oh,' Molly said. 'You never said anything.' Katy smiled tightly but did not reply. Molly, stepping into her blue dress, tried again. 'Are you seeing anyone?' Katy looked startled, and Molly realized that this was probably not a normal topic of conversation for the young lady of the house and her maid.

'No, Miss Molly. My time is taken up here with the job Miss Florence so kindly offered me. I don't see many lads.'

Katy fastened Molly's last button, and returned her empty cup to the tea tray.

Molly suddenly found that she had to ask. It hadn't really occurred to her that there was another young girl in the house beside herself until now. Eddie spent far more time with Katy than with Molly.

'You see Eddie,' she pointed out, trying to make her smile look casual; playful, even.

Katy's face was scarlet, and she looked as if she'd rather be emptying the chamber pots than having this conversation with Molly.

'Yes, miss. He's nice enough. But I know his eye is elsewhere.' She bobbed a little curtsy and left a thunderstruck Molly wondering just how much Katy knew.

On Thursday evening, every place at the table in the séance room was filled, and the dark, airless room felt all the more oppressive with fifteen people in it, sweltering in the summer heat. Molly stood at her place with the prayer book, waiting for the sitters to settle. Jenny had not arrived for her duties with the trapdoor. Molly had waited until the very last minute, looking out of the window down the street in search of her friend, but with a full room downstairs she couldn't wait any longer. She would just have to miss out the shower of spirit gifts; it could always be done another night. But as Molly murmured her way through the opening prayer, inwardly she prayed that Peter King had not been as furious as his daughter had feared.

As the séance progressed and the time for Eddie's materialization arrived, Molly stood up from the table, solemn in the darkness. 'I shall now bring forth my spirit guide. Please,' she added, 'keep the circle together.' She lit a single candle to guide her to the cabinet and flung the door open so that the sitters would see, in the candlelight, that it was empty. Molly stepped into the cabinet, blew out her candle and closed the door.

Almost as soon as she started humming, she felt Eddie slip from behind the hidden door. Molly continued to hum, as the air of suspense built in the room outside. She waited for Eddie to move past her and fling open the door – which he liked to do as quickly as possible in order to startle a few of the sitters – but he did not. Instead, Molly felt his hands close over her breasts, caressing her. His lips found her throat, kissing the soft skin of her neck as she forced herself to continue humming so as not to break her spell on the sitters. Eddie slid a hand down her stomach, pressing her through her skirts while Molly tried not to gasp.

On and on Molly hummed her tuneless song as Eddie's hand slipped down her leg, gathering up her skirts, pushing under her petticoats. She felt the rough skin and tiny hairs on his hand, deliciously abrasive against her thighs, before he slid his fingers into her drawers and between her legs. Molly felt a cry of delight bubbling up inside her, and pressed her lips together in a desperate attempt to stop herself from calling out. Standing behind her with his arm around her waist and his fingers slithering back and forth between her legs, Eddie pulled Molly back against him, pressing down on her core with his fingers while grinding himself against her buttocks. Molly felt her body shiver with a pleasure that seemed to burst from her body, out of the cabinet, out of the séance room, out of the house.

Eddie slowly slipped his hand away from her, his fingers slick with the scent of her arousal. Pulling the veil over his head, he threw the cabinet door open and stepped out into the room, brushing against sitters and leaving Molly in the shadows of the cabinet, her heart pounding with blood that tingled as it rushed through her.

When the séance had finished and the sitters had been shown out by Katy, Molly left Eddie in the back of the cherrywood cabinet and walked up to Florrie's bedchamber. Her aunt was quite still in her chloral-induced sleep. The low light of the gas lamp threw thin shadows over her, stroking her face like dark fingers. Molly felt a sob threatening to tear her throat and she knelt beside Florrie's bed, burying her face in the blankets. Holding Florrie's cold fingers in hers, Molly pressed her aunt's hand to her lips. Under her petticoats, her thighs were still damp, and she thought of the ecstasy she had felt with Eddie in the cabinet barely twenty minutes ago, while Florrie lay insensible upstairs.

Molly kissed her aunt's hand. 'I'm sorry,' she whispered.

Jenny arrived late that night, hammering on the back door. Eddie, who was now occupying one of the servants' attic rooms, went down to investigate – a butcher's knife from the kitchen in hand – and let her in. Molly was woken by a tap at her door and Eddie letting Jenny into her room, averting his eyes from her in her nightgown. After he had closed the door, Molly sat up, rubbing sleep from her eyes.

'Jenny, where have you been? I've been worried sick about you!'

Jenny's eyes glimmered madly in the light of the candle on Molly's bedside table. 'Joe's gone. I told him yesterday, and he said everything would be all right, and that he would speak to Pa tomorrow – well, today – but when I went in to work he wasn't there!' Her eyes, already red and swollen, filled up again, and tears ran down her cheeks. Molly put her arms around her friend.

'And you've been looking for him?' It was pointless to spout platitudes and say she was sure Joe would turn up. He was gone; they both knew that.

Jenny nodded. 'I've been everywhere. All the pubs, his house, his mates' houses . . . he's gone. His ma just said he wasn't there, and then she slammed the door in my face.' She gulped, and set herself off coughing. 'I didn't come straight here; I went back to ours first. To tell Pa.'

Molly tried not to cringe. 'And?'

'And he went mad. It got worse when he found out that Joe had gone, though. I can't go back tonight – can I sleep here until tomorrow, Mol? He'll have calmed down a bit by the time I get back from the mill.'

'Of course you can,' Molly soothed. 'But don't go to work tomorrow, you're in no state. You can stay here until you're ready to face your pa.'

Jenny looked at her with an expression Molly had never seen on her friend's face before. 'I have to go in. I'll lose my job if I don't. Anyway, I'll need money for the baby, won't I?'

Molly's face burned. 'Of course. I'm sorry, Jenny, I'm still half asleep. Come here.' She threw back the bedcovers, and Jenny pulled off her grubby clothes and climbed in beside her. Molly blew out the candle and took Jenny's hand in hers. Staring at the ceiling in the dark, Molly wondered once again how she had become this girl who could say such foolish things.

The following morning, Molly awoke to find that Jenny had already left. She stood silently as Katy dressed her. Jenny would be back that night if Peter King threw her out. *But who will you get to cook and clean for you then, you drunken old sod?* Molly thought to herself.

As she walked downstairs to take breakfast, she bumped into Eddie as he emerged from the cellar door. With a hand on her shoulder, he whisked her on to the top step of the cellar stairs, closing the door behind them. Molly had barely looked into the cellar since they'd moved in, and now she blinked in the darkness, taking in the black shapes of shelves and the dank, mossy smell.

'Where did you go last night?' Eddie snapped. 'I sat for ages in the back of that bloody cupboard and you just walked off!'

'Don't you take that tone with me,' Molly hissed. 'I don't recall telling you to wait for me.'

Eddie backed off, stung. 'I'm sorry, I just didn't expect you to leave me alone in there.'

'Why? We didn't have an arrangement, did we?'

'I thought . . . I . . . I don't know!' Eddie faltered. 'I'm sorry, Molly. I didn't mean to start a row, I just thought that

I might have upset you last night. Gone too far, like. We've got plenty of time for that, after all.'

Suspicion curdled low in Molly's throat and she glared at Eddie.

'Oh, we have, have we? And when were you going to include me in these plans?'

Eddie threw up his hands. 'For God's sake, Mol! What's wrong with you this morning?'

Molly softened. She reached up and stroked Eddie's cheek. 'I'm sorry. I went up to see Florrie after the séance. It just felt . . .' She tailed off.

'Come on,' Eddie sighed. 'I'm going up to sort the fire out. Why don't you see her before breakfast?'

Molly nodded. She felt like the only person in the house who ate anything these days. She knew that Eddie and Katy must be taking their meals downstairs in the kitchen, but Florrie had not eaten anything for over a week, and Molly always dined alone.

They paused at the top of the staircase before going in to see Florrie. Eddie leaned towards Molly, whispering in her ear.

'You do realize that you'll have to keep your hands off me while we're in there? I might have to complain to your aunt otherwise.'

Molly smiled, shrugging the weight of their argument off her shoulders. 'Shame.'

'Hussy.' Eddie grinned, pulling her towards him. Molly pressed her lips against his, pushing all thought from her mind as she gave in to the throbbing pulse that ran down her spine. As they kissed, neither of them heard the soft creaking of Florrie's bedchamber door.

Walking very slowly up the landing, Florrie was determined to reach her niece's room. It wasn't that she needed anything – as soon as she lay down these days her eyelids would droop and she would sink into a long, dreamless sleep. But just now she had woken from one such slumber and the walls of her room had seemed to be closing in, narrowing to a point around her. Her chest rattled as she fought for breath and she felt as if she were not in her own body but perched absurdly on the top of her head, teetering down the landing on disembodied legs, like a circus stilts-walker. She reached out for the brass knob of Molly's bedchamber door once, twice, three times, before she saw her ashen hand land on it. Then she felt herself falling.

A dull thudding sound on the landing above jerked Molly and Eddie apart. Looking over Eddie's shoulder, Molly felt all the blood drain from her face. And then she began to scream. Sprawled on the landing, two steps above them, was Florrie. She lay on her front, her neck twisted at a strange angle so that her sightless, glassy eyes were looking straight at her niece. The bluish tinge that had coloured her skin in the last month had turned almost grey, and watery fluid oozed from her mouth and nose.

Eddie span around, and jumped when he saw Florrie. Reaching down, he pressed his grubby fingers against her neck, hesitating when he found no sign of life. Turning, he gathered Molly in his arms, covering her eyes as he raced down the stairs two at a time. Molly keened like a snared animal – nothing coming out of her came even close to words.

In the parlour, Eddie dropped her on to the sofa as Katy came skidding upstairs to see what the commotion was.

'Get Dr Hartley!' Eddie shouted hoarsely. Katy nodded and skittered away, out into the street. With shaking hands, Eddie pushed Molly's face away from him, trying to cool her feverish brow with the back of his hand. Her skin was a translucent white, and blue veins snaked across her cheeks and down her neck.

'No!' she whispered, nibbling at her lips. She shrank into herself, and began to shriek. 'Nononononononono!' Then she fainted.

5

Through the blurry veils of sleep, Molly felt herself sliding back into her body. The scents of herself danced on the air around her: the creaminess of her skin, the saltiness of sweat and tears, the muskiness hidden beneath her clothes; all over-laid with the sharply sweet perfume of her rose handcream. She felt lost, floating in the ether, and she sniffed gently after her body, chasing it down. A warmth spread over her, and she could feel the softness of her pillow against her face as she slowly began to wake.

Then she remembered, and the image slammed into her brain: Florrie lying on the landing, her face ugly and twisted by death, her sightless eyes telling Molly everything they had seen, before the light faded from them for ever. Molly's whole body stiffened and went ice cold, and she knew that this was no nightmare.

The next thing she was aware of was the sound of herself screaming, and a dull pain as she scrabbled against her pillow, bending two nails back. She was biting the pillow, causing her to drool out from the corners of her mouth. Then a sensation of hands gripping her and turning her on to her back. Molly fought wildly, scratching out at the air with her eyes closed. She would not open her eyes. She would not see her aunt's glazed stare burning into her again.

'Miss Molly!' Katy's voice.

Molly's eyes flew open and met those of the terrified maid. Molly swallowed hard, blinked and looked down. She lay in bed in her chemise and under-petticoat. Her blankets were on the floor; she must have kicked them off. Katy's trembling fingers were clamped around Molly's wrists. 'I'm all right, Katy.' Molly's voice shook, and she didn't even believe it herself. 'Let me go.'

'I – I – I don't think I should, miss,' Katy stammered. 'Dr Hartley said to give you some more of your medicine if you were upset again when you woke.' She nodded towards a little blue glass bottle on the bedside table.

Molly recognized the granules inside as chloral, just like those Florrie had been given as she lay dying, while Molly was wrapping herself around the servant.

'No!' She wrenched a hand free of Katy's, grabbed the bottle of chloral and flung it at the wall. But the glass was tough and it just bounced off the skirting board on to the rug.

Katy jumped up to rescue the bottle. 'I really think I should, miss. Dr Hartley said—'

'Leave her be, Katy.' Jenny stood at the door, looking in horror at her best friend, wild-eyed on the bed, clawing at the maid. 'She's slept long enough.' Katy curtsied and pushed the bottle of chloral into Jenny's hand on her way out. Jenny set the bottle down on the dressing table and walked slowly towards her friend. She sat down on the bed and reached out and pushed Molly's hair away from her face.

'How are you feeling, Mol?'

Still disoriented, Molly looked blankly at her friend. She couldn't even bring herself to find words for how she felt. Instead, she rolled her eyes and smiled weakly.

Jenny clasped her hand. 'I'm so sorry, Mol. I came as soon as I heard. It can't have been much of a surprise though, can it? She'd been ill a while.'

Of course, Molly thought. *She'd been ill for a while, and Eddie and I just pushed her over the edge. He and I were kissing practically outside her bedchamber door.* 'No,' she said. *No indeed*, she added silently. *Florrie had a sick heart and I shocked her. Her death isn't much of a surprise at all.*

Molly was allowed out of bed the following day, having managed to convince Dr Hartley that she didn't need more medication. She'd sat up at the window for as long as she could manage the previous night, frantically trying to avoid sleep. When the morning came, she was exhausted, and unconvinced that her attempt to present herself as a young woman in the throes of reasonable grief, rather than one battling hysterical heartbreak, gut-wrenching guilt and the insanity of sleep deprivation, was convincing. But it must have been somewhat believable because the physician did not insist on further bedrest, and Katy brought up the bath so that Molly could wash away the sweat that had soaked into her hair during her frenzied sleep terrors. Afterwards, Jenny brushed Molly's wet hair loose down her back, and Katy dressed her in her underthings before taking a black crape house dress from the wardrobe.

'I ordered the mourning clothes from Gretchen,' Jenny murmured, by way of an explanation. 'I think I got it right.'

The stiff dress rustled as Molly stepped into it and allowed Katy to fasten up the back. She looked across to her reflection in the mirror, the respectable mourning dress made a parody of by her ashen face and the purple shadows around her eyes.

'Oh!' Katy gasped, scurrying over to the mirror and throwing a dust cover over it. 'I am sorry, miss. I should have done it ages ago; I covered all the others . . .'

'It's all right, Katy,' Molly said wearily. 'It doesn't matter.' But inwardly she chilled a little.

Leading them downstairs, Katy paused at the door of the drawing room, which stood ajar. She had barely opened her mouth to speak when Jenny silenced her.

'Not now, Katy,' she said, steering Molly away from the room. 'Plenty of time for that if she wants to.' She put an arm around Molly's shoulders. 'I think she could do with a cup of tea; I'll take her down to the parlour.'

Katy bobbed the awkward half-curtsy she always gave to this girl who looked as common as she herself did but who spoke to Miss Molly as an equal, and hurried off down the stairs ahead of them. Jenny led Molly away, but not before she had caught a glimpse, through the crack in the door, of Florrie lying in her open coffin, her greyish hands clasped upon her chest.

At some point during the week that Florrie's body lay in the drawing room, Jenny informally moved in. Nobody remembered when and how the decision was made but Jenny seemed better able to comfort Molly, during one of her teary outbursts or catatonic stupors, than either of the servants.

Molly had never exchanged more than a few words with Katy, and she would hardly so much as look at Eddie. Whenever he came into the parlour or Molly's bedchamber to collect the coal scuttle or stoke the fire, her eyes would briefly flick over him before staring into the flames; or else she would suddenly become intent on sugaring the cups of tea she and Jenny were drinking. Jenny alone seemed to be able to get Molly to speak and act normally, and besides, she was glad to escape the increasing tension that her rapidly swelling form was causing at home.

And so, one night, Jenny didn't return home. Katy suggested that Eddie could go for her belongings, but Eddie had not needed to be told that Jenny had next to nothing worth collecting. She wore the darker of Molly's old dresses and, at night, the two girls slept together in Molly's bed, where Jenny could shake her friend from the clutches of a nightmare when she woke to find her struggling against some invisible assailant.

Molly, meanwhile, found herself flinching away from any reflective surface. The curtains of the house in Ribblesdale Place had all been drawn and the mirrors veiled to mark Florrie's passing, but the surviving spirit medium quickly averted her eyes from the rippled images on the surface of her bathwater or her drinks, or the distorted smears of faces reflected in the gleaming copper pans in the kitchen. One afternoon, when Jenny had persuaded her to come outside to see how the summer flowers were blooming, Molly caught herself warily studying the drops of dew on the plants, as if she would see Florrie's sightless eyes in them, staring straight through her.

*

The day of Florrie's funeral dawned bright and hot. Sweat prickled Molly's skin underneath her corset. Once she had dressed in the thick black gown, Katy handed her a matching veiled hat and a reticule containing a black fan. The house was quieter this morning than it had ever been; Katy had gone about her duties making barely a sound. On her way downstairs, Molly passed the drawing room with some sense of relief – Florrie's body had been collected by the undertaker in preparation for the funeral procession. She had avoided going anywhere near her aunt's corpse, and as she was now the mistress of the house, there was nobody to insist on decorum. It had been the same when Molly insisted on wearing her white rosebud brooch with her funeral outfit: despite Katy's furrowed brow and pointed offering of some of the new jet and amber pieces, Molly was learning not to listen.

Jenny was waiting in the parlour with a pot of tea, and Molly sat and gulped down the hot, sweet liquid. She hardly seemed aware of its temperature, although she constantly fluttered her fan around her face and neck in a vain attempt against the cloying heat outside. The two girls did not speak; there was nothing to say. Naturally, all séances had been cancelled until Molly's two months of mourning were up. Life in the house had virtually ground to a halt.

Molly knew the hearse had arrived even before Eddie came into the parlour, in borrowed black, to escort the girls to the mourners' carriage. She had heard the horses' hooves clopping along the cobblestones, getting ominously louder. As she stepped out into the harsh July light with Jenny and Eddie behind her, she caught sight of the polished coffin resting on the bier in the back of the hearse. An image of Florrie's dry eyes sinking back into her skull flitted into Molly's mind, and her knees buckled. She felt Eddie's arm hook around her, holding her up, and realized that the last time he had held her was on the morning Florrie had died.

Florrie was buried in the new cemetery just outside the centre of town, after a service at St John's Parish Church. Molly locked her jaw into an expression of frozen stoicism as she led the mourners into the church. She made a half-hearted attempt to follow the service, and snuffled through the sickly-sweet perfume of the bouquets and wreaths, searching for the scent of Florrie's violet water. But there was nothing, only the competing odours of lilies (from Florrie's wealthier clients) and the straggly little clumps of harebell picked by her aunt's old friends.

The procession filed out of the church and into the carriages, and wound through the roads towards the cemetery. Molly cast her eyes around for any sign of Florrie. *If you can see me now*, she said silently to her aunt, *then show me. Even if you hate me now, then please, at least* . . . She felt a lump rise in her throat, crushing the breath from her, and she gasped a little, blinking her stinging eyes. Jenny hooked an arm through hers and twisted her naked fingers around Molly's gloved ones, squeezing her hand.

The hole was ready and waiting when they arrived. Molly found herself swaying as Florrie's coffin was lowered into the dirt, as if she were about to tumble in after her. She stepped back from the grave's edge and felt Jenny press a small wreath into her hands – the wreath Molly had insisted on ordering despite the florist's raised eyebrows. Molly knew that there would be plenty of white lilies, and she insisted that the florist use the blooms she had selected.

The pall-bearers backed away from the grave, and Molly, half-blinded by her black veil, tossed the first flowers on to the coffin. They landed with a hollow thud that made her legs tremble. She watched the other tributes rain down upon Aunt Florrie's coffin, burying her own under a weight of perfume and petals. *Cinquefoil*, she thought, remembering her aunt and her *Language of Courtship: Maternal Affection; Asphodel: My Regrets Follow You to the Grave.*

Back at Ribblesdale Place, Katy had prepared sandwiches and cake for the wake, and the mourners piled into the drawing room to scatter crumbs, inspect the furniture, and offer their condolences to Molly, who sat in an armchair in the corner while Jenny tried to persuade her to eat something.

'Remember you haven't had any breakfast, Mol,' Jenny said softly. 'You're only going to faint again if you don't eat something.'

'Oh, I should imagine that she can hardly take a thing.' The voice of Marianne Meadowcroft startled them both. 'I can assure you that Molly and her dear Aunt Florence were ever so close. It's not something one gets over in a morning.'

Jenny bristled. 'I understand that,' she said in a forced tone. 'Molly and I grew up together, and she is very dear to me.'

Marianne looked at Jenny, her thinness exaggerating the bump in her belly, her skinny wrists sticking out of the sleeves of the charcoal-grey dress she had borrowed from Molly. 'Ah yes,' Marianne said with an unconvincing smile. 'I had forgotten. I was about to ask you for more cream.' She wove away through the throng of mourners, leaving Molly and Jenny looking awkwardly at each other.

Katy was nowhere to be found when the last mourner left the house early that evening, and Jenny had gone in search of a splash of brandy for Molly's tea, so it was left to Molly to walk the last of the visitors to the door (Mrs Southworth from the draper's, who had spent the afternoon fingering every piece of cloth in the house: curtains, tablecloths, antimacassars, even the spare odds and ends that Katy had covered the mirrors with). Outside, the sky was a dusty blue, and a dying ember of the sun was dropping down behind the trees, leaving heavy clouds hanging over the silhouettes of the chimneys opposite the house. Molly stared at the path just in front of the door, and again she waited for the scent of violets. *Come on, Florrie, old girl, you must've got the hang of this materialization lark by now*. Again, nothing. All she could smell was the smoke and muck of the town, the scent of cut grass from the gardens on the Square barely masking the sickly rottenness of the gutters. Molly turned and walked back into the house.

Aunt Florrie was not watching over her, Molly was fairly sure of that – neither as a loving and beatific guardian nor as a vengeful wraith. Ribblesdale Place was as it ever was, the house was as it ever was, and Molly was as she ever was; except without Florrie, of course. She could no more feel Florrie's presence than that of any of the nameless 'spirits' they had mucked about with in the séance room. Molly waited for fresh tears, but they did not come. The muscles in her back and shoulders ached, and she shrugged, trying to shake off a phantom weight. Her feet stung and, underneath the layers of crape, her body itched.

The first thing she did was unlace her boots. The new, stiff black leather had been chafing her all day, and soft blisters on the soles of her feet made her flinch with every step. Without bothering to find her house slippers, she tiptoed, on throbbing feet, to the table, which was still laid with the remains of the wake food. She picked up a slice of plum cake and bit into it, allowing crumbs to fall on to the rug. In the off-colour light of the gas lamps (Katy must have lit them as the evening darkened) shadows flickered and danced like revelling ghosts. Out of the corner of her eye, Molly caught the unfamiliar shape of a length of muslin veiling the mirror above the fireplace, and started slightly. Stepping up to the mirror, she drew the cloth back a little, just enough to see her reflection.

And it was her face she saw, of course. Not that of the late Florence Tranter. Molly stared back at her reflection, at the girl she'd become in the past few months. Her skin was pale, speckled and unlined. The softness of her cheeks conflicted somewhat with the stubborn set of her jaw. But her eyes – the eyes Molly had widened so often to convince clients of her charm and trustworthiness – stared levelly back at her with a new, steely quality. Despite the illogic of it, Molly found herself staring back, willing them to break their gaze first.

'Miss Molly?'

Molly jumped and suppressed a shriek, her hand releasing the mirror's cover, which swung silently back into place. 'Good heavens, Katy, you almost frightened me to death!'

Katy was standing in the doorway, looking as if she had seen something she shouldn't and expected to be punished. Molly was just about to launch into some apologetic babble about straightening the cloth over the mirror, when she stopped herself. She was the mistress of the house now, and she would not explain herself to the maid.

'Was . . . was there anything you needed, miss?' Katy had remembered herself, it seemed.

'Yes, I shall spend the rest of the evening in my room, I believe. Please ensure that the fire is lit in there, and bring me a tray of chocolate. I shall eat supper with Jenny in there, too. You don't need to make anything special. Something left over from this afternoon will do.'

'Of course, miss – I mean ma'am,' Katy corrected herself. Clearly Molly was not the only one adjusting to the new hierarchy in the house. 'Thank you, ma'am.' Molly nodded and tried a smile, and Katy scurried off. Molly smoothed her dress and padded from the room in stockinged feet.

6 Autumn 1856

Molly's two months in black crape passed swelteringly in the midsummer heat. It was something of a relief, though, not to be expected to carry out her spiritualist duties during this time. She sat in the parlour, fanning herself against the heat and resenting the drawn curtains, while a pile of calling cards from Florrie's former clients – their corners folded to express sympathy – piled up on the silver tray in the hall. But although Molly occasionally flinched at her memories of her aunt, the restlessness of youth soon had her fidgeting and pacing the rooms, desperate for something to break the monotony. And so it was with some relief that she awoke on her first day out of mourning and dressed in her blue gown to go for a walk with Jenny.

As they stepped out of the house, Molly put up her parasol against the morning sun and sniffed at the fresh autumn air, crisp and clear, without the mugginess of summer. The shifting seasons were almost palpable. They walked around the corner to the gardens on Winckley Square, tiptoeing carefully over the uneven cobbles as they crossed the road, giving the dustman's cart a wide berth. The iron railings around the public gardens had been freshly painted, and the gate propped open so that no one could get into a mess trying to open it. The flowerbeds were still full, though some blooms had begun to shed their petals, while others had paled in colour and smelled somewhat overripe. Cool breezes fluttered the foliage on the trees, causing a confetti of slightly burnished oak leaves to fall at their feet.

'Eddie says you've still barely said a word to him, Mol,' Jenny said, breaking the silence and looking a little awkward.

Molly cleared her throat. 'I wasn't aware that there was anything I was meant to discuss with him.' She walked briskly ahead, kicking a small stone along the path with the toe of her boot.

'I thought that you were . . . well . . . making a match of it,' Jenny said in hushed tones as she caught up. 'Eddie seems to think that you had an understanding . . .'

Molly's temper – ever the subject of knowing smiles and jokes about tempestuous redheads – flared. 'Oh, he did, did he? Because I don't recall saying a word to him about any such arrangement.'

Jenny faltered. 'Oh. Only he said . . . never mind. It doesn't matter.'

Molly's eyes narrowed. 'What doesn't matter? What did he say?'

'Oh, don't worry about it! We were talking last night, that's all; about the house being yours now and all that. I won't be able to stay for ever, not when I've a baby on the way, and I was worried about you; about whether you'll manage all right on your own. Eddie said that you two had a bit of something going, and that you might not have to be alone for much longer, so I assumed—'

'I suppose everything would have worked out perfectly for him,' Molly interrupted. 'I've just inherited the business, and all of a sudden Eddie's thinking of wedding bells.'

'So there's nothing going on?' Jenny asked. 'I mean, he's even been staying up at the cemetery, hasn't he? He's done that for you, at least.'

A moment of dizziness came over Molly, and she drew several deep breaths. A couple of nights after the funeral, she and Jenny had caught Eddie slipping out of the front door, and Molly had forced herself to ask him why. He had looked at his boots and muttered something about the night watch at the cemetery. Molly had looked blank and Jenny had taken her elbow and looked at her.

'D'you remember back when we were little 'uns, and folk talked about John Cutts?' she'd said.

The memory of the big man who always smelled of ale and had pale clay stains on his boots had come flooding back to Molly, and she stared at Jenny. John Cutts was a local man about whom there were many whispers, particularly of money slipped into his pocket in exchange for a little digging in churchyards and cemeteries after dark. Not even the bodies of those that were hanged and the poor sods who couldn't afford a burial were enough for the surgeons, people said, and ghouls like John Cutts – chillingly known as the Resurrection Man – could make a pretty penny from rummaging either in the pit that held the remains of those too poor to afford a little solitude in death, or in private graves if that was where the fresher pickings were to be had. Eddie had been guarding Florrie's grave, a nightly vigil until she would be too soft and rotten for the surgeons to use.

'I know what he's been doing,' Molly said now, her heart pounding as if it would come loose, 'but that is no reason to marry anyone I did not plan to marry, and I never had the slightest intention of marrying Eddie Rathbone.'

'No,' Jenny began, 'but—'

'Molly dear!' They were distracted by the voice of Marianne Meadowcroft, who was hurrying towards them with a maid in tow carrying her reticule.

'Marvellous,' Jenny murmured under her breath. 'It's her ladyship.' Molly stifled a giggle and elbowed her friend.

'I thought you must be coming out of mourning soon. It's delightful to see you out, dear girl.' Marianne fussed about, admiring Molly's gown and ignoring Jenny.

She snatched her reticule from her maid and started digging through it, pulling out a calling card which she thrust into Molly's hand. 'You simply must come to my dinner party tomorrow night. It'll be so good to see you again.'

Molly eyed Marianne's card. She already had three of them, but Marianne seemed to have a limitless supply. 'I'd be delighted,' she replied.

'Good,' Marianne said, fussing with the clasp on her tortoiseshell card case. 'Dinner will start at eight.' Then she was gone in a flurry of lavender water and swirling skirts.

'What do you want with her, Mol?' Jenny asked with a slightly frosty glare. 'You know she wouldn't look twice at you if you weren't a spirit medium.'

'Yes, and I haven't been a spirit medium for the past two months, have I?' Molly replied testily. 'We can't afford for me not to be back in business as soon as possible, and I can drum up trade at Marianne's dinner party. People forget – they won't have spent the last two months watching their diaries and waiting for me.'

She stuffed Marianne's card into her reticule. Lately, Jenny had begun to seem like a moral chaperone standing over her. A few days ago, over breakfast, she had looked critically at Molly when she had mentioned arranging the first séance after her mourning period, and had told her that they had enough money to manage for some time yet, without Molly having to give up her morning chocolate. What Jenny proposed to do after the last of the money had run out, she did not say. Molly looked up at the sun, high and white in the sky.

'It must be near lunchtime,' she said, and turned to head home.

The following evening, Molly dressed carefully in a dusky-pink evening gown that highlighted the blushing undertones of her skin and her twinkling green eyes. She descended the stairs amid the rustling of petticoats, holding the hem of her skirt clear of her new cream slippers. Her hair was coiled up on top of her head, revealing her pale neck and throat and the white rosebud brooch pinned at the collar of her gown. Katy was waiting at the door to drape Molly's cream shawl around her shoulders while Eddie stood outside with a hansom cab hired to take her to the Meadowcrofts'. Eddie's hands rested on Molly's waist as he helped her into the cab, but she no longer felt the lick of delight that such contact would have given her only a couple of months ago. Now Eddie's touch made her feel trapped, as if his every look, every word to her, were designed to seduce her into handing the spiritualism business over to him. The warning Florrie had given her on her sixteenth birthday came back with fresh resonance, and sometimes Molly wondered if Eddie had seen Aunt Florrie hobbling towards them, that day on the stairs. As if she could fall into his arms, now, when her last view from his embrace had been her dead aunt's face!

The Meadowcrofts lived on the other side of town, in a large terraced house not unlike Molly's own. Molly had a suspicion that Marianne was none too pleased about the similarities between her own home and that of a family of self-made spinsters, but it seemed that as long as spiritualism was fashionable nothing would be said. As Molly was handed down from the cab by the driver and began her walk to the Meadowcrofts' front door, she spotted a twitching curtain on the second floor. Squinting through the greenish evening mist, Molly could just about make out the voluminous moustache and oiled head of Richard Meadowcroft, Marianne's ill-suited husband. Lacking even his wife's icy charms, Richard had once attended a séance with her, after Florrie had fallen ill.

'I just had to see it for myself,' he had announced, squeezing Molly's fingers a little too hard. 'Marianne told me that the medium's young niece had taken over, and I couldn't pass up the chance to see how one so young and lively –' here he'd made a poor attempt to maintain discretion while staring at Molly's bosom '– could possibly speak with the spirits of the dead.'

Molly had quickly excused herself.

Now, as she listened to the footsteps echoing down the

hall towards the door, she reminded herself to avoid any close proximity to Richard, so as to escape any further greasy pawings.

Inside, Marianne was entertaining a few of the guests in the drawing room, plying the ladies with milky tea and talk of her nettle troubles in the garden, while Richard held court with the gentlemen, pouring ever increasing servings of port into their glasses and occasionally braying at their remarks. The Meadowcrofts' manservant stood in the doorway and waited for a lull in the conversation before announcing Molly – 'Miss Molly Pinner; sir, madam' – and retiring. The gaze of every man and woman in the room fell on Molly at once, almost like a physical blow. She felt the inscrutable eyes of the women picking apart every stitch of her evening dress, while the men stared at her through a haze of port. As she tilted her head and acknowledged the Meadowcrofts and their guests, she caught sight of a man lounging in an armchair with his back to the firescreen, looking back at her with a touch of devilish mirth glittering in his eyes.

In his late twenties, or perhaps his early thirties if life had been kind to him, the man had warm brown eyes and hair to match, creamy skin that glowed in the firelight, a solid, well-built frame and a slightly lofty expression. He straightened up a little in his chair and crossed his legs, putting a boot up on the fender. Molly's eyes slid down to take in the shape of his leg through his breeches, and she blinked, mentally shaking herself before she could disappear into a more feverish reverie.

'Of course, our dear Molly doesn't know anybody here!' Richard Meadowcroft cried, a little too loudly. 'Molly

Pinner: meet George and Pansy Hart, Peter and Beatrice Colman, and William Hamilton.'

The name stirred something in the back of Molly's mind, but she soon disregarded it as the chestnut-haired man sitting beside the fire stood up and took her hand. *This is the one who's here alone?* Molly thought incredulously. She tried to smile and chewed the insides of her cheeks as William Hamilton bent to kiss the back of her hand. His lips delicately pinched a tiny fold of her flesh, and Molly ordered her legs not to tremble.

'No connections to Lady Emma, I assure you,' Hamilton said with a playful smirk. A spicy smell drifted from his carefully groomed hair and scrubbed skin.

Molly, realizing that she was supposed to acknowledge his reference, silently scrambled through every lesson in school and every book of Florrie's she'd ever read for a mention of a Lady Emma. Failing to recall anything, she settled for a knowing smile and a daintily repressed laugh. It seemed to work, for at that moment the Meadowcrofts' manservant announced that dinner was served, and William Hamilton offered Molly his arm to escort her into the dining room. She took it, trying not to press her fingers too arduously into his sleeve.

Of course, at the dinner table, Molly found that she was to be seated opposite William. Marianne and Richard occupied the two seats at the head and foot of the polished mahogany table, and the Harts and the Colmans sat opposite one another. Molly peered at William from under her lashes as the manservant handed her into her seat. She suppressed a shiver of excitement as she watched William's long fingers curling around his soup spoon.

The first two courses passed uneventfully. Molly's demure and ladylike manners excused her from speaking too often, allowing her more opportunities to steal glimpses of William Hamilton. She was sure, however, to keep one ear on the conversation at all times, so that she might smile at George's Hart's jokes or look appropriately scandalized while Peter Colman held forth on the number of beggars he and Beatrice had encountered on their last shopping trip in town.

'Of course, we have a very gifted guest here with us tonight,' Marianne cooed. 'Molly here is a spirit medium, no less.'

A series of exclamations erupted around the table. Pansy Hart was full of questions; her godmother had attended a number of séances and had provoked Pansy into a delirium of curiosity about materialized spirits and tilting tables.

'And so what happens once your guide has materialized from the cabinet?' she asked Molly.

'He moves among the sitters,' Molly replied, holding up her head and meeting the relentless gaze of the party guests. 'Sometimes he touches one of them; sometimes they just feel a breeze as he passes.'

'Really?' William Hamilton asked, his brows raised and his eyes burning into Molly. 'I would have thought that shedding this mortal coil might prove problematic when trying to touch a person.' He pressed his fingertips together, and regarded her with a calm stare.

'Oh really, Mr Hamilton!' Marianne said nervously.

'It's perfectly all right, Marianne,' Molly replied, licking her dry lips. 'To answer your question, Mr Hamilton, the spirit takes a temporary form from ectoplasm extracted from the medium's body while she is in the materialization cabinet.'

William Hamilton's gaze was unwavering. 'Is that the case? And can all bodies produce this *ectoplasm*, or is it something peculiar to those with talents of mediumship?'

Molly was acutely aware that everyone at the table was waiting for an answer, whether or not they considered ectoplasm a fitting subject for the dinner table. She cleared her throat. 'No, it is a talent exclusive to those born with the ability to commune with the spirit world.' She looked back at William, who nodded and pursed his lips, lacing his fingers together in front of him.

'I see,' he replied, with barely a hint of a smile. 'Then what a talented body you must have.'

A chorus of politely repressed chokes and splutters erupted around the dinner table, and Beatrice Colman looked as if she would swallow her dessert spoon. The tension at the table was palpable – clearly the Meadowcrofts had not anticipated a debate on the validity of mediumship between Molly and the obviously disbelieving William Hamilton – but then Beatrice announced that the very idea of spirits loose in one's house made her feel quite faint, and Molly's shoulders loosened in relief as the topic of conversation was changed. But as she sat poking her peaches and cream around the bowl with her spoon, she couldn't resist another glance at William Hamilton. When she looked up, he was looking straight back at her, his eyes gleaming appreciatively.

After dinner and drinks, Molly had been hoping to slip

away to hail herself a hansom cab at a suitable distance from the house, but found herself accompanied by all the other guests when she made her excuses and waited to be escorted to the door by the manservant. Amid a flurry of apologies about morning engagements and journeys to make the following day, the Colmans and the Harts bustled out to their waiting carriages, leaving Molly to walk down the front path with William Hamilton. The autumnal evening air was cooling in anticipation of the coming winter frosts, and Molly dug her hands deeper into her fur muff and shrank down into the collar of her evening gown as she pulled her shawl tighter about her shoulders. Without even looking, she could feel William's presence beside her, and found that she was unconsciously drawing close to the warmth of his body. A flush crept up her neck as she thought of the heat of him under his clothes, and she stole a look at his solid frame.

'Miss Pinner, it seems that your carriage is not awaiting you. Terribly bad form when one is collecting a solitary young lady.' Hamilton gestured to his own carriage, which stood – very conspicuously alone – by the side of the road. Molly flinched and turned to face him guiltily, as if her fantasies of him would be plain to see.

'Oh, yes.' She made a show of tutting and appearing inconvenienced. 'I suppose I shall have to find a cab.' She had the distinct feeling that William did not believe for one moment that she possessed a carriage.

'Nonsense. How could I let a young lady walk the streets in search of a way home when my own transport is perfectly serviceable?' He gestured to his carriage, while taking hold of her hand and pressing it to his arm. 'Come now.' He strode off, and Molly had to shuffle along in her best boots, slipping slightly on some wet leaf mulch. William's driver, Ashton, a short, stocky young man with fair hair and a professionally detached expression, held the door of the carriage open while his master offered Molly his hand before hopping in beside her. The driver shut the door of the carriage with a bang, and Molly felt the vehicle swaying as he climbed back up on to his seat and set the horse off trotting over the cobbles. She was suddenly very aware that she was alone with William Hamilton. She turned to look at him and her stomach churned as she watched him pulling off his gloves, one finger at a time.

'Ah . . . your driver does know where he's taking me, I presume?' she asked.

'Of course. When Marianne said that you were a spirit medium, I presumed that you must be the one in Ribblesdale Place. That is you, isn't it?' He seemed to be sitting awfully close to her.

'Oh, yes. I am the only medium in Preston, since my aunt passed away.'

William nodded. 'I see. Gifted, ectoplasm-producing bodies must be a rarity among young women.'

Molly felt a smile spreading irresistibly across her face. 'You seem to be more interested in mediums' bodies, sir, than the extraordinary spirits which speak through them.' She turned, doe-eyed, to face him, her lips parted slightly, as if the very idea shocked her beyond belief.

William stared back at her, and the blue light of the moon shone through the carriage window and flashed across his face. 'I certainly am.'

Molly knew that she should look away, break the momentum between them, but an almost forgotten ache pulsed through her body and she could not. Instead, she cleared her throat, trying to act as if this were just another casual conversation.

'There is no great mystery about the body, Mr Hamilton. The spirit world is another matter, and it surprises me that it does not concern you more.'

'Don't be surprised,' he whispered. 'I am not particularly interested in matters of the spirit world. Not for as long as I have the bodily one to preoccupy me.'

Molly was not sure who moved first, but William Hamilton's lips met hers with an almost bruising force. Dispensing with the notion of delicate, courtly kisses altogether, he placed a hand on the back of Molly's head, pulling her deeper into his kiss. She felt a tugging at her neck and was startled to feel his fingers pulling apart the fastenings of her dress, and his cold hand moving down the warmth of her throat and chest. The carriage bumped over uneven cobblestones, jolting her further into William's embrace. His lips slipped down her neck, and an experienced hand plunged down the front of her corset and gathered her right breast into its palm, pressing against the soft flesh. William's fingers closed around Molly's nipple, which responded with an almost sharp sensitivity to his caresses as his lips slipped down to her neck.

The carriage jolted again, and Molly felt herself rocking with the movement, and a dampness as she was ground again and again into the plush of the carriage seat. Just as William was reaching down to the hem of her skirts with his free hand, the carriage came to a stop and shook as the driver jumped down. Startled, Molly pulled herself away and gathered her shawl about herself as quickly as she could. William sat back in his seat, the picture of respectability, apart from his gloves which he had discreetly positioned on his lap. When Ashton threw open the door and handed Molly down, she hurried into the house with only the smallest nod to William.

Shutting the front door with a bang, Molly fell face first against it, laying her brow against the impassively cool wood. She was frantically rearranging her underclothes and fumbling with the buttons of her evening dress when Eddie's voice broke the silence behind her.

'Molly?' Practically jumping out of her skin and suppressing a shriek, Molly span around with one hand clasping her shawl together.

'Eddie, what on earth are you playing at? You almost frightened me to death!'

Eddie's stare was cold. 'Why didn't you send word if you were going to be back early? I could have had the cab come sooner.'

Discreetly kicking the rumpled hem of her skirts straight with her toe, Molly forced an airy smile. 'Oh, I thought it would be a pity to inconvenience you. Especially when I was offered a lift home.' She tried not to think of what that lift home had involved. Eddie knew her facial expressions when aroused.

'I see that. Who from?'

'A Mr William Hamilton. I met him at dinner this evening.'

'And his wife?' Eddie still hadn't moved from where he stood, blocking the hall. Molly was starting to feel cornered.

'No. He is not married.'

'You accepted a ride home from an unmarried man? What the hell were you thinking?' Eddie's voice was a harsh whisper, as if he were fighting the urge to bellow and throw things. Molly could hear footsteps overhead – Katy, or perhaps Jenny – and her eyes flitted to the ceiling. She had had enough of this interrogation.

'I don't see how that has anything to do with you,' she hissed.

'You don't . . . of course it has something to do with me!' Eddie grabbed her arm and started to pull her towards the parlour door, but his fingers dug into the tender muscles and she wrenched herself free.

'Get off me!' Molly's voice was louder than she had intended, startling them both. She dropped it to a venomous whisper, eager to escape Eddie and this conversation before Jenny or the maid came running. 'You forget yourself, Eddie Rathbone. Who I socialize with, and what I do with them, is none of your concern.'

'So there *was* something happening. God, Mol, what are you playing at – are you trying to get yourself into trouble?'

'How dare you!' Molly hissed. 'How can you even ask that of me? Whether or not anything happened between William Hamilton and myself, it is not your place to comment on my behaviour. Firstly because you work for me –' here Molly observed a satisfying shrinking in Eddie's posture: so he had indeed been planning more for himself '– and secondly because you are in no position to comment on my chastity. Now let me pass; I wish to go upstairs.'

Eddie's face was like slate, and as he looked down at Molly, his eyes caught the disarray of her clothes at her neck; her shawl hanging open to reveal the buttons of her dress – some in the wrong buttonholes and others left open. With an icy expression, Molly gathered her shawl about her once again.

'I said let me pass, Eddie.'

The manservant reached towards Molly, hooking a finger under her chin and pulling her head up as he used to when he kissed her. He stared at her exposed neck and uttered an exclamation of distaste before pulling his hand away from her face and stalking off into the parlour. Molly picked up her skirts and ran upstairs with the heels of her boots rapping loudly on the varnished wood.

Once she was safely shut in her bedchamber, Molly pulled off her shawl and threw it on to the chair by her writing desk. Tugging at her laces, she kicked off her boots and walked in stockinged feet to her dressing mirror. Turning her head this way and that, she looked at her neck for whatever it was that had so upset Eddie. Then she saw it: just above her collarbone, a misshapen bruise on the pale skin of her neck where William had kissed her, ruddy in the shadowy light of the gas lamp.

7

Late the following morning, Molly was taking tea alone in the parlour. Jenny, whose belly was so swollen that she was having trouble getting clothes to fit, continued to get up before the rest of the household and go to work at the cotton mill, despite her nausea and aching ankles and Molly's insistence that she needn't continue to work.

'If it's your keep that's bothering you, don't worry,' Molly had said the previous night. 'You help me out with the séances; you don't need to keep working at the mill as well. Besides, you don't want to hurt yourself again, not in your condition,' she added, nodding discreetly towards the scar on her friend's hand, which had come about when a younger, less attentive Jenny had been cleaning the back of the cotton-weaving machinery and had her hand crushed between the iron frame and the moving loom (or 'the mule', as the cotton workers called it).

Jenny had seemed uncomfortable, and mumbled that everything would be fine. But she was getting more and more tired, going to bed practically as soon as she'd eaten her supper. Lately, Molly had found herself distracted during séances when the shower of spirit gifts came, knowing that

Jenny was nodding off over the trapdoor upstairs. Around the house, she wore Molly's old clothes, but she still donned her shapeless smock to work at the mill, fearful of damaging Molly's cast-offs. When Jenny undressed for bed at night Molly could see a livid red mark around her friend's stomach from the waistband of her skirt.

Molly was swirling the dregs of her tea around the bottom of the cup when she heard the doorbell. Katy's shoes scuffled along the floor as she hastened to answer it, and Molly straightened her clothes. Her ivy-green house dress was at least presentable for visitors.

'Beg pardon, ma'am; a Mr Hamilton to see you.'

Molly, startled, sat bolt upright in her chair. She stole a glance out of the window, ensuring that Eddie was still filling the coal scuttles from the bunker outside.

'Show him in.'

She had adopted an elegant, if somewhat contrived, posture, standing by the mantelpiece, by the time William Hamilton was shown in. She smiled in a suitably cordial manner, and inwardly in a rather less ladylike manner, as William bent to kiss her hand.

'I was wondering if you would care to come for a walk, Miss Pinner,' he began. 'It's a mild enough day for the time of year, and I was passing by and thought that you may like to feel the benefit of it, what with winter approaching us so quickly.'

'Oh! Yes, I'd be delighted, Mr Hamilton,' Molly replied. She nodded to Katy to fetch her shawl, and excused herself while she raced upstairs and changed her clothes herself.

Walking into her bedchamber just as Molly was pulling on her boots, Katy looked a little surprised.

'Oh, ma'am, you should have said. I'd have helped you change!'

'It's quite all right, Katy,' Molly replied, pulling her shawl from the maid's arm and arranging it about her shoulders. 'I wanted to be off quickly, that's all.'

Katy looked – as she so often looked – as if she expected to be upbraided for not doing her duties sufficiently. 'Would you like me to get Eddie to chaperone you, ma'am?' she asked nervously.

Molly tried not to let her horror at the thought show on her face. 'Oh, no. Eddie is busy, and I shan't be going far. Mr Hamilton and I will be fine.'

Katy was starting to look alarmed by now. 'But ma'am . . .'

'That will be all, Katy,' Molly interrupted, in the imperious tone she had been perfecting ever since Florrie died. 'Thank you.' She swept out of the room in a swirl of damson velvet, and headed downstairs to meet William.

William's carriage was parked just outside the house. The coat of black paint looked fresh, and the roan mare harnessed to the front was young and muscular. William lifted a hand to his driver to indicate that he should stay put, and offered Molly his arm. They walked around the corner towards Winckley Gardens, the public gardens on the Square. There was a definite autumnal chill in the air, and their breath formed little clouds in front of their faces. William held the gate open for Molly and she stepped through before taking his arm again.

'So, how is the life of a spirit medium?' William asked.

'Not so bad,' Molly replied, doubting that this was why William had asked her to accompany him. 'I have been rather busy holding circles for all my clients who missed me while I was in mourning for my aunt.'

William nodded. 'Ah, yes, of course. I had forgotten. My belated condolences.'

Molly nodded and waved it away. 'Yes, thank you.'

'So,' William said, guiding Molly around the curving path and through a scattering of acorns that crunched underfoot, 'you aren't in contact with her then?'

Molly gasped. 'My aunt?'

'Forgive me.' William smiled. 'I should not be asking questions of the spirit medium and forgetting the young lady underneath. I meant only to ask if your . . . abilities permit you to converse with those whom you have lost.'

Shaking the image of Florrie from her mind, Molly nodded and forced a smile. 'I understand. No, I am not in contact with her. In fact, I am not in a constant state of commune with every person who has ever departed this life.'

William held up his hands. 'I am sorry. There is no reason why you should be concerning yourself with such things at all times.'

Molly couldn't help but smile. 'Indeed,' she said, looking up at William. 'Especially when I am talking to one who has already professed his preference for bodily matters over spiritual ones, and in no uncertain terms.' She was pleased to see William catch his breath, and she met his gaze as if to dare him.

William smiled again and glanced around the deserted

gardens. In an instant, he had an arm around Molly's waist, pulling her off the footpath and into the trees. He backed her up against the thick trunk of an oak tree, and Molly could feel the rough irregularity of the bark digging into her through her velvet suit. William's lips covered her own, then trailed down to the collar of her jacket, nipping at the soft skin of her neck. Reaching down with one hand, he pulled up a handful of her skirts, pushing layers of petticoats aside and sliding his fingers into Molly's drawers. As she felt the firmness of his fingertips against her core, Molly gasped. She could feel a relentless throbbing pulsing through her body, much as she had during her tryst with Eddie in the materialization cabinet. Only now there was no feeling of being trapped by the close, wooden walls of the cabinet, and no dying Florrie lying just a few feet away.

While William fumbled impatiently with his breeches, Molly heard a leisurely footfall and murmured conversation pass right by the tree William had her pressed up against. A delicious little shudder passed through her. At that moment, she wanted William's body against hers with a ferocity that she had never felt before, even with Eddie. She couldn't even bring herself to care about the people taking a morning walk so close to where she and William were hidden. Having freed himself from his breeches, William crushed his body against hers, pushing her legs apart with his knee, lifting her up and pressing her against the tree trunk. Molly trembled, willing her body to relax as William plunged into her. A moment of surprise; a bright, sharp flash of some strange sensation running through her body; and a quiet little yelp, quickly muffled by William thrusting his tongue into her mouth. Again and again he ground her back into the bark of the tree, suppressing a groan with each thrust. Molly found herself growing damper and instinctively drawing her legs up around William's waist and further apart.

With his usually immaculate hair now flopping forward into his eyes, and an expression that was almost a grimace, William slammed his body into Molly's – once, twice, three times – before falling forward on to her, his head on her shoulder. He let loose a shuddering sigh, and Molly cried out as the churning bubble of tension that had been building low and deep inside her exploded. After a couple of tiny, pulsing thrusts, William pulled out of her, releasing a warm, yeasty smell that mingled with Molly's muskiness. There was also a sharp odour, which, as she glimpsed a thin reddish coating on William's manhood, Molly realized was her own blood.

Flustered, William straightened his collar and smoothed down his coat until he was as presentable as when he had appeared in Molly's parlour. Once again, he offered Molly his arm and they headed for the gates, Molly taking stiff little steps and hoping that the dampness on her thighs was not soaking through her petticoats and the velvet of her walking skirt.

'I won't be able to call on you until next month,' William announced in a somewhat husky voice, before clearing his throat.

Molly, a little startled, stopped staring blankly at the carriages and people bustling around Winckley Square and turned to William. She hadn't really been expecting a conversation. 'Oh?' she asked in a tone that sounded more confused than curious.

'Mm. I have to go away to Sheffield for a couple of weeks, unfortunately; business, you see.'

'I understand,' Molly replied. 'Ah . . . what is your line of business, if I may ask you that?'

'I recently inherited my father's cotton mills,' William said as they turned the corner into Ribblesdale Place and stepped the footpath. 'He died last Christmas.'

'I'm sorry to hear that,' Molly forced herself to say. She tried not to think about her aunt, but flinched at the thought of what Florrie would say if she could see how well her niece was sticking to her advice about men. A bolt of pain shot through her as she stepped over a puddle, and she winced before resuming her careful tottering.

William shrugged. 'I hardly saw the man,' he said dismissively, 'but I was his only surviving child, and so I ended up with three mills: one here in Preston, one in Sheffield and one in Manchester. I try to let my managers do most of the work – I don't know a bloody thing about cotton – but sometimes I must put in an appearance, I suppose.'

Molly nodded, but she barely heard him. Parts of her body she was seldom even aware of were clamouring for her attention: her legs aching, her lips tingling, a hollowed-out sensation between her thighs.

They came to a stop outside Molly's house and William bent to kiss her hand. 'I'll pay you a visit when I get back. Perhaps we could have dinner?'

Molly nodded, hoping that Eddie was safely out of the way.

'I can't invite you to my house, I'm afraid,' William was saying, 'I'm just renting rooms at present. Hardly suitable for guests.' He tipped his hat to Molly and strode off to his waiting carriage.

Molly managed to creep back inside without attracting the attention of either of the servants, and walked on aching legs up to her bedchamber. She couldn't have Katy helping her to change in this state. William's remarks about his cotton business and his offer to take Molly out to dinner after his trip away nagged at her, although she couldn't be sure why. Sinking down on to the chair in front of her dressing table, she flinched, and as the aching reminded her afresh of what had just passed between them, it occurred to her that William was evidently not planning on their little dinner party being a cover for a repeat performance of today – at least not if he was concerned about his rooms being unfit for formal dining.

My God, he's actually courting me. The thought came over her like a bucket of icy water, and Molly's skin tingled with shock. The young girl from Ashgate Lane hadn't yet managed to think of herself as an attractive marriage prospect for a man like William Hamilton. She might be a well-placed young lady, a businesswoman, no less, but she still felt like a fraud when she dressed in her tailored clothes and ate a good breakfast served by her maid. When she responded to William's advances she wasn't playing the part of Miss Molly Pinner, spirit medium. She felt truer to herself backed against a tree in Winckley Gardens than she had at Marianne Meadowcroft's dinner party.

Molly sat down on the bed and winced at the tenderness that still hummed between her legs. She reached over to the bowl of water Katy must have left for her to wash her hands when she came back from her walk, and splashed her hot cheeks and forehead. Shifting around, she tried to get comfortable, pulling her clothes away from her body to stop them clinging to her skin. Suddenly, the thought hit her: if William planned to marry her, then surely the most effective way to ensure her agreement would be to get her pregnant. The stickiness between her legs was suddenly unbearable.

Snatching up the bowl of water, Molly dropped down on to the floor, her back against the door so that Katy could not open it from the other side. She pulled the layers of her skirts out of the way and yanked impatiently at the ribbon holding her bloodstained drawers around her waist. Once she had finally wrenched the tightly knotted ribbon free, Molly squirmed out of her drawers and kicked them aside. Forgetting the wooden floorboards beneath her, she scooped handfuls of water from the bowl and washed herself clean of blood and William's seed, flinching every time her fingers brushed against her smarting flesh.

Then she grabbed her discarded drawers and surveyed them critically. The very obviously positioned bloodstain was drying in a shade of purple-black; Katy could hardly fail to notice when she next did the laundry. She might only be the maid, but Molly did not want her knowing about this. Bunching the drawers in her hand, Molly scrubbed at the darkened patch on the wood floor where she had sat sloshing water on to herself. Once she had soaked up the worst of the water, Molly cast her drawers into the grate, where they fizzled and hissed on the coals. Picking up the brass poker, she pushed them into the flames and watched them blacken and shrivel.

*

Jenny arrived home late from the cotton mill that night, ravenous and exhausted. Molly, who was already in her nightgown, rang for Katy to warm up Jenny's supper and bring it upstairs to Molly's bedchamber. The bed in Aunt Florrie's room had not been used since her death, and although Katy had washed the sheets and aired the mattress, it had not crossed Molly's mind that anyone should sleep in there, nor had Jenny ever suggested having her own room. Now, however, as Molly watched Jenny undress for bed, trying not to look horrified at the fiery seams of red scrawled all over her taut belly, it occurred to her for the first time that they would have to find space to keep a baby.

'So,' she began, once Jenny was sitting up in bed, supported by pillows and ready for her supper, 'how far along are you now?' Her friend's heavy new body looked awfully clumsy, and Molly wondered how she was going to manage at the mill for much longer.

'Seven and a half months, according to Sally Marsden at work,' Jenny said with an apprehensive grimace. She shifted and sat up straight as Katy came in with a plate of mutton and potatoes.

'Who's she, then?' Molly asked. 'Why would she know? You're the one having the babe.'

'Midwife,' Jenny said through a mouthful of potato as Katy walked out of the room with her arms full of clothes to take down to the laundry basket. 'Brings in a bit of extra money, she says.'

'And she can tell when your time's due?'

'She can get a good enough idea. And she delivers babies when they do come. She's wet-nursed a couple of times for quality families before, but she says she's too old for that now; can't keep up enough milk.' Jenny swallowed and set about attacking a rather leathery piece of meat with her knife. 'She does other things around those areas, too,' she added.

Molly turned the chair at her writing desk around to face Jenny and sat down gingerly, trying not to let her discomfort show. 'That right?' she asked, as she started plaiting her hair for bed. She had a faint recollection from childhood of a woman who could not only deliver babies, but tell women how not to get one, or how to stop one.

Jenny nodded. 'Not that she makes that common knowledge, of course. She only told me when everyone at the mill found out how Joe had left me expecting. Sally offered to help me find a way out of it.'

'Why didn't you?' Molly heard the incredulous tone in her voice. She knew that a woman who could barely feed herself, never mind a child, sometimes had to do such things. It wasn't something that was discussed more than it had to be – the threat of the hangman's rope had that effect on people – but Jenny was half dead with exhaustion every evening now. How did she expect to bring up a baby if she still insisted on working at the mill?

'Sometimes I ask myself that.' Jenny swallowed the last of her supper and took a gulp of chocolate. 'Like when I'm hauling bolts of cloth about at work and I keep tripping over 'cause I can't see my feet, or when the skin on my belly's itching and driving me half mad. But other times it don't feel so bad. I'll manage.'

'You always have.' Molly downed the last of her chocolate and pulled back the bedcovers, nudging Jenny to get her to make room for the two of them.

'*We* always have.' Jenny rested her head on Molly's shoulder. 'You're doing brilliantly, Mol.'

Molly choked down a teary gulp and nodded hastily.

'So,' Jenny said, changing the subject, 'Eddie said you went out for a walk with a gentleman this afternoon.' She grinned impishly. 'Is this why you're not interested in Eddie any more?'

'What?' Molly gasped, incredulous. 'Sometimes I think all that boy does is follow me around. Who's been telling Ed—' She broke off. '*Katy*.'

'She probably didn't mean anything by it.' Jenny yawned. 'If he asked where you were . . .'

Molly toyed irritably with the end of her plait. 'I wish I'd never looked twice at Eddie Rathbone sometimes. He wants to know everything I do and everyone I see all the bloody time.' She thumped the pillow twice before flopping down on to it.

'Men get that way,' Jenny murmured. 'Why d'you think your aunt never wanted to marry?'

In her sulk, Molly barely flinched at the mention of Florrie. 'We're not married though, are we? We never were. And I never said we ever would be; I mean, as if I—' She stopped herself and fell silent.

'Oh, forget about Eddie,' Jenny sighed. 'Tell me about this gentleman you're being courted by, before I fall asleep.'

'Oi! I'm not being courted!' Molly nudged her friend. 'He's just the one who gave me a ride home from Marianne Meadowcroft's dinner party the other night.' She tried not to think about exactly what that ride home had involved; Jenny's gaze was a little too intent.

'Sounds like he's courting you to me.'

Molly bit her tongue before she could ask exactly what Jenny knew about respectable courting. 'All we did was go for a walk,' she said. The half-truth felt heavy in her mouth, and she began to wonder what she herself knew about respectable courting. She turned over to face Jenny. She still felt tender, and her legs ached where they joined her body.

'Who is he then?' Jenny's eyelids were starting to fall. Concluding that Jenny wouldn't know or care about William, Molly told her.

'His name's William Hamilton. He's got a carriage and a few mills.' Jenny's mouth flew open and she stared at Molly. 'Ah . . . I forget how many mills,' Molly lied. 'Not many. Anyway, it doesn't matter . . .'

Jenny spoke slowly. 'Well, I know at least one of those mills. He owns the one I work in.'

'Oh!' Gooseflesh broke out down Molly's bare arms – *Hamilton!* How had she not recognized it before? – and as she continued, her voice was too bright: 'How strange! So many mills in Preston and all the time—'

'You're seeing the man I work for?' Jenny interrupted, matching Molly's forced tone.

'I've told you a dozen times, I'm not seeing him!' Suddenly Molly's stunted conversations with William and even her increasingly hostile exchanges with Eddie felt easy compared to this discussion. 'Anyway,' she forced herself to say, 'what difference does it make?'

'Oh, none, I suppose,' Jenny sighed. 'Let's just get some sleep.'

They curled up together under the neat white linen, and Molly listened to the howling of the October wind. The looser strands of climbing ivy that grew up the wall outside Molly's bedchamber whipped against the glass. Jenny's breath was too rapid and shallow for her to be sleeping, and as Molly tried to settle in beside her, she felt as if she were trying to bed down for the night with a tense and sweating carthorse. She turned her back to Jenny, huddled herself around an armful of blankets, and tried to sleep.

8

On Halloween morning, Molly stirred from her sleep as the sounds of Katy bustling around preparing breakfast began to bleed into her dream. She yawned and rubbed the gritty sleep from her eyes before sitting up and wrapping the bedsheets around herself. She could hear Katy's scuffling footfall on the stairs as she started to climb the two flights up to Molly's bed-chamber. Suddenly, Molly remembered what day it was, and made a mental note to send Katy out to buy a few things for the Halloween séance that night. Then another thought seeped in, and she froze.

If tonight was Halloween, her time was two weeks late in coming. She sat motionless, silently searching her body for the signs that would put paid to the nagging doubts she had been having for the past week and a half. But there was no metallic-smelling stickiness on her thighs, no clammy dampness on her nightgown, no rolling ache turning over and over in the echoing space inside her.

'No,' she whispered to herself, 'I can't be.' She had only done it once with William, and although she'd never asked Jenny how many times it had taken for her to get in the family way, Molly had done everything she could to avoid it. An hour or so after she'd first washed her privates clean that day after her tryst with William, a faint ghost of a memory about salt water had drifted into her mind, and she'd sneaked down to the kitchen to mix up a cup of brine before slipping quietly back upstairs to wash herself again. She smothered herself in the brackish water, ignoring the sting, and blinking through the salt water that flooded her eyes as if in sympathy.

Now, as she accepted a tray of tea and toast from Katy and started to nibble at the edges of a piece of toast, she shook inside, and hardly dared to pick up the cup in case her trembling caused the tea to spill on to the clean white bed linen. The house suddenly felt very small, as if its walls were closing in on her.

Molly cleared her throat. 'Katy?'

'Yes, ma'am?'

'I've decided to go out today and buy the things for the séance tonight myself. I'll wear the green velvet.' It was a Friday, not really a séance day, but Molly knew that Florrie would certainly find a way to return from the grave and haunt her if she did not hold a circle on the one day of the year that even sceptics believed marked a thinning of the veil between the worlds.

Katy bobbed her head and started searching the wardrobe for Molly's green walking outfit. 'Will you be wanting me to carry the shopping, ma'am?' she asked.

Molly felt a ripple of irritation at the thought of the maid trailing around after her all morning, but somebody would need to carry the shopping basket, and better it be Katy than Eddie. She told Katy that she would need her, and slipped out of bed to be laced into her corset. The stiff boning slid closer to her as Katy pulled at the laces and the familiar squeezing began to press and shape her body. All of a sudden, Molly felt very bloated.

'Tighter,' she instructed the maid.

The town was bustling that morning, and Molly, clad in her thick velvet walking suit, wove in and out of the crowds like a plush snake, with Katy scurrying behind with the basket. Often she would see regular clients smiling politely or nodding in a discreet greeting, and she would return their attentions with a milkier, daytime version of her enigmatic medium's smile. First, Molly popped into Gretchen Houldsworth's shop to check on the dresses she'd ordered for the Christmas season: two for herself, a ruby-red brocade and an oyster silk, and what was to be Jenny's first custom-made dress, albeit a loose and flowing one that would accommodate her pregnancy and whatever body she was left with after it. Molly fingered the limp blue beginnings of Jenny's dress and pronounced everything to her satisfaction before leaving with a pair of silk evening gloves.

'Come on now, Molly, stay for a cup of tea!' Gretchen implored her, but Molly said she had to be going – busy night to prepare for and all.

'So it must be. I'd quite forgotten. Bye then, love!'

Molly left Gretchen's shop and walked up towards the parish church, worrying slightly that her new dresses were being made to measurements that might not fit her by the time they were delivered. She picked up her pace, calling back to Katy that she'd just go to the market before they headed home. They turned left and headed across the square, past the town hall and over to the heavy black canopy that hung over the market. The air was crisp and clean as long as you steered clear of the gutters, and the autumn winds blew the wet, earthy smell of leaves through the town in little gusts, sending the signs hanging outside the shops flapping and the detritus on the cobbles swirling. As Molly and Katy stepped under the market canopy, the white daylight fell away, and the breeze started to nip at Molly's cheekbones. She dug her hands further into her muff and made her way around the stalls, picking out loaves of bread and currant cakes and lengths of ribbon, and waiting for Katy to pay and pack them into her wicker basket. She asked the woman on the fruit stall for pineapple, thinking that she rather fancied some for pudding.

'Too cold, ma'am,' the woman said, pulling her greyish shawl tightly around her shoulders. 'Can't get 'em to grow in this weather, even in greenhouses. Not properly, anyhow.' She offered Molly some dried, sugared pineapple, but Molly shook her head. She had always found the sugared kind much too sweet.

While chattering away to merchants she had known since childhood, Molly cast furtive glances around for any substance that might provide a solution to the problem growing inside her. She studied the spice stall as if trying to remember an old family recipe, but could not see anything that looked as if it might help her. As she turned and headed for home, she spied a toothless gin-peddler handing a brown glass bottle stoppered with a rag to a girl of about Molly's age. The girl walked away, pulled the rag from the bottle neck and tossed it into the gutter before taking a belt of the liquor inside. Molly knew that gin might solve her problems, but she also knew she would never be able to get hold of any without questions being asked. There had to be another way, a way that would seem innocuous to onlookers. She called Katy to her side. The maid scuffled up to walk alongside her, her basket overflowing with fruit and flowers and pies, as well as a couple of cream cakes Molly had taken a fancy to.

'I'll have a pot of chocolate in the parlour when we get back, Katy,' she said, smiling tightly. Her breath made little clouds in the air in front of her mouth, and as she walked on she could feel the wet steam on her nose and cheekbones. 'It's so terribly cold.' The maid bobbed her head, and they walked the rest of the way home in silence.

Molly's other problem was Eddie. She'd barely spoken to him since their argument after William had first driven her home. Thinking of that night as she drank her chocolate and took lunch in the parlour, she grimaced, bunching her fists in her lap and pressing them into the pit of her stomach. Eddie was still acting as her spirit guide for the séances, but Molly felt more trapped than ever when closed in the cabinet with him. She could feel him pushing out from behind the secret compartment, rigid and formal, all disapproval and wounded pride. Sighing, Molly flicked through a spiritualist periodical lying in her lap, determined to find something else she could introduce into the séance.

She would only get rid of her spirit guide if she could find a new way of thrilling her sitters. Licking frothy chocolate from her lips as she set her cup down, Molly looked again at the paper in her lap. 'Dancing Table Showcases the Power of the Spirits', said the headline above an ink drawing of a circle of sitters whirling around a table with their fingers pressed to its top. Molly thought of the polished wooden floor of the séance room. It had to be worth a try.

Eddie sat on the floor of the séance room, a grubby sheet catching the shavings he was whittling off each of the table legs.

'Not too much,' Molly said, eying the table's new, rounded feet. 'Not enough to be conspicuous; just enough to let the table move across the floor without scraping.'

Eddie looked at her, irritation in his eyes. 'I know, I know.'

Molly drew herself up straight and glared at him.

'Eddie,' she said. Then she rolled her eyes; it was useless to stand and battle with the manservant's pride when she had a far greater problem to deal with. 'When you're finished with those, give the floorboards another coat of polish, please, in time for them to be completely dry for tonight.'

Eddie tested the rounded-off edge of the table leg with his finger and scratched at a little knot in the wood.

'I'm going up to my room now,' Molly added. 'Don't disturb me unless it's absolutely necessary – and that goes for Katy, too.'

By Bonfire Night, Molly still hadn't bled. When Jenny came home that evening, she mentioned that a Guy Fawkes bonfire was to be held at Moor Park on the other side of town, and that some folks from work would be attending. Tired though she was these days, Jenny's eyes lit up with childlike enthusiasm at the thought of fireworks, and Molly quickly warmed to the idea. She might be able to get a moment with this Sally Marsden woman. Besides, Molly had enjoyed Guy Fawkes Night when she was a child, and she had fond memories of bonfires she and Florrie had gone to. She remembered the smoke stinging her eyes and her little jaw working tirelessly on the bittersweet bonfire toffee.

It was arranged over an early supper that Molly and Jenny would hire a cab and go over to the bonfire, with Eddie as chaperone (on Jenny's insistence; she was becoming very protective of her unborn child). Molly chewed a mouthful of gammon and swallowed forcefully. Nearly everything she had eaten over the past couple of days caused her mouth to flood with viscous bile, and she'd secretly brought half of it straight back up again; usually outside at the back of the house if she could get there, or else out of a window into the gutter below. She didn't want Katy asking questions when she emptied her chamber pot. As it was, surely the maid would realize soon that her mistress hadn't produced any bloodstained rags for her to wash recently. All this sickliness didn't seem to be curbing Molly's appetite, though. In fact, she was already hoping that there would be parkin at the festivities tonight.

They stepped out of the hired carriage, both of them wrapped up against the biting wind, and looked across the park to where the bonfire burned in a bright orange blaze. Dozens of townspeople milled around the fire, holding their hands out towards the flames to ward off the cold, or watching the eddying smoke and laughing like heathens. The fire seemed to be getting inside everyone, and while Eddie paid the cab driver, Molly and Jenny scampered off towards the nearest stall to buy cups of warm cider and parkin, then looked over to where Eddie was buying ale at the next stall. Taking Jenny's arm, Molly pulled her friend away through the crowds. She needed to lose Eddie for a while.

As they walked away through the trees, Molly chewing on parkin and wondering if it had always tasted like coal, a young lad yelped at them to get back. Barely a foot in front of them, a firework exploded, causing little silver sparks to rain down. Jenny pulled Molly away with one arm, shielding her belly with the other.

'There's something I have to tell you,' Molly began. The sparks from the firework fizzled away before they could touch the grass. Jenny, shivering, gestured that they should walk back towards the fire. Molly looked at the people huddled around it. None of them seemed to be paying attention to the two girls. 'I need your help—' She got no further before she lurched away from Jenny, doubling over to vomit the barely swallowed parkin on to the grass. The cake suddenly looked to her like nothing so much as a flattened dog turd. Gasping for breath, she straightened up, with Jenny's warm hands on her back and a fire burning at the back of her throat. She heard a chorus of shouts from the people clustered around the bonfire, and through the scalding tears squeezing out of the corners of her eyes, she watched as the guy was hurled into the flames. A wretched little bundle of rags, squeezed and shaped with knots of rope into something that looked vaguely like a small and deformed man, the misshapen sacrifice smouldered in the fire, until someone took a stick and pushed it into the heart of the bonfire. Jenny's eyes burned into Molly, as intent and glittering as the fire.

'What is it, Mol?' Molly was sure she already knew. She cleared her throat and spat in a rather unladylike manner to get rid of the sharp taste in her mouth.

'I think . . .' she began, before another wave of nausea broke over her and she threw up more than she even knew she had in her stomach. When she stood up again, her face was tearstained, and not just from the effort. She wiped her mouth with the back of her trembling hand, forgetting her kid gloves. 'Help me,' she tried again.

Jenny's arms were around her. 'How long?' she whispered in Molly's ear.

'Can't be long,' Molly replied, her voice sticking on a sob. 'I've only missed my course once. It was due early October.'

Jenny took hold of her friend's shoulders and held her out at arm's length, looking her up and down. She wiped a tear from Molly's pink cheek and tucked a few escaped curls behind her ears.

'William Hamilton then, I suppose?'

Molly nodded. Her face was rapidly going pale, even this close to the bonfire.

'I can't . . .' she stammered, choking on frightened tears, 'I can't . . .'

'Molly?' It was Eddie. The two girls span round to face the manservant, who was staring at Molly in the flickering firelight. *Curses*, Molly thought. *How long has he been there?*

'Molly's taken ill,' Jenny announced smoothly. 'Maybe she's had some iffy cider. I think she needs her bed.' Gratefully, Molly turned towards her friend, huddling against her shoulder so that she didn't have to meet Eddie's eye. As they left the park, the grass crunched under their feet with the beginnings of a frost. Eddie hailed a passing cab while Jenny stroked Molly's sweaty hair and murmured in her ear. The girls got into the cab first, just as a fresh flurry of fireworks shot into the sky, blowing the heavens above the park apart in a shower of light and noise. Eddie watched Molly as Jenny settled her into the seat nearest to the window, and his gaze was as icy as the weather.

Back at home, Jenny ushered Molly upstairs to bed, where they peeled off their clothes and washed their faces in the basin of water Katy had brought up. Molly wetted her lips with the water and spat into the bowl, trying to get rid of the foul taste in her mouth.

'Why didn't you say something if you thought there was a chance?' Jenny asked from the bed.

Molly climbed in beside her, shivering a little in her nightgown. Her arms were sprinkled with gooseflesh, the freckles on her face shot through with red flecks from the strain of vomiting.

'I didn't think there was.' Jenny looked at her, and Molly knew that she was remembering having the same thought herself, months before. 'Besides,' Molly added, 'I did wash . . . you know, down there.'

'Did you wash inside yourself, too?' Jenny asked. Molly's face was blank.

'How was I supposed to do that?' she squeaked incredulously.

Jenny sighed and shifted on the pillow. 'A couple of the women at work do it so they don't have any more than they can feed, but they say you have to wash inside yourself too, using a rag on a stick or something. That's where most of it goes, after all.'

Molly's head span at the thought of stuffing herself with a wet rag, especially while tender and bleeding as she had been that day. 'I used brine, though,' she said. 'That's supposed to help, isn't it?'

'No, you ninny – salt was what they used to say would help if you wanted a boy! Sally says it's cobblers, though.'

Molly was suddenly gripped by a vision of herself trapped between William Hamiltons I and II: the first owning her home and business; the second in the wings, waiting to take over. How could she have been so stupid?

'I think you were supposed to *eat* salt for a boy, though, not wash with it,' Jenny was musing.

'Let's just get to sleep,' Molly muttered. She blew out the candle on the bedside table and burrowed under the blankets. Her friend's warm arms wrapped around her, and Molly huddled closer to her, resting her forehead on Jenny's. 'Thank you,' she whispered. Jenny kissed her on the cheek and was soon asleep.

Molly lay belly-to-belly with her friend, trying to take comfort from Jenny's familiar presence and her slow, sonorous breathing. But then she felt a stirring against her stomach through the thin cotton of her nightgown: a rippling pressure pushing against her. With a little gasp of shock, she realized that it was the baby in Jenny's belly, kicking out against the barrier of its mother's flesh and into Molly's. She pulled away, repressing a shudder, and turned her back to Jenny.

9 Winter 1856

William Hamilton's carriage pulled up outside the house in Ribblesdale Place late in November. As he stepped down on to the pavement, a box of sugared almonds tucked under one arm, he was startled by a gruff voice behind him.

'Oi!'

William span around to discover a wiry, dark-haired youth. He cleared his throat. 'Yes?' he asked, his tone chilly.

'I'm Molly's . . .' Eddie hesitated, '. . . manservant.'

'Then I worry for Miss Pinner –' William emphasized Molly's formal title, as if to remind Eddie of their relative positions '– that she has such ill-mannered staff. Now, if you'll excuse me . . .'

Eddie glared at the back of the gentleman's head. His chestnut hair smelled of macassar oil, and his shaven jaw of barber's foam. The manservant rubbed his fingers together, grinding soot and soil into dark smears on his hands. 'Wait.'

William Hamilton turned to face him again. 'Make it quick then,' he sniffed. 'It is rather cold out here, in case you hadn't noticed.' He glared at Eddie's grubby shirtsleeves and pulled his coat about himself.

Eddie's face twisted into a strange expression. 'Molly has been . . . somewhat *unwell* while you have been gone . . .'

Upstairs in her bedchamber, Molly was sitting on her bed beside a pile of books taken from Florrie's room – the first time she had been in there since her aunt's death. She had retrieved every book on flowers and plants Florrie had owned, and now she sat frantically thumbing through the pages and indexes, searching for something that would halt her pregnancy. The search was proving fruitless, though; all of Florrie's botanical texts seemed to be gardening primers or dictionaries of symbolism, more suited to someone wanting to know how to grow a plant or interpret its meaning. Frustrated, Molly slammed *Garden Blooms of the English Countryside* closed, sending up a cloud of dust from the yellowing pages. Panic dropped inside her like a stone. A tap at her door made her jump, and she started to shove the books under her bedsheets before remembering that they were perfectly innocent in appearance. Katy popped her head around the door.

'Mr Hamilton in the parlour to see you, ma'am.'

Molly drew a deep, shuddering breath as the maid walked back down the landing. Everything would be fine. William could not see through the flesh of her belly to the traitorous little being that clung there. She would simply behave as any young woman would when her suitor returned from a trip away. Straightening her dress, Molly headed downstairs to the parlour.

William was standing by the fireplace waiting for her, his hat in one hand and a box tied with a red ribbon in the other.

He froze as she walked in, a dozen emotions chasing around his face.

'William?' Molly hoped she sounded suitably unsuspecting.

'Molly . . . I . . .' He had crossed the room in moments, snatching up her hands in his. He was still wearing his gloves, and the cold leather made Molly shiver. William made a little exclamation of frustration, as if he had forgotten something, and guided Molly to an armchair. He dropped down on his knees in front of her and Molly shifted under his gaze.

'I know about . . .' he gestured awkwardly towards her stomach, and her heart sank . . . 'your condition.'

Molly willed herself to speak, to deny everything, but the words stuck in her throat.

'I . . . I'm not . . . I was only sick for a while,' she tried.

'Don't upset yourself, my dear,' William was saying as he fussed with her red curls, pushing them away from her waxen face. 'It isn't good for either of you.'

A wave of tears scalded behind Molly's eyes, and she willed them not to overspill. She looked down at her skirt, avoiding William's eye.

'Oh, Molly, please don't be distressed, we'll sort everything out,' he said.

For a moment Molly's heart leaped giddily inside her. Was he going to help her get rid of it? Then he drew himself up on to one knee and she cursed herself for a fool: why on earth would he want to do that when he held her and all she owned captive?

'No one need know that this happened out of wedlock,'

William was whispering. 'If we marry soon they won't be able to tell the difference. I'll apply for the licence today.'

Her head still spinning, Molly struggled to think what licence William could possibly be talking about, until she realized with increasing nausea that he was referring to a marriage licence. The part of her mind that remained back in the tiny terrace that she and Florrie had started out in still saw the banns as the first step to marriage. She nodded weakly, and William pressed a kiss on to her hand before pulling her towards him and kissing her cheek. She watched the tip of his tongue flick out and over his lips, and she realized that her face was wet with salt tears. He gathered her into his arms and held her possessively, crushing her face into his chest as he had done that day in the Square gardens. William stood up, but gestured for Molly to stay sitting.

'I'll be back this evening,' he told her. 'Don't worry; everything is going to be just fine.'

Molly's bottom lip quivered, and she hated herself for acting every inch the moneyed young lady. She hadn't been raised to cry and swoon when things got difficult.

Remembering his gift, William handed the box of sugared almonds to her. 'Oh, I quite forgot – I brought you these.' All the confidence he had shown in the back of his carriage and in the gardens seemed to have evaporated as he toyed with his hat, passing it nervously from hand to hand. Was he afraid that she would claim he had forced her? Was that why he was so keen that they wed? Even in her panic, Molly could not begin to consider the idea. *William has always been good to me*, she thought, *and we never did anything that I wasn't happy to do.*

William patted her hand awkwardly, then turned and left without waiting for Katy to show him out. Molly sank further into her armchair, twisting her fingers into the ribbon on the box of almonds. The slippery red satin was well woven; perfectly symmetrical and smooth. Careless of the neatly brushed fabric of the chair, she pulled her feet up and huddled herself into a ball, her arms wrapped around her folded knees. Again and again she repeated William's words to herself – *everything is going to be just fine. Everything is going to be just fine.*

When Molly rang the bell for a pot of tea she was too muddled to realize that the heavy steps she could hear coming down the hallway were not Katy's. When Eddie strolled into the room, she stared at him, uncomprehending.

'I wanted Katy,' she said, confused. Eddie knew that if Molly rang, it was always the maid she needed.

'I know,' Eddie replied. He seemed to be looking straight through Molly, a smile hiding behind his lips. 'I just wondered how Mr Hamilton's visit went.'

The realization chilled Molly to the bone; then, just as quickly, she felt her face flush in fury. '*It was you*,' she muttered, her lips stiff.

'I've been watching you throwing your guts up nearly every day for two weeks,' Eddie said, his voice husky. 'I saw you with Jenny at the bonfire. I know you've been alone with that Hamilton bloke at least twice. And I ain't stupid.'

'And just what does it have to do with you?' she hissed.

Eddie grinned like a gargoyle. 'Oh, nothing. You've made

that very clear. I just wanted to do my duty by my mistress. I wouldn't want your reputation destroyed, ma'am.'

Katy's footsteps could be heard on the stairs. Molly flew out of her seat, her eyes fierce. 'I see. Then you won't be surprised that I want you out of my home right now.' She was satisfied by a shocked expression on Eddie's face, and wondered why he hadn't expected this.

'Did you think I'd be afraid that you'd talk?' she snarled. 'Do you think William Hamilton would stand for a disgraced former servant slandering his wife?'

Eddie paled. 'Wife?'

She watched the alarm spreading across his face. He would need employment, after all, and without references he would struggle. Molly found she was able to regain some of her composure.

'Yes, wife. William has asked me to marry him; what did you expect?' Scrutinizing Eddie's horrified expression, Molly suddenly understood.

'You thought he'd drop me like a hot coal, didn't you? You thought he'd deny all knowledge and you'd be able to step in and save my reputation.' A bitter taste flooded Molly's mouth, and she fought the urge to spit.

'You rang, ma'am?' Katy walked into the parlour and stopped as she took in the sight of Molly and Eddie standing rigid with anger in the middle of the room. Molly swallowed hard before turning to the maid and requesting tea. When she turned back to Eddie, her green eyes glittered. He might have delivered a heavy blow, but who would ultimately be the worse for his actions?

'Collect your things, Eddie. You can leave as soon as you

have everything.' Katy gasped and looked across at Eddie, and Molly turned on her: 'I said tea, Katy, unless there was something you wanted?'

'No, ma'am. Ever so sorry.' Katy gave a curtsy and scurried away, her head down. Eddie stalked from the room, and Molly heard his boots pounding the stairs as he ran up to his attic room in the servants' quarters to gather his belongings. Molly's gaze darted around the silent parlour, like a trapped animal looking for a way out.

Eddie left the house barely ten minutes later. Molly heard the front door slam and watched from the window as her former manservant, former friend and former lover stomped down the road with a small brown pack on his back that must have contained all his worldly possessions. Eddie looked lost, which, she supposed, he probably was. None of his family were alive, as far as Molly was aware. But a bitter surge of anger soon drowned any regrets: thanks to Eddie Rathbone's spite, she had been found out and would almost certainly be trapped into marriage.

I am betrothed to William Hamilton, Molly said silently to herself. It was inevitable now; she might as well get used to it. *I am to marry a man with a chain of cotton mills and a carriage. I may be able to stay in my house. I may be able to continue as a spirit medium.* She pressed her face into her hands, digging her wrists into her eye sockets and rubbing at tears that had long since dried. *I shall have to ask my husband if I may*, she added bitterly. *Mrs W. Hamilton; Molly Hamilton; Molly Hamilton, Spirit Medium.* Her inner voice grew tiny and weak. *I'm so sorry, Aunt Florrie*, came the silent whisper. *I lost it all.*

William was as good as his word, returning early that evening having applied for the marriage licence. Molly was curled up on her bed when Katy tapped at her door with water to wash before supper. She sat up and waved Katy away, brushing the creases out of her skirt. She felt as if she had swallowed a cannonball: a round, leaden weight in her stomach that held her down and slowed her movement. She dragged herself over to her dressing mirror to neaten herself up; it was nearly time for supper, and she supposed that William might as well stay, although she flinched at the idea of her betrothed and her best friend – his employee – sitting down to a meal together.

Molly refastened the clip that held her hair off her face, and pulled a few tight curls loose so they framed her forehead. She splashed her cheeks with cool water and patted them dry. Taking one last look at the ghost girl in the mirror, Molly straightened the brooch Florrie had given her – *A Heart Ignorant of Love* – and left her bedchamber in a swirl of pink.

Downstairs in the parlour, William was waiting for her. He greeted Molly formally with a stiff kiss on the cheek, and Molly found herself missing the passionate William Hamilton she had known before. It was bad enough that Eddie's meddling had pushed her into an unwanted marriage, but the thought of marrying this new William appalled her. She reached out a finger to smooth the rich brown hair around his face, but William caught her hand in his and held it loosely at his side. Forcing a cheerful tone, Molly asked if he would like to stay for supper. He accepted, and Katy scuttled away.

As soon as the maid had left, and the parlour door swung to behind her, William hooked an arm around Molly's waist and pulled her into him. She accepted his kiss with a dizzying feeling of relief, and felt her legs quiver underneath her.

'It occurred to me that I'd hardly touched you since I found out about the baby this morning,' he whispered in her ear.

Molly bristled at the mention of her pregnancy, and felt the old panic swallow her desire.

'I don't want you to think that I'm angry with you,' William continued. He pulled Molly's sulky chin up with a finger, and his brown eyes burned into hers, his pupils large and dark. 'I couldn't be more pleased.'

Molly bit her tongue. Of course he was pleased. They'd shared their pleasure in the gardens, but only he would continue to gain: a wife, a child, a house . . . and Florrie's business.

William fumbled in his coat pocket and retrieved a tiny black velvet-covered box. Snapping it open, he drew out a small, delicate gold ring, and Molly found herself curling and uncurling her naked fingers. William took hold of her left hand and slipped the betrothal ring on to her finger and Molly felt the gold band tighten. Her hands felt hot and dry. She made a show of holding her hand out in front of her face to inspect her new ring, and saw a little emerald set in the centre, winking mischievously in the gaslight. A playful stone, a passionate stone, a stone of wickedness and desire. Surprised, she turned open-mouthed to her fiancé, who smiled his crooked smile back at her.

'I looked at the usual rings, the proper ones.' His voice was low. 'But none of them reminded me of you. And then I spied this amongst the rubies and diamonds, and all I could think of was our walk, that day in the gardens.'

Molly couldn't help but smile finally to see the devilish smirk she knew. She looked again at the glittering green gem. It was a beautiful ring, but it weighed heavy on her hand, dainty though it was. Her fingers felt awkward and clumsy.

'You made the right choice,' she whispered. William was standing very close to her, and his breath was hot on her jaw. She looked up and faced him; his mouth was not even an inch from her own. The house was quiet, save for the distant sounds of Katy clattering pots and pans in the kitchen downstairs. Molly snuffled delicately at the warm, thick scent of him; she could almost taste it, musky on the back of her tongue. William moved his face closer to her, and she could feel his every breath tickling her lips as they brushed against his.

She thought of their hasty coupling in the gardens, and the rough pushing of his body against hers, pressing her breath out as she was backed against the bark of the tree. She thought of the shuddering deep in the pit of her belly, and of the trickles of blood. She imagined the child forming inside her: a reddish clump of meat and bone taking shape, and how it would be shaken if William were to grab hold of her now and consummate their betrothal as she knew he wanted to. Some sixth sense in her could feel his hardness gathering in his breeches, and his fingers itching to grab hold of her, to pinch and knead her, to let his hands fill with her body. She nuzzled her face against William's, letting him catch the perfume of her face cream. Sliding her body close to his, she pressed the curves of her breast and hip against him. Molly remembered mutterings about women who lay with their husbands while they were expecting, only to have the child shaken loose from their womb and lost. If William were to push her down on the sofa now, would he shake her hard enough to lose this one? Would she feel it loosening its grip, feel its weight dropping down through her body? Molly let her eyelids flutter and close as she felt William's hands tighten on her waist.

'No, Molly . . . I mustn't.'

Her eyes flew open, incredulous. 'William?' His lips were still brushing against hers; he was still clutching possessively at her, but he lowered his gaze and would not look at her.

'This is all I thought about while I was away,' he was muttering. 'I fully planned to come back and find time for us to be alone together. But I can't make demands on you now, not while you're carrying my child in your body.'

'But you're not making demands!' Molly forgot the last traces of her pretence of maidenly virtue. 'Don't you think I thought about you while you were away? That I lay awake at night . . .?' She let her voice trail off, allowing William to imagine her in her nightgown, craving and feverish. She felt his fingers on her waist instinctively slip down to hold her around her hips, ready to grind her body against his.

'But still, I wouldn't want . . .' he began.

Molly bit her lip delicately and looked up at him as if she

would pull him towards her with her gaze alone; as if he would fall down on her like a man caught in a whirling current. 'It's felt so long since you left,' she murmured in his ear. 'I've missed your touch.'

With a furious gasp, William grabbed hold of Molly and held her tightly. She clawed at the buttons on his breeches, tugging awkwardly at them. He had grabbed a handful of her skirts, and she could hear him groaning deep in his throat as she struggled with his breeches. Finally she had him undone, and impetuously put her hand on him, squeezing and gripping the unfamiliar organ. She swallowed down a little shriek of excitement as William pressed her to him, snatching her hand away from his breeches and pushing himself up under her petticoats, pulling her drawers aside. She felt him brush against her, hovering just outside, barely entering her. A deliciously bittersweet ache pulsed down through Molly's body, and she heard herself cry out in desperate delight.

That was all it took. William seemed to snap out of his reverie instantly, his face a picture of shock and concern.

'Did I hurt you?' he asked, trembling with frustrated lust.

Molly felt as if she would weep. 'No!' she cried. 'It was pleasure, not pain. Here, let me touch you . . .'

But William stepped back, fastening his breeches and straightening his waistcoat. 'I'm sorry, Molly. For a moment I was so transported that I forgot the delicacy of your condition.'

'I don't feel in the least delicate!' Molly protested. 'Please . . .'

Having tucked himself safely away, William laid a shaking hand on her shoulder and gently pecked the tip of her nose. 'It isn't worth the risk, my dear,' he replied, brushing her skirts down with the back of his hand. 'There's too much at stake.'

Molly tasted suspicion, like poison, in her mouth. 'Well, we are both business people,' she said icily. 'We know when not to take a risk.' She wondered if William had considered what they had risked that autumn day when they took their walk together.

'Yes, you're a sensible girl,' he replied, squeezing her hot little hand with his trembling fingers. 'You've certainly kept this place going well since you lost your aunt. So the spiritualism business must bring in plenty to keep you, then?'

At that moment, Katy appeared. Supper was ready.

'After you,' William said cordially. Molly smiled prettily and led the way, but once her back was turned to William, she felt her face harden like slate.

10

Two weeks later, Molly lay in the bathtub in her dimly lit bedchamber. It was late in the evening and the December winds shrieked off the glass of the windows and speckled them with rain. The bathwater, which Molly had instructed Katy to make as hot as she could bear, was getting cold, but Molly sat there letting the chill spread through her. A coating of gooseflesh started to break out over her arms as she trailed her fingertips through water made cloudy by her flower-scented soap.

Jenny would be walking home by now. Molly thought of her heavily pregnant friend trudging through the rain, with her head down and her eyes darting from side to side, looking for danger in the darkness. Molly twisted her betrothal ring round and round on her finger. A droplet of water landed on the emerald and glimmered and undulated in the gaslight. She let her hands sink under the cool water and rest on her belly, which was starting to push itself out into a hard little bump. She pressed her hands down, but that only brought an alarming discomfort, deep and low in her body, as it had the many times she had tried it before.

Angry red stripes lined her torso where the bones of her

corset had been digging into her. Katy knew that Molly was betrothed to Mr Hamilton, but Jenny was the only person in the house, other than Molly, who knew why, and so Molly had been sure to force any discomfort from her face each morning as her maid laced her. Now, as she finally climbed out of the bath, patted herself dry on the sheet Katy had left, and snatched up her nightgown, Molly felt the familiar ache deep in her breasts. She dropped the nightgown down over her head and looked across at her reflection in the dressing mirror. The loose white cotton flowed over her body, hiding her new shape, and for a moment Molly let herself forget about the pregnancy, and think about William's carefree smile when he had dropped by for tea that afternoon to bring her up to date with his marriage preparations.

'The licence is in hand,' he had said between sandwiches, 'and my solicitor assures me that we hardly need a marriage contract at all, given that you have no family to give you away. The house and the business will automatically be taken as your dowry.'

Molly had swallowed hard, and William squeezed her hand.

'I do hope you're not feeling too delicate,' he said in a muted tone. 'You're strong and healthy, and I'm sure it will pass in time. You'll be blooming soon enough.'

Molly pushed away her plate. 'William?' she asked, trying to stop her voice shaking.

'Yes?' He was looking at her left hand again, and Molly wondered why he admired the emerald ring every few minutes.

'I have a request, if it would be . . . acceptable for you?'

She forced her voice to sound light and merry, as she imagined was appropriate for a bride-to-be. 'As you know, my background is a rather mean one, and there's rather a difference in station between myself and my oldest friend from my girlhood . . .'

William was looking thoroughly perplexed. Molly had planned for him to meet Jenny before now, but her friend had excused herself from taking supper with them on the day of Molly and William's engagement.

'The strange thing of it is, well, my friend is an employee at your Preston mill.' Molly fancied that she could see William trying not to look confused at the prospect of his fiancée's closest friend being one of the shabby little brown-clad drabs that scuttled like mice around the machinery in his mill. Still, she pressed on.

'She's pr— expecting a happy event also,' she finished delicately.

'Oh.' William blinked. 'I see. Really?'

'We've been like sisters since childhood,' Molly added, hoping that another reminder of her background would ease things.

'I understand.'

Molly doubted that, but smiled regardless as he continued.

'Well, I'm sure it will be very nice for you not to be alone in this, but why on earth are you telling me?'

'Because it is in your power to allow Jenny – my friend, that is – to remain at home until her child is born. I worry about her, she's eight months gone and still bleaching cloth . . . I just don't think it can be good for her, or the baby.'

Molly looked up at William from under her eyelashes. 'She's got no one else.' At this, she saw William's eyebrows rise, and she knew he must be wondering about the baby's father. Molly was regretting having started such a conversation with a man who seemed so confused by any forbidden passion other than his own. She took his hand in hers, squeezing his fingers.

'Could you spare her?'

William let out a lengthy sigh, and gripped Molly's hand so tightly she had to suppress a squeak. 'I suppose so. She can do some things around here while she's at home; earn her keep and all that.'

Molly's face fell in shock, but then she remembered. This house was as good as William's now. Jenny could only stay with William's permission, whether she was working or not, and anything he granted Molly now would be considered a favour, a mark of the benevolent husband. She decided not to argue; it was as well to get into the habit.

'Oh, she will. She helps me with my business.'

William nodded, and turned the conversation back to the subject of setting a date for the wedding. Molly glanced around the deserted parlour, listening to the clatterings downstairs where Katy was working in the kitchen. If she could play the part of the grateful fiancée effectively, she might be able to kill two birds with one stone.

'Thank you,' she murmured, dropping her voice into her throat as she did during the séances. Her medium's voice was almost a purr. 'You're so good to me, William.' Molly drew her hand away from his and slid it slowly under the white lace tablecloth. She chased her fingers down the front of his breeches, trying to keep a triumphant smile from her face as she heard his shuddering breath. As her fingers closed tightly around him, William groaned and threw his head back. Still he did not reach for her. Molly gently squeezed him, sliding her hand up and down before reaching down with her left hand and gently rolling the emerald up and down his organ until he gasped quietly. Still he did not lay a hand on her.

Molly drew herself closer to him, letting her hot breath flow against his neck. William's eyes were closed, and a strained expression was building on his face. Molly felt herself aching for him; her body crying out for his touch. Her hand moved under the veil of the tablecloth as William writhed in her grasp. When it all became too much to bear, she snatched one of his hands up in hers and pressed it between her legs, the firm tips of his fingers sending jolts of ecstasy through her petticoats.

In that moment, William let loose a strangled cry and Molly felt a slippery dampness in her palm. He sank back into his chair, breathing heavily. She felt him growing soft, and he opened his eyes with a satisfied sigh.

'You're quite welcome,' he croaked.

Molly forced a smile and William changed the subject again, while she pressed herself as hard as she could into her seat, in a frantic attempt to take away the frustrated throbbing.

By the time Jenny came in, Molly had dozed off. She was woken by the creaking floorboards under her friend's feet.

'Sorry,' Jenny whispered in the fading light of the bedside candle.

Molly propped herself up on one elbow. Strands of hair tangled around her face, her curls like Medusa's tresses. 'It's fine. Do you want me to ring for your supper? You must be starving.'

Jenny shook her head. 'I'm too tired to eat. I just want to sleep.'

'Still,' Molly protested, 'it can't be good for you to go to bed on an empty belly again.' She briefly considered suggesting that Jenny take supper with herself and William soon, but decided against it for now.

'Not much emptiness in my belly, Mol,' Jenny groaned. 'Honestly, I just need to rest. That bloody mill's killing me.'

'Then I have some news for you.' Molly wasn't entirely sure how Jenny would react to the favour she had requested on her behalf, but she had no intention of seeing her friend continue to grow so gaunt. Her arms and legs were bony; apart from her belly, Jenny seemed to be wasting away.

'I spoke to William this afternoon,' Molly said carefully, 'and told him that I need your company now more than ever. I think he likes to be reminded of my condition,' she added sulkily.

Jenny nodded.

'. . . and he agreed that you can stay at home until your baby is born. So you don't need to wear yourself out.'

'And my job's still there when I go back?' Jenny asked warily.

''Course it is, silly! I wouldn't get you sacked as a favour, would I?'

Jenny smiled weakly. 'No. No, 'course you wouldn't.

I just don't want to stay here on . . .' She hesitated. 'On his charity.'

'You wouldn't be, you'd still be helping me with the séances.' As soon as the words had left her lips, Molly regretted them, but Jenny didn't fly into a rage.

'Oh. Yes. Well, it's less tiring than working for him at the mill, I suppose. And I'll need my strength come January.'

Molly tried to ignore the suggestion that the spiritualism business was now a part of William's small business empire. 'True.' She tried a laugh. 'Still, rather you than me when that time comes!'

Jenny's smile was strange. 'You've got your own time to come now, Mol,' she whispered quietly, turning to face her friend as they lay side by side on the pillow.

That night, Molly did not sleep for a long time.

On Thursday afternoon, she was sitting in the parlour with half her mind on that evening's séance and the other half on the drawings of wedding gowns being shown to her by Gretchen Houldsworth. William had come round for supper the previous evening and announced that the wedding was all arranged for the 21st at the parish church. It would be a small affair, given that neither bride nor groom had any close kin living. Molly had been planning on wearing one of her better dresses for the occasion, but William had laughed and assured her that he would buy a proper wedding gown. Molly had smiled her spirit medium's smile and deliberately avoided looking at Jenny, who had not spoken since William had arrived, except to whisper awkward thanks for her freedom from the mill.

'. . . and this one has a lower collar. It'd look well on a young thing like you, and we could do it in this lovely cream silk we got in just yesterday,' Gretchen was saying. 'I think it'd suit you better than a white dress, Molly.'

'Pardon?' Molly was instantly alert, hoping that she wasn't blushing.

Gretchen hardly seemed to have noticed. 'With your colouring. Pure white might make you look a bit washed out. The cream'll bring out your hair better.'

'Oh . . . yes. Yes, that one will be fine,' Molly said, snatching a cursory look at the dress sketches before Gretchen bundled them away in her bag.

'A good choice, I think. God, Mol, I can hardly believe that you're marrying a gentleman!'

'He's not exactly a gentleman,' Molly murmured. 'He's a businessman.'

'And how far have you come to be seeing much of a difference?' Gretchen said. 'It's more than any of the girls you grew up with'll ever manage. Caroline nearly went green when I told her. Of course, she's still waiting to find herself a young man, but still . . .' The dressmaker smiled and patted Molly's hand. 'I'm sure your Aunt Florrie would be happy to see how you've landed on your feet.'

Molly tried not to think of what Florrie would have said about her betrothal, and kept her false smile on her face until Gretchen had hurried off to her next appointment.

William was certainly keen to start planning for his move into the house in Ribblesdale Place. In the weeks leading up to the wedding, he hired men to bring over everything he could live without until Molly and he were married, including his many boxes of books and papers, and a wooden desk that Molly admired the moment she laid eyes on it. In thick, heavy oak and varnished to a glossy sheen, it seemed so much more honest than the spindly furniture that Florrie had insisted on buying for the new house. William had instructed the men to deposit his possessions in Molly's bedchamber, and when Molly turned to him with an alarmed expression, he met her gaze calmly.

'Well, it isn't the master bedroom, is it, Molly?' he said. 'I know it must be an inconvenience to you now, but you won't be sleeping in your girlhood room much longer.' His gaze was heavy on Molly's face, and she trembled as he slipped one unseen hand on to the small of her back.

'I'll be needing to set up an office in the smaller room,' he continued, his fingertips leaving imprints of heat on Molly's back as he dropped his voice to a whisper. 'Of course, we'll need to plan another room in a few months' time.' Then he hopped, carefree, into his carriage and left Molly ducking out of the way of the team of hired men heaving William's furniture into her house.

After the men had left, Molly stood in her absurdly cluttered bedchamber, stroking the smooth top of the desk, reminded of the seemingly sturdy cabinet in the séance room. She shivered with delight at a thought that drifted unbidden into her mind like one of her veiled ghosts, a fantasy to replace that of her and Eddie in the séance cabinet. She trailed her fingers across the desk, inhaling the hints of William's tobacco and the soapy smell of his skin ingrained in the wooden surface, and toyed with the idea of her body being crushed between William and the hard wood.

Smiling slyly to herself, she slid into the upholstered chair, running her hands along the strong arms as she lowered herself into their grasp. She reached out to the drawer in the desk and idly pulled it open. Nothing but a pot of ink and several tatty pens. Molly picked up the cleanest one and rolled it down the back of her hand. Every sensation seemed heightened by her frustrated lust. The more William denied her, while desire burned in his eyes, the more Molly found herself cursing her pregnancy.

She and William were formally betrothed, making her as good as his wife already. He had never said as much, but Molly's suspicious sixth sense was leading her to wonder if the house she lived in was William's property even now. He had already arranged all the legal matters regarding the marriage, of course.

She dug her fingernail into a little knot hole in the bottom of the desk drawer, her face twisted in concentration. There was nothing she could do: even if she were to break their betrothal now, the fines William could claim for the inconvenience might well strip her of the house and the accoutrements essential to her spiritualism business. Besides, her reputation would not survive a broken engagement. Molly rattled the desk drawer in a fit of rage. She would be William's wife, and all she could do to observe her aunt's dying wish was to keep her new husband sweet and hope that, in practice, if not in law, he would allow her to keep control of her family business.

At least she desired William and was fond of him in some

way, as she suspected he was of her. Molly couldn't exactly claim to love him, but she had always felt a connection to him, beginning back in the Meadowcrofts' drawing room, when the bright-eyed stranger had gazed at her as if she alone in the crowded room could hear his silent, and slightly ribald, compliments. Inwardly, though, she cursed herself for the pleasure she took in a match which she knew Florrie would disapprove of. Nor could she come to terms with the child growing inside her. If she and William could have remained childless, she might have enjoyed the pleasures of marriage. With a young Hamilton in the nursery that would be out of the question.

Suddenly, Molly noticed something that she had been missing completely, what with the aches in her body and the thoughts that had been needling her. The bottom of the desk drawer rattled with a hollow sound as she scratched at the knot hole, and when she tapped on the wood, she could hear the echoing of an empty space. She laughed at her own ignorance – how could she have missed it? Hooking her nail into the tiny hole, carved and stained, she now saw, to look like a knot in the wood, Molly pulled at the bottom of the desk drawer until it came away in her hand. In the compartment underneath lay a sheaf of papers: deeds to each of William's mills, proudly printed with the 'Hamilton Cotton' heading. There was also a bunch of keys (William's master keys to each mill, no doubt) and a small, velvet-covered box, identical to the one which had contained Molly's emerald betrothal ring.

She picked up the box. Her face was grim, her hand did not tremble. She snapped the box open and saw the two plain gold bands – one small and dainty, the other large and thick. Molly sat in silence, listening to Katy's mouselike scratchings from the kitchen and Jenny moving about in the parlour below, before dropping the box back into the drawer.

On the morning before her wedding day, Molly sat in the parlour with Jenny, sharing a pot of tea. Molly's fingers tested the warm, smooth surface of her cup over and over again, and she stared out of the window, standing and pushing the delicate lace curtain back with one pale hand. A light dusting of snow had spread on the cobbles in the street below, and the road was busier than ever, with grocers' delivery carts carrying Christmas fare.

'Did I tell you that William wants us to be away for Christmas?' she asked Jenny.

Jenny pressed a hand on her swollen bump, wincing at a particularly strong kick. 'You did,' she replied. 'But why in God's name does he want to be at the seaside in the middle of December?'

Molly couldn't stop herself grinning, and rolled her eyes slightly. 'I don't think he's ever been to Southport in winter. I don't think the fact it'll be bloody freezing has occurred to him. He just thinks it'll be nice for us to spend our first Christmas alone together.'

'Oh aye?' Jenny's grin was mischievous, but Molly exhaled gloomily.

'I doubt it's for that reason. He's terrified of doing something to the baby.' She tutted, irritated, and Jenny looked at her, her expression indecipherable.

'Anyway,' Molly said, by way of changing the subject,

'what are you going to do with yourself, then?' She looked at her friend, and a lump started to form in her throat. For as long as Molly could remember, she had seen Jenny every year on Christmas Day. Back in Ashgate Lane, the girls used to meet up after dinner – which, to all but the poorest families, was usually roast chicken and bacon – and exchange little presents or slices of fruit cake. Christmas back then smelled of slightly burned food, prepared by people who were not used to cooking so much meat.

'I'll have a bit of dinner with Katy,' Jenny replied. 'There's bound to be food that needs using up while you're away.'

Molly nodded vigorously. 'Yes, take whatever you like.' She hoped that Jenny would find the goose, which she had bought before she knew about her extended honeymoon.

'Is Gretchen bringing your dress today?' Jenny asked, swallowing a mouthful of tea.

Molly nodded. 'So I've got my something new, and the corset I'm planning on wearing has been worn once or twice, so that'll do for something old.'

'Have you got something blue?' Jenny asked.

'Yes, Gretchen said she'd bring some garters with blue ribbon woven through them. She's got the wedding list on the brain, I think.'

'Well then,' Jenny said, fumbling in the pocket of her woollen winter dress, 'take this.' She flipped a coin over to Molly, who caught it in one hand. It was a silver sixpence.

'Where did you get this?' Molly asked.

'It was the sixpence my ma had in her shoe the day she got married. She gave it to me before she died. So I could carry it at my wedding.' Jenny smiled ironically.

'But I can't take this, you've got the baby on the way!'

'I know – I ain't giving you money, missus!' Jenny batted Molly's arm playfully, and for a moment the two girls smiled at each other in the carefree way they used to before money had come between them. 'It'll do for something borrowed, too. I don't know if there's anything in it, but I don't want you to end up like I did. Best try for all the luck you can get on your wedding day.'

Molly took Jenny's hand and squeezed her fingers. The silver coin was clammy between their palms. In the distance, the bells of the church on Fishergate clanged portentously.

'Thank you,' Molly whispered.

11 Christmas Week 1856

The following morning, the morning of her wedding, began early for Molly, when Katy bustled into the room to draw the curtains and set out a tray of tea for the bride-to-be. Jenny, who had been getting used to sleeping late, grumbled under the covers beside Molly as the white December sunshine streamed in through the window. Molly hauled herself into a sitting position, tugging at her long nightdress, which had tangled around her ankles. She had spent her last night as a single woman curled up with her childhood friend, whispering into the blackest hours. This morning would be the last on which she would awake in this room. Molly suppressed a shiver at the thought of sharing a marital bed with William in her dead aunt's old bedchamber.

'Mrs Houldsworth will be round shortly to dress you, ma'am,' Katy was saying as she scurried around the room, getting all her usual duties done so that she could prepare the house for the wedding breakfast while everyone else was at the church. 'I brought you a little toast so you won't feel faint before you get back and have your proper breakfast.'

'Thank you, Katy.' Molly smiled nervously. The maid had become much more capable in the past few months, she had to admit. Molly took a bite of the buttered toast, but she could barely swallow. She chewed her mouthful laboriously, wishing Katy would leave so she could throw up in the window box on her sill.

Gretchen Houldsworth arrived at half past nine, and Katy was excused so that she could prepare the dining room. As Gretchen and Caroline tugged at the laces of her corset, Molly stood silently and hoped they would not notice her swelling belly. The fewer people to know about this pregnancy, the easier it would be. Not that a pregnant bride would come as a surprise to Gretchen. Jenny sat in the corner in a buttery-yellow gown borrowed from Gretchen's shop, the only presentable dress she could fit into. She tried on each of Molly's pairs of boots in turn, squeezing her swollen ankles into the tight leather, never looking up to notice how tightly Molly was allowing her dressers to lace her.

Once Molly had been dressed in her underthings, Gretchen and Caroline held out the wedding gown for her to step into. She toyed with the lacy cuffs on her sleeves as the dressmaker's quick fingers fastened the tiny buttons running down the front of the gown. Caroline shook out the skirts of the dress and smoothed them down over the petticoats, and Molly stared, bewildered, at the elegant, princess-like bride being pieced together in her mirror. With the soft, creamy silk flowing over her tightly laced figure and the veil tumbling over her face, Molly looked ethereal and otherworldly, as if she would float across the floor rather than taking steps like a mortal woman. She stepped into a pair of white heeled boots as Gretchen and Caroline held her skirts out of the way.

Molly teetered awkwardly on the extra inches the boots lent her, while the dressmaker and her daughter laced them up. These were the highest boots she had ever worn; had they been a couple of inches higher, they would have put her on a level with William. She tried a few steps, swaying precariously.

'Take little steps,' Gretchen advised. 'They're not easy to walk in if you're not used to boots this high, but they make the gown look particularly elegant. You won't be walking far in them, anyway.'

Molly held her head high and tried walking in a straight line, in a suitably dignified manner, in preparation for her walk down the aisle.

William's carriage arrived at ten o'clock to collect Molly and Jenny. William himself would already be at the church. As Molly stepped carefully into the carriage, holding her gown clear of the slushy snow melting in the gutter, marriage to William suddenly seemed alarmingly real. All her mental preparations of the past few weeks paled as, in the bright light of this winter morning, Molly realized that before midday she would be a married woman. Ashton shut the carriage door with a bang, and Molly jumped. Jenny pulled a hand from the fur muff she had borrowed from Molly, and gently arranged the curls tumbling around her friend's face.

'How are you feeling, Mol?' she whispered. 'Not sickly, are you?'

Molly shook her head, gripping her bouquet of bridal roses tightly, and bit her lips to stop them trembling. Her face was even paler than usual, and her freckles stood out like a dusting of cinnamon on a bowl of cream.

They pulled up outside the parish church and Molly and Jenny were handed down from the carriage by Ashton. The wind blew in icy gusts, sending a light snowfall spinning around and down to the cobbles beneath their feet. They stepped cautiously up the church path towards the heavy wooden door and slipped quietly inside.

Though forbidding in appearance from the outside, St John's was spacious and neatly laid out internally, having been refurbished just a couple of years previously. It was well lit by the large, ornate windows, and rows of empty pews lined the aisle, flanked by great stone pillars. Molly gazed up at one of them now, her eyes trailing up to the arches of the roof. Jenny smoothed Molly's dress as she had watched Caroline do, and wiped a few snowflakes from her friend's hair. She quickly kissed Molly's cold cheek, took the white fur-lined cape from her shoulders, and pulled the veil down over her face before walking into the main body of the church to take her place for the ceremony. Molly squared her shoulders and stepped out into the aisle, walking alone towards her future husband, who stood at the front of the church with the vicar and a man Molly had never seen before. She assumed he must be William's best man. Jenny's silver sixpence chafed the soft skin on the sole of her foot: Molly tried not to wince as she approached the three men.

The ceremony was over quickly; there were no hymns and nobody to give Molly away. The couple stood at the altar before a great stained-glass window depicting the Crucifixion, their vows echoing around the cold church and bouncing off the stone walls. Molly pledged herself to William in a tremulous whisper from beneath her veil; nothing like the persuasive, lilting tones she used in the séance room. She sounded every bit the frightened orphan and, part blinded by her veil, she couldn't even look at Jenny. William's tone was confident and assured as he took Molly to be his wife, and his grip on her hand was firm as he slid the wedding ring on to her finger. She took William's gold band and set it on his hand in a trance.

'I now pronounce you man and wife,' the vicar intoned. Molly didn't recall ever having met him.

'You may kiss the bride,' he informed William dourly, as if he were advising him of the sum total of a debt accrued over many years. William lifted Molly's veil without any hesitation, and pushed his face into hers. His kiss was measured: just strong enough to look sincere, but nothing to suggest to the sour-faced clergyman that the gentleman in front of him had ever pushed his pale, delicate-looking bride up against a tree in a public garden, or released himself into her palm in a sunny parlour. When he pulled back from Molly he beamed in her face, and Molly gave a shy smile that she supposed would look appropriate on the maidenly girl she was playing this morning. The vicar looked upon the newly-wed Hamiltons as if he were not entirely pleased with the work he had done. Molly wondered if William were as unobservant a Christian as she, or if the vicar had perhaps heard of her ungodly line of work. Then they were called into the vestry to sign the marriage register, and Molly signed herself as Molly Pinner for the last time (and earned another hard look from the vicar when forced to give her father's name and occupation as *Unknown*).

Molly and William walked out of the church behind Jenny and the blank-faced best man, and Molly took William's proffered arm as she stepped on to the crunchy snow in her new boots. Suddenly she was engulfed in a fierce hug from her left side, and she jumped, suppressing a little shriek, and nearly slipped on the snow. In an instant, William had caught her under the elbow and set her on her feet again, and Molly turned to see Jenny, her arms flung around her shoulders and a smile frozen on her face. William glared across at her.

'What the hell are you playing at?' he hissed, before remembering he was in the grounds of a church.

'I – I was only congratulating Molly, Mr Hamilton,' Jenny stammered.

William's eyes rolled. 'And a fine thing it would be if your congratulations caused Molly to slip and hurt herself!' His voice was so low now that only the three of them could hear it. His best man and Ashton stood by William's carriage at the gate, trying not to stare at the scene erupting in front of the church.

'I take it you are aware that Molly should be treated carefully,' William was saying in withering tones. He glanced at Jenny's rounded shape as if he pitied the babe whose mother took such risks. 'Please be a little more careful with my wife in future.'

Only Molly could see how hard Jenny was trying not to cry.

'I'm fine, William,' she said soothingly. 'It was the snow

underfoot, not Jenny's fault at all. She knows how to look after me, I assure you.' She slid Jenny a discreet, comforting smile. William tossed his head.

'Very well,' he said. 'Come along, Molly, I don't want you getting chilled.'

Back at the house, Katy had cleaned until the place was spick and span, lit all the fires against the snowy chill in the air, and prepared the dining room for the formal breakfast. It occurred to Molly that Katy had not only mastered all her own tasks around the house, but Eddie's too. Molly's stomach rumbled at the smell of freshly baked bread. Katy appeared in the hallway in her best dress and curtsied to the wedding party, and Molly found herself being pulled forward on William's arm. Silently, she reminded herself once again that William was the head of the household now.

The wedding breakfast was a plentiful meal of bread, cheese and ham. Jenny sat opposite her, while William and his best man (Robert Thorpe, a businessman of William's acquaintance) took the head and foot of the table. Throughout the meal, the men talked of business and some of the regulars at their gentlemen's clubs, ignoring Molly and Jenny for much of the time. Molly wolfed down as much as she could, while sneaking glimpses of William, trying to determine whether or not her table manners were suitably ladylike. When she finally began to feel full, she took an extra roll of bread and ham and bit into it a few times so that she was able to leave food on her plate and declare that she couldn't eat another thing. She felt the fatty taste of ham rising in her throat again and swallowed hard, praying that she wouldn't be sick. She had no quick way of excusing herself in the middle of her own wedding breakfast. Molly slid Jenny a rueful smile and grimaced in an attempt to relay her rising nausea to her friend. But Jenny's eyes had been fixed on her plate throughout the entire meal and she remained silent and unresponsive.

After the breakfast, Molly changed into a travelling dress for the trip to Southport. Once the men had talked among themselves – about the cost of labour in the workplace and home, and how treacherous the roads were likely to be for the journey to Southport in this weather – William checked his pocketwatch and exclaimed at the time.

'We had best be leaving, Molly,' he announced, 'if we want to be in our lodgings by nightfall.' Molly rang for Katy to fetch her luggage, which was waiting in her old bedchamber. Jenny slipped out of the drawing room and followed Katy upstairs.

Draining the last of their drinks, William and Robert Thorpe exchanged juddering handshakes, Thorpe smiling slyly at William and stealing such lecherous glances at Molly that she almost pulled a face at him. Then Katy rattled downstairs with the last of the cases, and Molly, William and Robert Thorpe (Jenny was still nowhere to be seen) followed the maid out into the hall.

Outside, Ashton was loading Molly's cases into the box on the back of the carriage. William's were already safely strapped in and secured. William and Robert exchanged a final handshake and Molly was swept outside on her husband's arm, huddling into her warmest shawl. She looked back over her shoulder to see if Jenny was in the doorway, but only Katy stood there now, quiet and respectable in a manner that Molly knew would please William. No waving or throwing of shoes. Ashton held the carriage door open for Molly and she stepped inside, stealing a glance up at the window of her old room. Jenny's face peered from behind the gauzy curtain and Molly held her gaze for as long as she could before disappearing into the carriage, with William following.

William slung a careless arm around her waist and Molly felt a warm flush rise as she remembered the first time they had ridden in the carriage together. She put her feet up on the hot brick Ashton had set on the floor, and wrapped herself in the blanket that had been left for her.

'Comfortable, my dear?' William asked. Molly nodded and felt his arm tighten around her waist, the tips of his fingers pointing down to curve over her belly. Looking into his dark eyes, Molly sensed the restraint in his hesitant caresses. As the carriage jolted over the uneven, slippery roads, Molly felt another surge of ham-scented breath in the back of her throat, and she willed away the queasy sensation. William's hand on her belly moved slightly with the rocking of the carriage, and Molly remembered the job she still had to do.

The light was failing as the Hamilton carriage trotted along the coastal road into Southport. Molly lifted her head from William's shoulder where she had been dozing, and looked out of the window and across to where the grey sea rolled like a giant in a restless sleep. A few lonely gulls whirled above the wind-tossed tide, occasionally plunging down and snatching fish from the waves. The ocean winds buffeted the carriage as if they would blow it over, and Molly heard the clicking of the horse's hooves slowing as Ashton reined her in for this last, dangerous leg of the journey.

William stirred beside Molly. 'We should get to the guest-house by suppertime,' he said, rubbing his eyes in the dim light. 'We can explore and do a little shopping tomorrow.' He drew Molly closer to him, and she knew he was contemplating the notion of a chaste wedding night with as little enthusiasm as she; perhaps he was even trying to convince himself that to caress her a little would not be so very bad for the growing heir. Molly looked up at him, her eyes wide and sparkling. If she knew William at all, she knew that his sense of propriety could not hold out against his sensualist's craving for indulgence for long. William gathered her closer to him until he had pulled her up on to his lap. She sat lightly, allowing the rocking of the carriage to press her body tantalizingly into William's.

As the carriage wound its way into Southport, through streets with large, well-lit shops and ornately carved arches, William drew Molly's copper curls away from his face with one hand, while he traced the shape of her thigh through her dress with his other.

'There are a lot of old buildings here,' he was muttering into her ear. 'Those white ones with the black boarding date back to the Tudors.'

Molly vaguely remembered something from school about a king who went through a string of wives, a couple of whom ended up headless; but she couldn't be sure that they were the same Tudors William was talking about, so she just nodded and made an interested *hmm* sound.

'These are more recent,' William continued, indicating one of the tall white buildings with detailed carvings over the doors. Molly was getting a distinct feeling that he was expecting her to gasp in awe at his knowledge. She would not. William knew that Molly was no wide-eyed schoolgirl, for all that she couldn't tell one dead king from another. She turned in his lap to face him, ostensibly so that she could tidy his hair with her fingers in preparation for their arrival at their lodgings. As she did so she pressed the curve of her breasts, more ample these days, against William's jaw, to remind him of the desires he was trying to fight.

Molly felt a lick of triumph as he turned his face into her chest, nuzzling the soft velvet of her dress. Discreetly, as if he were trying not to be noticed even by himself, he loosened the first few pearl buttons so he could push his face into the neck of her gown and against the soft, creamy-smelling skin of her throat. Molly closed her eyes in delight as William's face moved down to her corset and he rubbed his nose and mouth against the tops of her breasts through the thin linen of her chemise. His fingers plucked hungrily at her underclothes and she relaxed into the rocking of the carriage, allowing herself to move with William. But just as his tugging started to become more urgent, the carriage slowed and Ashton pulled the horse to a halt. They had arrived at their honeymoon lodgings. Cursing silently, Molly fastened the top of her dress while William drew his coat about him.

The lodgings William had booked for them were in a neat guesthouse, a few streets from the seafront. As William guided Molly over the frosty gutter, she looked up at the guesthouse. It was a spacious-looking building, in the style William had identified as dating from the time of the dead king and his dead wives.

A very formal-looking woman of middling years answered the door, and looked past the driver as soon as he announced the Hamiltons' arrival. Ashton stepped aside while Molly and William went into the hall out of the cold. Molly gazed around at the plush decor of the hallway while the woman who ran the guesthouse sympathized with William over the cold and tiring journey he must have had. Would the gentleman and his charming bride care for some warm refreshments? William said that they would take supper in the dining room, if that was convenient (of course, it was), and asked if their luggage could be taken up to their room. The woman immediately rang for a porter and offered the distinguished young newly-weds a drink by the fire while they waited for the porter to take up their luggage.

While they waited, Molly and William sat by the roaring fire in a parlour so formal it looked more like a drawing room, William with a glass of port, Molly with wine and water. She sipped carefully at the tart-tasting wine, watching William swallow his port down in three gulps. Molly had not drunk wine very often, and already she was beginning to feel the combined warmth of the drink and the fire melting through the icy feeling in her blood. She looked across at the Christmas tree in the corner, hung with strings of beads. Someone had sprinkled the tree with flour to look like snow – an old trick of Florrie's, when they'd had the flour to spare – and its thick, dusty smell mingled with the sharp scent of pine. There were little red velvet bows scattered across the branches and Molly watched the strange shadows the tree cast on the wall in the flickering gaslight. Her eyelids felt heavy. She was only a couple of months gone, but she became tired so easily these days.

'Tired?' William asked, startling her. She wasn't aware that he'd been watching. 'It has been a long day.'

Shaking her head and stirring herself from her dreamy state, Molly set aside her glass of wine. If her plan stood any chance of working, she had to be alert for any shifts in William's mood.

'No,' she replied, smiling softly and nodding towards the tree. 'I was just thinking about Christmas. I remember the first time we had a Christmas tree; I must have been about five or six, and I was fascinated. I thought it was actually growing up out of the parlour floor.'

William chuckled affectionately, and Molly felt quite shy. She hadn't expected that she would be discussing her girlhood with him, but she might as well continue now.

'I did, honestly,' she said. 'I used to lie on my front on the floor beside it, looking at the bucket it was standing in and trying to work out where the roots grew into the floorboards. What about you?' she asked. 'What were your family Christmases like?'

William smiled, his eyes wide and dark in the dim light. 'The thing I remember most is the coin in the plum pudding,' he said. 'My earliest memory is poking through my pudding bowl with a spoon, with my mother watching over my shoulder to make sure I didn't swallow the sixpence by mistake. She always made sure I got the slice with the silver coin in it.'

It was Molly's turn to laugh. She couldn't imagine William as a small boy.

'Did your mother have Christmas trees when you were older?' she asked. 'My Aunt Florrie loved them. She just got the smallest one she could find, so we could fit it in the corner of the parlour.' She didn't add that Florrie had to scrimp and save for the rest of the month in order to buy a tree at all.

William looked thoughtful. 'The only time I remember having one was when we were entertaining guests,' he said. 'Once, when I was about fourteen, some relatives on my father's side stayed with us over Christmas, and we had one then. My mother loved it, but Father called it new-fangled foreign nonsense, and he was always complaining about the mess it made.'

'Oh,' Molly said hesitantly, unsure what else she could say.

'We still had wreaths and holly branches in the drawing room, though,' William added quickly. 'I liked those too.'

Molly watched him pick up the decanter of port and pour himself another measure. She wasn't sure exactly how much liquor it would take to melt his resolve. After slipping up to their room to change clothes, they went down for supper. In the few moments it had taken to change, Molly barely had a chance to admire the luxurious room, or the soft-looking linen on the double bed, but she had made sure to undress without stepping behind the screen.

They were one of only a few parties dining in the guesthouse that evening, and Molly's mouth stung in anticipation as she realized how hungry she was after a long journey with no lunch. The first course was a smooth vegetable soup with a sprinkling of coriander on top, quite unlike the chunky broths Florrie used to make, but it smelled delicious. Molly took a bread roll from the plate in the centre of the table, and had already broken three small pieces off and dropped them into her bowl before she realized that William was looking somewhat surprised.

'Oh . . .' she said, instantly aware that she had broken a rule of etiquette previously unknown to her. 'Is something the matter?'

William still looked a little confused, but his tone was amiable enough. 'It is not normally the done thing to put one's bread in the soup,' he said, quietly tactful. 'No matter, though; no one saw.'

'Ah.' Molly picked up her spoon and scooped up the offending bread pieces, popping them into her mouth one by one. 'I'm sorry.' She was not sure that she could see the point in serving bread and soup together if one was not allowed to eat them together, but she was getting quite used to such strange rules.

William waved his hand dismissively. 'It's perfectly all right.' Lowering his voice, he leaned conspiratorially towards her, his eyes sparkling. 'Actually, I was just thinking it looked rather tasty.'

Relieved, Molly beamed mischievously. 'It is. Try it.'

William considered for a moment before shaking his head. 'Not tonight. When we get home, certainly.' As soon as he said this, he paused, smiling gently at Molly. She felt her cheeks flush as she realized what he meant: they shared a home now.

When the main course arrived, Molly was delighted by

the plentiful portions of roast beef with crispy roast potatoes and plump carrots and greens. William poured thick brown gravy over each of their plates, and she wolfed down as much as she could, and drank mostly water. After a dessert course of cake, and then one of cheese (offered only to William), they were ready to leave the dining room. William held out his arm to Molly and they headed up the stairs.

William's tension as they stepped into their room was palpable. Molly casually strolled over to the bed, on which a perceptive and discreet maid had folded and laid out her best nightgown next to a deep-green robe that must belong to William. The thick curtains at the window had been drawn against the cold night air. Molly undid the buttons running down the front of her evening dress and slipped it from her shoulders. She could feel William's gaze on her but she made sure she did not look up at him just yet. She stepped out of her petticoats and draped them across a chair with her dress. Peeling off her camisole and stockings, she reached around to undo her corset laces. She heard the rustling of William shedding his jacket and waistcoat and smiled inwardly as she unhooked the front of her corset.

Molly stood with her back to him, dressed only in her chemise and drawers. She shivered a little in the thin linen and slid a discreet look over her shoulder. William stood watching her in just his breeches, his face flushed with drink and desire. Feeling her own lust rising giddily, Molly forced herself not to look at his bare arms and chest. Instead, she stretched lazily and drew her chemise over her head, then, pulling gently at the ribbon in the waist of her drawers, kicked them off. William wouldn't have got this from any well-bred young lady on his wedding night, Molly was prepared to wager.

She turned around, naked, and made to turn down the bedsheets as if she had simply forgotten to put on her nightgown. She heard the sharp hiss as William drew a breath. In a moment he had scrambled across the bed and snatched her up, his hands on her waist, his half-naked body bearing her down on to the bed. He reached down to free himself of his breeches and Molly squirmed as the back of his cold hand pressed between her legs while he fumbled with his buttons. She would not cry out in pleasure – not until this was done.

William let loose a shuddering groan as he pushed into her, and Molly slid herself down underneath him until he was fully inside. Having done this only once before, she was quite tender when William thrust deeply. At this rate, the maids might get the bloodstained linen they were expecting. Then she allowed herself to feel the weight of William between her legs, ran her hands down his back and felt the coarse stubble of his face rough against her neck, and something inside her melted in delight.

12

Molly discovered that after a short doze, William was eager to roll on to her again, and in his drowsy state, late at night, he had lost all fear of causing her to miscarry. She had smiled sleepily as she felt him reach for her in the darkness and lower himself on top of her. If those women she'd heard about really had lost their babies after going just once with their husbands, then this had to work. Molly didn't relish the idea of William seeing her blood on the sheets in the morning, but it had to be done, and this way it would look natural. She could not be blamed for permitting her husband his conjugal rights, after all.

But when she woke, blinking groggily in the light streaming through a gap in the curtains, she couldn't feel anything approaching what she'd expected a miscarriage to feel like. She was a little tender and stiff from wrapping herself around William all night, and she could feel a gentle aching, like a light bruise, between her legs, but nothing that might suggest premature labour. Molly slid her bare feet out of the bed and turned her side of the blankets back carefully, so as not to wake William. There was no blood. Still naked, she stood and put her hand down over her belly. The bump was still jutting out just under her belly button. Everything looked and felt normal. Shivering with the realization that she was still very much pregnant, Molly reached out for her nightgown.

'I can see my son.'

Molly span round to see William lounging on his pillows, awake and watching her.

'Sorry, didn't mean to startle you,' he continued lazily. 'I haven't seen you without your clothes on – well, apart from last night.' He smiled wickedly. 'I hadn't realized that you were starting to show. I suppose my new bride's dress bill will be bigger than most, then?'

Molly paused as she walked back to the warmth of the bed. She knew that look in William's eye; she'd seen it often enough now.

'I didn't hurt you then, last night?' William asked. 'I couldn't help myself.'

Molly couldn't resist a smile. William's suggestive expression always did that to her. 'Do I look hurt?' she asked in her medium's voice. William reached out and took her hand, drawing her into bed beside him. He ran his hands over her breasts and belly, and she felt his hardness against her leg.

The maid was not required to tend the fire that morning, and the Hamiltons ate breakfast late.

Southport at Christmas was like a fairytale town turned to ice. As the Hamilton carriage trotted up and down the parades of brightly lit shops, Molly peered out of the window at the warmly wrapped people scurrying along the footpaths carrying bags and boxes. Molly and William spent their days shopping and dining out, only slipping back to their lodgings to change or sleep. But whenever they returned to their room, muffled sounds of pleasure and the creaking of the big bed could be heard throughout the guesthouse. After a chambermaid walked in on them while they were supposedly changing for dinner, the guesthouse staff were somewhat cooler towards them for the rest of their stay.

If it hadn't been for the worry of her pregnancy and the sense that she had betrayed Florrie, Molly could almost have enjoyed married life. In William, she had found a partner as hedonistic and passionate as she; one who wasn't averse to caresses in the back of the carriage as well as in the bedroom, and who enjoyed food and wine as well as she did, although his choices of restaurant were somewhat intimidating. Still, Molly made sure not to drop her bread in her soup bowl for the rest of the honeymoon.

Growing more confident that he would not affect his developing child, her husband indulged his passions with unrestrained ferocity. Once, after another of William's references to her protruding stomach as 'his son', Molly asked if the Hamilton women usually had boys first.

'Oh, I'm not sure,' William had replied quickly. 'In any case, it's not so important. We have time.'

On one of their shopping trips, when Molly was being shown a parade of dresses and measured for others, she had gritted her teeth in irritation when William casually suggested that the salesgirls show Mrs Hamilton some of the looser styles of gown as well as the more structured, fitted ones she had picked out.

'Never know when she may need something with a little more room in it,' he had smirked, clearly amused by the assistants' discomfort at his hints of forthcoming pregnancy for his new bride. Molly tried to ignore his obvious delight in her condition and her mind raced to find a new solution.

On Christmas Day they dined by the fire in the guesthouse and William presented Molly with a string of pearls and a cape of russet-red fox fur. In their room, Molly allowed him to wrap the pearls around her throat. She looked into the dressing mirror at the strange picture of herself as a wealthy young lady with her handsome husband. She gave William a cane that he had admired in one of the Southport shops, and an encyclopaedia with a rich red leather binding. William did not seem to care that Molly was more spirited and less well behaved than the women they encountered while out dining and dancing; if anything, he seemed to want her all the more for it.

One night, when Molly awoke in the small hours with a desire to use the pot, she realized that she and William had fallen asleep, naked, in each other's arms, and was somewhat surprised to see a closeness developing between herself and her husband. Molly could not imagine feeling the pain she had experienced when Florrie died if she were to lose William, nor did she worry over their relationship as she worried over the breach that had developed in her friendship with Jenny. But she was beginning to lose her conviction that William was plotting to trap her. However, she thought, unconsciously placing her palm on her stomach, she could not feel the same about the Hamilton who would grow up to disinherit her.

Part Two

13

Molly and William travelled back to Preston just after Christmas. The carriage ambled to a halt outside the house in Ribblesdale Place and, as she stepped down from the carriage, Molly could hear a faint scuffling from inside as Katy prepared to open the door. Ashton took the cases down from the back of the carriage and William offered Molly his arm and strode confidently towards his new home. As they approached the doorstep, he stopped and glanced up at the front of the house.

'This is the first house I've ever owned,' he murmured. When Molly turned to look at him, he was smiling softly. Shifting his arm down to her waist, he hugged her discreetly. 'It's nothing like I expected it would be.'

As they reached the door, Katy flung open the polished wooden door and bobbed a breathless curtsy. William snatched Molly up off her feet and stepped inside. Katy scurried out of the way as William set a startled Molly down on her feet.

'What was that for?' she squeaked, abandoning any idea of a dignified return home.

'It's traditional,' William replied casually as he gestured

to Ashton to bring the cases inside out of the light rain that was starting to patter down from the dismal grey sky. 'It's so you don't trip on your way in and bring us bad luck.'

Molly looked baffled.

'And in any case,' William continued, 'I'm meant to be the first to set foot in the house.'

Molly was about to question the possibility of this romantic notion, given that she had been living in the house long before she had even met William, but suddenly Jenny's voice piped up behind her.

'Mol?'

Molly span round and couldn't resist flinging her arms around her friend. So distended was Jenny's belly that she could barely clasp her hands around her shoulders. Molly's skin prickled at the thought of stretching so far herself, and she wondered how a skinny little scrap like Jenny was able to carry so much extra weight.

'Good grief, Jenny! How much bigger are you going to get?' Molly asked.

'Sally Marsden says it can't be more than a couple of days now,' Jenny said. 'She came round to check on me over Christmas and stayed for dinner. She'll come over when my time comes and deliver my baby.'

Molly saw William stiffen slightly at the mention of dinner guests in their absence, but she was determined that William and Jenny would not clash before they'd even got through the door properly. Improvising rapidly, she offered to show Jenny her new clothes if she came upstairs with her to unpack, but William caught hold of her arm.

'You don't need to unpack your own cases, Molly. You

have Katy to do that for you.' When Molly had first introduced her maid to William, he had been somewhat surprised that Molly referred to her by her first name. It had not occurred to her that she might do otherwise; Florrie had never called the staff by their surnames.

'In any case,' he was saying, 'I arranged a surprise for you while we were away.'

Out of William's sight, Jenny's eyes rolled slightly.

'Come, and I'll show you.' Molly was swept upstairs, glancing apologetically back at her friend.

Molly was still half expecting to walk into her old room, but when William stopped outside the door of Florrie's bedchamber, she silently reprimanded herself for continuing to think of the room as belonging to her dead aunt. William pushed open the door of their new master bedroom to reveal a complete redecoration: Florrie's dusky-pink walls had been replaced with a warm burgundy, with cream skirting boards and heavy wooden furniture. With some relief, Molly noted that the bed in which Florrie had spent her final weeks had been replaced with a strong king-sized one with thick posts and heavy linen. There was a new dressing table for Molly on one side of the room, with little drawers for her pots of creams and perfumes. A fire had been lit in the grate, and the flames licked the shadows into a hundred dancing shapes. It barely looked like Florrie's room at all. Molly inhaled quietly, sniffing for the last traces of Florrie's violet-scented lotions and balms; but all she could smell were the aromas of pine cones on the fire and brand-new bedsheets.

'Well?'

Molly realized she hadn't yet acknowledged the surprise.

'How did you arrange all this before we left?'

'I ordered everything before the wedding. Do you like it?'

Molly realized that William was standing very close to her, and she trailed her fingers across his waistcoat. He kicked the door closed behind them.

'He's stopped worrying about the baby, then,' Jenny remarked the following morning, as she and Molly sat in the parlour with a pot of tea.

Molly's old room had been papered in deep green while they were away, and before lunch William had taken the opportunity to have Ashton set up his new study to his liking. Molly winced as she heard the scraping of furniture against the floorboards, and hoped that Ashton wasn't scratching the varnish.

'What?' She had been gazing out through the lacy curtains, and the sudden sound of Jenny's voice had startled her.

'William,' Jenny continued. 'I thought he got you up there pretty quickly. Katy had to wait until the creaking had stopped before she asked Ashton to bring your cases in.'

Molly prickled slightly. She had the feeling that she was being scolded for her behaviour with her husband in her own bedchamber. And the notion of sparing the servants' blushes was simply ridiculous.

'And what if we were?' she asked, glaring at Jenny. 'If Katy's horrified by the thought of William and me together, she'll not last long as a maid; and Ashton drove us around on our honeymoon, so I don't think we'll offend him too much either. And, come to think of it, I don't think you're in a position to read me any lectures.'

Molly felt the angry flush around her ears and the back of her neck. She knew she would regret quarrelling with her friend later, but the fury was bubbling unbearably in her head.

'I don't think it's such a terrible thing to do with *my husband*,' she hissed. She watched Jenny's pale-blue eyes flick down to her heavy body, and instantly regretted her words. 'I'm sorry,' she murmured, kneeling on the floor beside Jenny and resting her head in her friend's lap. 'You know I don't care that you won't be married when your baby's born. I know you and William don't really get along, but he has given you time off work to have your baby; not many girls get that.'

Jenny rested a hand, motionless, on Molly's red curls.

'I know. Everything's just been so different since he came into the picture.'

Molly looked up into Jenny's face.

'It's been difficult for me, too. I still have trouble realizing that when people say "Mrs Hamilton" they're talking about me. William's taken to marriage so easily, but . . .'

Jenny nodded. 'It's just the way he looks at me sometimes. Like I'm a part of your old life that he wants rid of. I know he thinks less of me than he does of you. Even though you were pregnant when he married you.'

'Yes, well,' Molly muttered, getting to her feet and brushing off her skirt. 'That wasn't meant to happen.'

'But you're married now,' Jenny said earnestly, 'and no one will know the difference. It's not a problem now, is it?'

Molly looked at Jenny, sitting back against the cushions with her hands resting on her belly. She hesitated, trying to find the words to explain her terror of her condition; a terror that hadn't miraculously dissolved as soon as William slipped the wedding ring on to her finger. Mercifully, though, Katy rang the bell for lunch, and Molly, grateful for a reason to discontinue the conversation, made a show of going to wait at the foot of the stairs for William to lead them into the dining room.

That night, Jenny stayed up later than Molly and William.

'I've been restless these last few days,' she explained, as Molly retired for the night, 'and it's moving about so much I can't sleep until I'm dog-tired.'

So it was quite late when Molly and William were woken by the sound of knocking on their bedchamber door.

'What the hell . . .?' William protested, irritably pulling back the sheets and searching for his robe.

Molly, blinking sleepily, suddenly realized who it must be. Katy would never disturb their sleep.

'I'll go,' she said, laying a hand on William's arm in a soothing gesture. 'It'll be Jenny.'

Ignoring the indignant rage on William's face, she scooped her nightdress up off the floor and wriggled it over her head. She walked over to the door and opened it a crack, to see Jenny standing there.

'What is it?' she whispered. 'William's fuming! Why are you knocking on our door?' A thought hit her. 'Oh – has it started? Is the baby coming?'

Jenny shook her head. 'No. But the bed's gone out of your old room. I just came up and it's gone – where am I supposed to sleep?'

Blinking in sleepy confusion, Molly turned to William, who sat up in the bed, staring pointedly at the door.

'Where's my old bed?' she asked. 'The one that was in my room?'

'Moved out, of course,' William said abruptly. 'Why would I need a bed in my study?'

'Ah,' Molly began, 'but Jenny still sleeps in there.'

'What?' William's tone was frosty. 'Might I ask why?'

Molly pushed the door a little further closed, dropping her voice.

'Because she's my guest. We used to sleep in there together. Where should she sleep now?'

'You have attic rooms, don't you?'

Molly suppressed a squeak of horror at the thought of telling Jenny to go and bed down on one of the pallet beds in the servants' quarters.

'But she's not—'

'She is a part of my staff,' William interrupted, 'whether she works here with you, or at the mill. I am certainly not going to have my plans for a study ruined. Will you ensure she understands, or shall I?'

'I'll do it,' Molly replied instantly, her voice small. She made to step out of the room to speak to Jenny privately on the landing.

'It's as well it's done now, anyway,' William muttered, burrowing back down under the bedclothes. 'She'll have to move out before that child of hers is born, and there's no sense in her getting settled in her own room. You can offer her the other attic room for now if you like, but don't be long.'

Molly nodded and slipped out of the room.

'What did he say?' Jenny whispered.

Molly swallowed hard. 'He says for you to take one of

the attic rooms.' She paused, twisting her fingers together. 'He's having his study in that room now.'

Jenny's hands instinctively flew to her belly.

'And where will he put your baby, then?' she hissed, glancing towards Molly's bedchamber door. 'Is it to join me and my child in the attic with the other servants?'

Molly, thrown momentarily by the mention of the baby she was carrying, shook her head in confusion. This did not seem like a good time to relay the rest of William's speech.

'I don't know . . . I haven't asked what he plans to do about a nursery.'

'You don't know what your husband is planning to do with your child?'

Molly's temper flared. 'No! It's months away yet. I'm not even thinking about it. And why is it such a bad idea that you move upstairs, anyway? It'll be quieter for the baby, won't it?'

Jenny looked at her coolly. 'Yes. And I suppose your darling husband can soon get it trained up as a chimney sweep once it's crawling.' She turned on her heel and swept up the landing towards the attic stairs, leaving Molly standing speechless and cold in her nightgown.

The following morning, the last of 1856, Jenny did not come down for breakfast. William barely noticed, but as he buttered rolls and drank strong coffee, Molly's mind was racing. Somehow she had to get Jenny to understand that she didn't see her unborn baby as a new servant in the making. When an idea hit her, she cleared her throat and addressed William as casually as she could.

'I need a few things for the séance tonight,' she began. 'I

thought I'd go out for them myself. I could do with a little fresh air.'

William scowled. 'You should be taking things easy in your condition – why not send Katy? Perhaps you shouldn't be working until you are delivered anyway.'

Molly remembered William's weight on her last night and in the early hours of the morning, and marvelled at the selectivity of his concern for her condition.

'I will be taking Katy to carry the basket,' she reasoned, 'so I won't be putting any strain on the baby. And there's no reason why I should stop working – not just yet.' She thought of Jenny, who had been hauling heavy bolts of cotton cloth around William's Preston mill in her eighth month.

'In any case,' she said, 'I simply must hold a sitting on New Year's Eve. There are certain days when the clients particularly want to attend a séance, and if I can't provide them with one, they'll go elsewhere. I've already missed too many circles this year, what with mourning for my aunt and our honeymoon.' She opened her green eyes and let her gaze burn into William. 'I know I don't *need* to work, but might I continue?' It galled her to ask, but still she dropped her gaze and looked up from under her lashes at him. 'I'm not like most other young ladies, after all. I have a gift.'

William grinned wickedly. 'You certainly do,' he said. 'Very well, but don't walk into town – take Ashton and the carriage. He can carry your purchases; you won't need Katy. She can stay here to clean the house; my new study will need tidying before I can use it.'

Molly nodded deferentially.

*

That afternoon, Molly was putting fresh candles into the holders on the séance table when Katy tapped at the door.

'Delivery for you, ma'am.'

'Oh yes,' Molly said, setting the freshly polished bell down on the wooden tabletop. 'Tell them to take it up to Jenny's room in the attic, will you? And bring a clean tablecloth up here after you've done that.'

Katy dipped her head. 'Yes, ma'am. But ma'am, this that they're delivering is for Jenny, then? Not for you?'

Molly glared at her. 'That is what I said, Katy. What would cause you to question it?'

'Nothing, ma'am. Sorry. I'll go and tell them to take it up to the attic now.'

Molly watched the maid retreat, letting out a sigh of frustration once she had gone. She jabbed a finger at the bell hanging on its little brass frame, and it let out a thin, reedy tinkling. Time was pressing on, and Katy was beginning to realize the truth. Molly knew what she had to do. She would speak to Jenny as soon as she had made her peace offering.

'Oh, Mol, it's beautiful!' Jenny's face lit up at the sight of the new cradle at the foot of her pallet bed. Molly popped her head around the door as Jenny tested the rockers with a gentle tap of her toe.

'I just wanted to say sorry.' Molly smiled awkwardly. 'You know I don't see you or your baby as servants, Jenny. But there's so little room now, and when William says something, I have to . . .'

'I know.' Jenny put her arm around Molly and pecked her on the forehead. 'I'm sorry I blamed you. You've got a new husband to deal with, and a baby of your own on the way. We'll be fine up here.'

Molly rested her cheek against her friend's.

'Anyway,' Jenny said with a smirk, 'it might be for the best. I don't want to have to explain to my baby what that racket is coming from your room at night!'

Molly giggled and swatted her. 'We do not make a racket!' She could feel the blush spreading across her face.

'You want to try sleeping with that going on!' Jenny laughed. 'Still, it'll have to stop soon. He can't keep doing that with you in your condition – what are you, three months now? You'll be too big for him to get on top soon.'

Molly, irked that once again the conversation had come around to her unwanted pregnancy, tried a smile. She had a feeling that it appeared as a grimace. Now was the time to ask.

'It's not going to be so bad, you know, Mol,' Jenny said soothingly. She was looking very closely at Molly. 'God knows I was terrified when I first found out – especially when Joe ran off – but it'll be all right for me, and for you too.' She stroked her bump, smiling softly. 'It's a miracle, when you think about it. Us both carrying our babies inside our bodies.'

Molly smiled tightly. 'Let's go downstairs and have some chocolate,' she said. 'Katy can set your cradle up.'

14 New Year 1857

The New Year's Eve séance went beautifully. Molly watched carefully as the seven sitters – all finely dressed and certainly able to afford the higher fee she charged on nights like this – stepped into the room. She quickly picked out Marianne Meadowcroft and Pansy Hart as the best matches for her own diminutive stature, before nonchalantly indicating for them to sit on either side of her at the table. Florrie had once told her these were held to be honoured positions, allowing the sitters proximity to the spirit medium while she performed her miracle. Others appreciated the opportunity to try to catch her out. In fact, the two people on either side of the medium had been invaluable to Florrie, as they were now to Molly.

'Ladies, please remove your gloves.'

Once the clients were in a circle around the table, Molly took her place. She blew out the candles, plunging the room into darkness.

'Please join hands,' she said in her most mysterious tone. She felt the warmth of Marianne's and Pansy's hands as they reached blindly for hers, and heard the soft swishing of their sleeves on the tablecloth. Carefully, silently, Molly drew herself away from the table, so that instead of taking her hands Marianne and Pansy grasped each other's. Leaning gently back into her place, Molly folded her hands in her lap for the time being.

'Let us pray,' she said.

As the placatory prayer came to an end, she reached out to the bell she had carefully placed within reach before the séance began and poked it. Suppressed gasps and sharp intakes of breath followed the sound. Molly smiled into the darkness.

'They have come,' she announced.

She instructed the sitters to lay their palms gently on the tabletop, keeping the circle intact by touching their little fingers with their neighbouring sitters'. She slipped back into her place in the circle, sliding her hands between Marianne's and Pansy's as soon as she heard the rustling of their dress sleeves. Molly eased her right wrist slightly upwards, allowing her to drop the little leather ball that had been hidden in the loose, lace-trimmed cuff of her sleeve. A thrill ran through her at the sound of the ball rolling softly across the tabletop, and then again at the surprised reactions of the sitters as they felt the ball touch their outstretched fingertips.

'This is an acknowledgement of our efforts from the spirit world,' she explained, her voice authoritative and calm. 'Allow the ball to move where it will, and please do not forget to keep contact with the person to your left and to your right.'

For the next ten minutes, the ball rolled around the varnished wooden tabletop, seemingly independently. In the darkened room, the sitters were unaware of the effect they had upon the ball, propelling it further with every tiny, startled movement they made. Unable to see it coming, they were startled afresh whenever it rolled in their direction, and thus they were quite enthralled by a simple trick.

A gasp of delighted dread from Marianne Meadowcroft told Molly where the ball was now. Through the velvety darkness of the séance room, Molly revelled in the quiet scandal of the sitters, and her stomach fluttered with excitement. Then the sitters fell silent, listening for any clue as to the whereabouts of the travelling ball, and Molly's stomach fluttered again.

The realization horrified her. Across the table, the ball had just bounced off the fingers of one of the gentlemen sitters, who quickly suppressed his exclamation of surprise. Low in Molly's belly, the bubbling sensation continued, and without thinking she pressed a hand against the bodice of her dress, trying to muffle the feeling inside. Then the ball bounced off another sitter, rolled towards Molly, fell off the table and bounced across the floor, much to the amazement of the sitters. One of the women screamed, and Molly returned her shaking hand to the tabletop, claiming that she had been temporarily possessed by a spirit.

Jenny was dreamy for the rest of the evening. She sat with Molly and William when they ate a late New Year's Eve dinner after the séance, and barely seemed to notice William's less than pleased expression. The baby was moving around a great deal, and Jenny constantly had a hand on her belly as she murmured to her unborn child.

'Look, Molly,' she whispered in awed tones, and a faint

shape rippled through her flesh as she held the thick wool of her new winter dress close against her body.

Molly stared at the strange, undulating movement, and suddenly her own bump felt very heavy. She had barely eaten a thing at dinner, although the movement in her belly had settled. She felt sick with fear. In her innocence, she had not known what the first movement of her pregnancy would feel like. She had heard that such movement occurred before the mother was even showing, before the babe even had legs long enough to kick with; but she had not imagined that it would happen so soon. Worse, her quickening in the séance room tonight had changed everything, for now it would be a capital offence to procure a miscarriage. Molly gulped from her glass of water. She had to act soon.

Across the table Jenny smiled, as if her child were already in the room.

When the clock on the mantelpiece had chimed midnight, Molly and William retired to bed, leaving Jenny sitting in the parlour, gazing out at the stillness of the frost that coated the cobbles in the street below.

'It's enough to make a cat sick,' William grumbled as he threw the blankets over them. 'What's the point in talking to a child that can't hear yet?'

'Oh, leave her be, William,' Molly said, wriggling down under the heavy bedclothes. 'It's just a fancy some women get when they're at the stage Jenny's at.' Earlier that day, she had eventually managed to persuade William to allow her friend to stay in the attic for a little longer, at least until she had delivered her baby and was strong enough to look for somewhere else to live, but he was still irritable whenever Jenny was around.

'That reminds me,' William asked, cupping a hand to Molly's belly, 'how are you feeling lately?' His palm felt very warm through the thin linen of her nightdress.

Molly had lost faith in the notion of procuring a miscarriage by lying with William, and her stomach churned a little at the memory of the stirring she had felt during the séance. Still, her husband was handsome in the faint light from the bedside candle.

'I feel fine,' she murmured, as William's lips covered her own. She felt him tugging her nightdress up around her waist, and a familiar lick of delight as he lowered his body on to hers. She wriggled underneath him and let out a quiet little cry, knowing that it always made him push deeper into her.

In the early hours, through a fog of heavy sleep, Molly heard a frantic tapping. Stirring, she felt the warmth of the bedclothes and William lying beside her, and burrowed her face into the soft pillow. She could smell the deep scent of her body and William's on the linen as she opened her eyes. The knocking was still there. Next to her, William stirred and Molly could see him in the faint light, blinking in a bemused manner. Irritation flashed across his face.

'That bloody girl again!'

Molly rested a hand on his cheek. 'Jenny?'

The door creaked open, and Katy's head appeared, her hair tied in a straggly plait for bed, a tatty shawl thrown on over her work dress.

'Beg pardon, Mr and Mrs Hamilton. I'm so sorry to wake you.'

'What is it?' William snapped.

'It's Jenny, ma'am,' Katy said, turning to Molly. 'She's started, ma'am; the baby's coming. She's asking for you.'

'Oh!' Molly gasped. 'Have you sent for Sally Marsden?'

Katy nodded and bobbed a sleepy curtsy. 'Yes, ma'am, Mrs Marsden is already here; I just got back with her. She says the time is very near, and Jenny keeps asking for you. She insisted that I come and fetch you.' The maid shifted awkwardly under the glower of the master of the house.

'I'll come straight up, Katy. Go and see if there's anything Mrs Marsden needs.' Molly swung her legs out of bed and began searching for a warm shawl.

'Molly, you can't go running off around the house at all hours of the night just because she's having a baby,' William was complaining. 'You have to keep your strength up for when your turn comes.'

Molly thought about arguing with him, but time was short and she couldn't afford to anger him.

'I know, William, but it's only this once,' she said soothingly. 'It's not as if I shall be up doing this every night. Besides,' she added, swallowing down the bitter taste in her mouth, 'it will help me to know what to expect.'

'That's what worries me,' William grumbled. 'I don't claim to know much about childbirth, but I'm sure it would not be very encouraging for a girl as young as you to witness it while in your condition. I don't want you unnerved.'

If only you knew how unnerved I am already, William.

Outwardly, she smiled. 'Oh, don't worry! Your son and I will be perfectly well. I shall come down immediately if I feel weak or faint.'

'See that you do,' William said, and flopped back on to his pillow.

Upstairs in her attic room, Jenny was lying on her bed, straining and biting down on a piece of wood. Sally Marsden, a sturdy-looking woman of middle years, with faded brown hair, turned around as Molly stepped into the room.

'Mrs Hamilton.' She bobbed an awkward, grudging curtsy.

Molly waved a hand and dismissed the formalities. 'Just call me Molly, Mrs Marsden. May I call you Sally?'

'Certainly may,' Sally replied with a shrug. 'If you like, you can sponge Jenny's face with cold water.' She handed Molly a bowl and a cloth, and ducked down to peer between Jenny's legs.

'I'll just see if I can feel it coming down now, Jenny,' she called out over Jenny's grunts and heavy breaths. Jenny, her teeth gripping the wood so tightly that Molly expected it to break, nodded irritably before closing her eyes and shuddering with fresh pain.

Molly dabbed at Jenny's red forehead and cheeks with the cloth, stroking the roots of her friend's sweaty hair while murmuring in a soothing voice. She stole a glance down to the other end of the pallet, where Sally Marsden knelt on the dusty floorboards between Jenny's splayed legs, pushing her hands up into the livid red of Jenny's stretched and straining body. Katy stood to one side, with fresh sheets and a bowl of hot water, staring with a look of almost comical horror at the spreading red-black bloodstain on the sheet underneath Jenny's long, skinny legs.

‘I can feel it coming,’ Sally announced. ‘With everything you’ve got next time, Jenny.’

Jenny barely seemed to hear her, but as the next wave of contractions struck her, a strange, violent movement, which seemed to come from her very gut, forced her up into a sitting position. At a quick gesture from Sally Marsden, Molly slipped behind her friend’s back so that Jenny could brace herself against her body. Jenny’s legs trembled uncontrollably with the effort, and a fresh flood of liquid, like dirty water, streamed from her on to the already soaking old sheet. She strained as if she would burst, and let loose a frenzied gasp. Molly pressed her face against the back of her friend’s clammy neck.

‘Nearly done, Jenny,’ Sally called above the racket. She snatched a sheet from Katy’s hands. ‘One more time.’

Jenny groaned and doubled over. Molly saw the muscles in her back through the wet nightgown, rippling in a manner that put her in mind of William’s horse. With a moan that sounded like all of her breath being torn from her, Jenny pushed one last time, and Molly saw a hard pink shape slither out from between her friend’s legs. Sally Marsden took it expertly in the sheet, and Jenny fell back into Molly’s arms as a choking cry filled the servants’ quarters.

‘It’s a boy.’ Sally smiled as she wiped the slimy little bundle down. Jenny lifted her head weakly and gasped a little as the afterbirth slithered out of her. Sally cut the murky red cord and wrapped the baby in another sheet before handing him to Jenny. Molly gently kissed her friend’s cheek and whispered her congratulations, then watched as Jenny wearily drew her legs together and took hold of her son. The baby was very red, with small, squinting eyes and wrinkled hands.

'Peter Joseph,' Jenny whispered as the baby wrapped its hand around her finger.

'After your pa and Joe? Why?' Molly gawped at her, but her friend barely seemed to notice. She was pulling her nightdress aside to offer the baby his first feed. Sally Marsden started to pack away her things and Katy bundled up the stained sheets and took them down for the wash. Molly slipped out of the room behind Sally, leaving the door ajar. She laid a hand on the midwife's shoulder, drew her to one side, and swallowed hard.

'Just a moment.'

Sally turned, her expression calm. Molly felt her hands trembling.

'I have need of you. I'm expecting.'

Molly could see that Sally understood she was not inquiring about her services as a midwife. She looked at Molly and waited for her to continue.

'I need you to . . .' Molly broke off and looked around them. The attic stairs were deserted, and even Katy in the kitchen could not be heard right at the top of the house.

'. . . finish it,' she whispered.

The woman she had asked to commit a hanging crime on her behalf did not even flinch, but merely nodded.

'Have you quickened yet?'

Molly nodded weakly. 'I think so. I was holding a séance yesterday, and something . . .' She motioned awkwardly toward her stomach. Sally's eyes closed briefly in acknowledgement of the familiar fear.

'Right. Well, we can't do it here,' she said. 'You'd have to come to me. You wouldn't know the place I use; I can meet you at the quays, if you like. Seven shillings.'

Molly hadn't seen the quays since she was a child, but she nodded. Sally's eyes were warm but she spoke firmly.

'You mustn't speak of this to anyone, especially not to your husband. I reckon he has no idea you're even asking me, has he?'

Molly shook her head, her eyes darting down the stairs to where William was sleeping.

'Don't try telling him you feel off-colour or anything before you come to meet me. It has to look like an accident. There's enough hangings happen at Lancaster Castle, and I've no intention of being one of them. D'you think you can lie to him? Not all women can.'

Molly thought of her cabinet of ghosts and the whirling séance table.

'I can do it.' It suddenly occurred to her that Sally had not even asked why a wealthy young lady, married to a successful businessman and living in a spacious house, should want to go through with such a risky venture.

'Don't you want to know why?' she found herself asking.

Sally shook her head. 'Nay, lass. It makes no difference to me; my job's just the same whether I'm sorting out a lord's wife or a lady of the night. It's not me as has to make the decision. You've got your reasons, and I don't need to know.' She looked Molly up and down. 'You're only a little thing yourself, aren't you? We'll try it without going in at first.'

Molly blinked and tried not to let herself think what Sally could mean.

'How far gone are you, anyway?' the midwife asked.

'Three months.'

'We'll manage it. Meet me this afternoon at three.'

Molly nodded, biting her lip.

'Sally?'

Molly and the midwife span around. Jenny was standing behind them in the doorway of her room, with the baby in her arms. Sally took charge of herself instantly, but Molly felt as if she might faint and fall down the attic stairs. Steeling herself, she looked across to where the midwife was wrapping a shawl around Jenny and ushering her back to bed.

'I can't get him to feed properly,' Jenny was saying.

'He just hasn't worked out how to latch on yet. Hold him to you like that . . . there he goes . . .'

Molly closed her eyes and listened to the bustling about in the servants' quarters as Sally settled Jenny and her son down for a feed, explaining how to change his linen as she did so. Molly leaned back against the wall, hoping that she hadn't overheard her conversation with Sally. When Sally came out of the room, she pulled the door closed behind her.

'This afternoon at three?'

'Yes,' Molly whispered.

Sally nodded. 'Go and see your husband for a while, then check on Jenny. Do whatever they would expect you to do.' She picked up her bag and set off down the stairs, saying that she would let herself out.

William stirred as soon as Molly slipped back into their chamber half an hour before Katy was due to come in to dress her for the day.

‘Are you all right? Is it over with?’

‘I’m fine,’ she soothed. Her medium’s voice made her sound much calmer than she was. ‘Jenny has a son.’

‘Mmm?’ William replied casually. ‘Then perhaps we shall be lucky and have one also. And if it is a girl, I’m sure we can manage to make another.’ He pawed at Molly through her nightdress, and she tried to forget the task she had ahead of her and closed her eyes, smiling in pretended arousal as William’s fingers traced the curve of her inner thigh.

After breakfast, she went up to see Jenny, an imitation of a carefree smile on her face. She had asked Katy to make up a breakfast tray for the new mother and carried it upstairs herself. Her friend was seated on the pallet bed with the infant sleeping in her arms.

‘He’s supposed to sleep in the cradle,’ Molly said with a grin. ‘Put him down for a while and come and have something to eat.’

Jenny gazed levelly at her. ‘Why are you meeting Sally today, Mol?’

An icy chill flooded over Molly, and the lie was past her lips before she could even consider it.

‘Oh, just to discuss the preparations for my time. She seemed good with you and little Peter, didn’t she?’

Jenny’s laugh was brittle. ‘For all that you do it for a living, Mol, you never could lie to me. You’re getting rid, aren’t you?’

Molly looked at the hem of her skirt, dusty on the attic floorboards.

‘Yes.’

'I don't believe you sometimes, Mol.' Jenny gathered her baby closer to her, and ignored the breakfast tray Molly had set beside her on the bed. 'I think you're starting to believe that you really do have an incredible gift. What makes you think you're so bloody special?'

'What? Why would I think that?'

Jenny's eyes flashed in anger. 'Because you've come all the way up from playing in the street and living in a two-up, two-down and now you've got this huge place and more clothes than I can count,' she hissed. 'Because you owned your own house and business when you were sixteen. Because you could dump Eddie Rathbone – who, by the way, is still looking for work, so I've heard – for a flash snob with plenty of money and one hand always up your petticoats. Because you're not happy just marrying a rich man – oh no, you have to keep making more money off those fools with more money than sense who think you can get the dead to move tables for them and shower them with flowers. And now you can't even let your own child get in the way. Who's going to be next, Molly?'

Molly slammed the door behind her, and Peter jumped in Jenny's arms and started to wail. Molly stormed across the room and stood barely an inch in front of Jenny, glaring down at her as she tried to hush the baby.

'How dare you?' she screeched, before remembering that William's study was on the floor below and dropping her voice. 'And I suppose it would all have been different if your drunken idiot of a father had been the one with the sense to get a business going properly and make enough money to get over to this side of town? I'll give you this – that baby is bald and red-faced and never stops making a racket; you named him well. D'you think you'd give away everything you'd worked for just to play nursemaid to a bloody baby if you were in my shoes?'

'*Your* baby!' Jenny protested. 'It's not—'

Furious, Molly continued, ignoring her friend's hushed anger. 'What more d'you want from me? I let you stay here and eat my food and all I ever asked for is a little help with the séances. I bought you that cradle, which you still haven't touched – don't worry, I didn't spit my bad-mother poison into it, you know – and I was the one who got you out of the mill so you could rest up before having that baby!'

'If I can do this, so can you!' Jenny whispered harshly. 'I had far more reason to get a miscarriage than you did, but I would never—'

'And do you want applause? You've brought this baby into the world when you hardly have enough to feed and clothe yourself, but you're reading me high-and-mighty lectures? I never told you what you should have done, Jenny. I never would have. But after a few months with a baby in your belly you look at me like you've wiped me off your shoe and tell me I'm heartless.' Molly's voice quavered. 'I've not stopped caring about you, Jenny. Since Florrie died, you're the person I've known and loved longest – the only person I love, actually. But you've been looking askance at me ever since I moved into this house. I can't stay in the gutter for you, and just because your baby is everything to you now, it doesn't mean it has to be that way for the rest of us.'

She heaved a sigh. 'And I will meet Sally today, and she

will help me to miscarry. You're not going to tell William, now are you?'

Jenny shook her head. 'I've no great fondness for William, you know that,' she said quietly, swaying side to side with the baby in her arms, 'and I don't want to see you and Sally taken up for murder. But I've not had a place in this house ever since William came, and I'll not watch you push your baby away and all. Peter and I will just have to move out. I'll get our things together.'

'Don't be silly,' Molly sighed. 'You've just given birth.'

Jenny shook her head. 'I'm not keeping Peter here any longer than I have to. You can keep the cradle, though God knows what you'll do with it. Set it up so it rocks during the séances and claim it's a ghost child, knowing you.'

A flash of anger shot through Molly's heart. 'Go, then! Get your little brat away from the awful woman who fed and clothed you the whole time you were carrying him, and got her dreadful husband to keep your job open for you! I'm sure he'll thank you when he's older and spent his life working in a mill on starvation rations instead of in a house where he'd have been warm and well fed. If you can't bring yourself to care more about *me* than what's growing in my body, just go. I wish I'd never bothered trying to help you.'

Molly slammed the door behind her, and ran down the attic stairs with unshed tears scalding her eyes and the sound of Jenny trying to hush the baby following hard on her heels.

15

When Molly heard Jenny's clogs on the stairs, she was curled up in an armchair in the parlour, willing herself not to cry. Her hands shook and her belly turned over and over as if she had the flux. She heard Jenny walking straight past the parlour door without pause, her baby grizzling. Downstairs, the front door slammed shut. Molly deliberately turned her back on the parlour window. She would not look out and watch Jenny walk away from her. Molly rested her head against the back of the armchair and felt a single hot tear running down her face. She closed her eyes and heard the venom in Jenny's voice, and saw the disgust in her expression, over and over again.

A hand on her shoulder made her jump, and Molly looked up to see William staring down at her.

'I was in the study. I heard shouting, and then the door. What is it, Molly?'

Molly cleared her throat. 'It's Jenny. We quarrelled and she insisted on leaving.' She paused and blinked hard. 'She's taken the baby and gone.'

'How very irresponsible of her,' William said, as if he were hardly surprised. 'But she must take her own risks in life; we've done her a great service allowing her to live here as it is. I'm far more concerned about the risk she may have put my wife and child at. You don't feel faint, do you, Molly? I could get a physician. I know a good one: Hartley, his name is.'

Molly tried not to show her horror at the thought of Dr Hartley in her home again.

'No, William. I'll be perfectly all right; it was unpleasant, that's all. In fact,' she improvised, 'I think I might feel better if I took a walk this afternoon. Just to clear my head.'

'Hmm,' William said. 'I suppose I could find time to take you out for a while. I have a lot of work to be doing, though; the Manchester mill lost a few workers over winter and I'm thinking about getting replacements from the workhouse. I need to look into the premiums and make my decision.'

'Oh, don't worry about that! You do what you need to do; I'll be fine. I shan't go far, I promise: just around the Square.' Molly tried a smile. 'Poor William. You work too hard. Once I've cheered myself up with a little stroll, we'll find a way to forget our troubles, shall we?'

William grinned, as she knew he would. 'Pity I can't come over to the gardens with you.'

'We don't need the gardens now,' Molly cooed. 'We have that wonderful warm bed you bought us.' She shuddered at the thought of the state she might be in by the time she saw her husband again.

'Later, then.' William smiled. 'Get Katy to accompany you.'

'Of course,' Molly lied.

Later that day, after William had gone back to his study, Molly sneaked down to the top of the cellar stairs and listened for Katy. The maid was clattering pans in the kitchen, probably washing the pots from breakfast. Softly, begging the steps not to creak, Molly crept upstairs and changed into a black velvet outfit left over from her mourning period for Florrie. The darker her skirts, the better: she didn't want any noticeable stains spreading across them on her walk home. She put on her plainest black hat and wrapped herself in a warm shawl, snatched up her reticule and parasol and quietly slipped downstairs and out of the house.

The bright white sunlight of the first day of January glared down from high in the sky, and Molly was relieved to be able to use her parasol. She shielded her face and hid in its shade, praying that she would not see anyone she knew. She wondered where Jenny was, and where she would sleep that night. Once Molly had walked as far as the bustling centre of the town, she slipped discreetly into the crowds and hailed the shabbiest old cab she could find. She couldn't afford to use one of the better cabs: she never knew when she might require the driver's services again and she didn't want to be recognized. These days, Mrs Molly Hamilton had no excuses for being seen at the quays.

'The quays, please,' she muttered to the driver, before slipping into the back of the carriage. If he wondered why such a well-dressed young lady wanted to be driven there, he never said so. Molly shrank back into the musty-smelling old seat as they jolted along the cobbles. She wished she were back at home.

16

The cab dropped her at the quayside, and Molly paid the driver twice, hoping that it would buy his discretion if he ever saw her again. She stepped down on to the cobbles and wrinkled her nose at the thick stench of tar from the ships. Preston's quays were small, constructed to allow the easy transport of goods and materials into the town, but still the place hummed with activity, from men unloading wooden crates to the traders and street girls touting for business. Molly felt a hundred eyes on her warm gown and the reticule clutched tightly in her hand. She looked down at the dark water lapping the stone edge of the quay.

Once, when she and Jenny were children, they had got into trouble at school over an argument about that water. Molly, who had recently seen men unloading boxes labelled 'SILK', had felt certain that the water must be one of the great oceans, and that the men on the boats were newly returned from exotic lands overseas. Jenny, whose pa sometimes went to the quays to collect orders of metal washbasins and buckets for his shop, assured her that it was just the Ribble, dammed to make it straighter so that the river could be used by local businesses. This debate had become louder and louder, until they were both scolded for talking in class, and sent for their palms to be caned at lunchtime. Back at home, Florrie had tutted as she bathed the welts on Molly's fingers, and told her she was a ninny for allowing herself to be caught.

'Jenny's right, anyway,' she'd said. 'It is just the Ribble.'

Now Molly looked up from the greenish water and blinked hard. If only all arguments were so easily resolved.

A young man in ragged, cut-off trousers climbing about in the rigging on a ship just in front of her tipped his hat and winked lasciviously. Molly dropped her eyes and looked away to her left, and a cluster of girls of about her own age, dressed in bright colours and cheap fabrics, stared at her and whispered behind their hands.

'There you are,' said a voice behind Molly. She jumped, and heard a raucous cackle from the group of whores as she span around. It was Sally Marsden, with a greyish bag slung over her shoulder.

'It's not far from here,' Sally said. 'Come on.'

With a firm grip on Molly's wrist, Sally drew her down the side streets, stepping precariously over the muck that had been tipped out on to the cobbles. The stone under Molly's feet was coated with a thin, greenish mildew, and she skidded even in her sensible flat boots. Finally, Sally indicated the rotten door of a tall, ramshackle building and pulled her inside. A toothless, grey old man sat in a chair just inside, his head tipped back, snoring. The smell of spirits drifted from his breath, and the reek of stale urine from his clothes. As Sally led her up the staircase, Molly put out a hand towards the banister, but drew it away when she saw how stained the wood was. They entered the first open room they came to. Sally closed the door and turned a rusty key in the lock. Molly eyed the tatty pallet bed and its yellowed sheets with ill-concealed terror.

'I know, I know,' Sally grumbled. 'But I don't do this part of the job from home. I can't bring that sort of danger back to my family. Nobody asks questions around here.'

Molly heard a rhythmic creaking from the room above, and nodded.

'Is it safe?'

Sally exhaled thoughtfully. 'I'm about as safe as you'll get, lass. I don't like to poke around inside unless I have to, and I won't feed you cotton oil or nothing like that. I'm trying to poison what you've got in your belly, not you.'

'So you haven't had any girls die?'

'I didn't say that. Not so many these days, but it has happened, and if you know enough to ask that question, you know there's a risk. Only you can say whether it's worth it.'

Molly thought again of the son William was so sure she was carrying; the son she would have to answer to when he was grown and William was gone, assuming childbirth didn't kill her first. She thought of herself as he would see her: the widowed mother whom he would have to keep until she died, but not someone to consider when making decisions about the house: *his* house. In rank, she would be just above the servants.

'What will you do?' she asked.

'I'll try giving you a brew first. It's mostly pennyroyal with a little rue. Tastes nasty, but it should set things moving. You'll stay here with me until it's all over, and I'll check everything's out. Then I'll tell you how not to get another, if you like. Extra penny, that.' Sally looked at Molly.

'If that doesn't work, I'll have to put something inside you to get it out. That's more dangerous, but for what it's worth, I've done a fair few now, so I'm less likely to poke a hole in something than most.'

Molly felt her throat fill with bile, and she choked down vomit. Sally was still watching her.

'So do you want to do it?'

Molly nodded. 'Yes.'

'Right.' Sally started rummaging through the bag she had been carrying on her shoulder and headed for the empty fireplace. 'I'll get the kettle on. Make yourself comfortable.'

Molly was staring out of the filthy, cracked window on to the street below when Sally thrust a tin mug under her nose.

'Drink up. Better if you do it quickly.'

Molly screwed up her nose at the sharp smell wafting from the reddish-brown liquid. She put her lips to the cup and tasted the tang of metal. After a deep breath, she took a huge gulp of the brew, and gagged on the fiercely bitter taste. It seemed to burn her throat all the way down.

'That's the rue,' Sally said, slapping her on the back. 'Just swallow it down and I'll make some tea to take the taste away.'

Molly choked down the rest of the foul-tasting liquid and thrust the mug back into Sally's hands. She hawked and spat on to the already dirty floorboards.

'That's right,' Sally said, swilling the kettle out to make the tea. 'Now, keep walking. The more you move, the quicker it'll come.'

For the next half hour, Molly paced the little room, gulping down Sally's tea and circling the room like a caged animal. The sky was darkening outside, and panic coiled in Molly's belly as she thought of William back at home. If he had finished with his papers by now, he would have started wondering where she was. And when he found that Katy was still in the house, and Molly nowhere to be found . . .

A deep, gut-wrenching pain – like the cramps from her monthly courses, but twice as strong – suddenly shot through her, and Molly doubled over, pressing her bunched fists against her tight-laced stomach.

'It's working,' Sally said. 'Next pain you get, push down and see if you can feel anything.'

When the next pain came, Molly gritted her teeth and pushed down. She felt a hot trickle run down her thighs and soak into the tops of her stockings.

'Oh, God!' she gasped.

Sally took her hand and drew her over to the side of the bed, where a cracked old chamber pot sat on the floor. While Molly curled over herself again and again, fighting down howls of pain, Sally pulled up her skirts and petticoats and tugged her drawers down. She guided Molly down on to the pot, where she sat with her red curls sticking to her sweaty face. She felt herself stretching and straining, and felt all manner of different liquids bursting and trickling out of her body.

'Can you feel a lump, low down?' Sally asked. Molly nodded and screwed her face up. Tears squeezed from under her eyelids with the pain and the effort.

'Then next time, really push and it'll be over. Your body's trying to hold on to the child, but you have to fight it.'

Molly took a deep, shuddering breath, her jaw set at a determined angle. With one last push and a throaty cry, she felt something hard poke out of her and fall into the pot. Molly wept for the burning pain between her legs. She dropped forward on to her knees and Sally took the pot from under her and poked around in it with a stick. Molly's eyes flicked over to the rich-smelling red-black mess in the pot. There was a pale, whitish clump in the centre, shaped like a sheep's kidney but with black eyes like boot buttons and little lumps where the arms and legs would have grown. She watched as Sally tipped the pot on to the fire and there was a suffocating reek of burning meat. The whitish lump fizzled in the fire like a Bonfire Night guy, blackening until Molly could not tell it apart from the burned wood and paper.

'Brandy.' Sally handed her a brown glass bottle. 'Drink a little. It's medicinal.' Molly tipped the sweet liquor down her throat and cringed slightly at the tart aftertaste of the alcohol. The burning smell in the grate had spread through the room and Molly's eyes stung from the smoke.

'Best tell your husband that you came over all strange and lost it,' Sally said. 'We'll not clean the blood off your legs – you wouldn't have had a chance to do that if you miscarried while you were out walking. If he gets a physician out to you, you'll have to think of something to tell him if he asks about . . .' She nodded towards the fireplace. 'He won't be expecting you to pick it up and keep it in your pocket, though. Just have something prepared to tell him.'

'He won't get a physician, will he?' Molly blanched.

'He's likely to. This'll probably be quite a blow, especially if it was your first. But I don't think they'd be able to tell what really happened. I've not been poking around inside so there's nothing to give us away.'

Molly scuffed the toe of her boot against the floor. 'You'll think I'm daft, but I never really thought about how this would affect William. I knew I'd never be able to tell him, but . . .'

'Aye,' Sally said. 'It takes men differently. All you can do is protect yourself. And me, of course,' she added with a grin. 'Is he the violent type? Is he likely to be angry with you for losing it?'

'No.' Molly's voice was small. 'He's always good to me.'

'Married for love, did you?'

Molly shook her head. 'I didn't want to marry; I wanted to keep my Aunt Florrie's business. She was a spirit medium.'

'I know,' Sally said. 'I knew your aunt back when we were girls. Knew your mother too.'

Molly sighed. Suddenly, she felt weaker than she ever had. 'What was my mother like?'

Sally looked at Molly, her head tilted to one side. She pursed her lips. 'You're a lot like her,' she said finally. 'You probably get told that a lot, don't you? But I don't just mean the way you look. You have some of her expressions.' She frowned. 'And she was always strong-minded, like you. This morning, at your house, I really saw it. Florrie brought you up grand, but you're still Lizzie's daughter.'

'Florrie never mentioned my father,' Molly said.

'She'll have had her reasons,' Sally said equably. 'Look, all I'm saying is that I don't think Lizzie ever took to the idea of motherhood. She was as white as a ghost the day she found out about you. If you don't see yourself with a babe, it's as well to do what you've done today. Don't go soft and get another on you just because you feel bad about deceiving your husband. It's easy to forget your reasons for doing this once it's done, but just remember what you were prepared to risk to be free of it.

'Here.' Sally handed Molly a clump of soft linen. 'This is what you use to avoid getting another one; this or something like it. Wet it and push it up high inside yourself; high enough so he can't feel it. It won't get lost or anything like that. Take it out once you're done.'

'What if we . . .' Molly shifted awkwardly, '. . . do it before I've had a chance to put it in?'

'Ah, it's like that, is it?' Sally smirked. 'Most girls know they'll only be bothered at night, so they put it in before bed. You can't walk around with it in all day. You'll have to do what the whores do, lass: wash yourself inside afterwards.'

With a flinch, Molly remembered the night she told Jenny she was pregnant and what her friend had said about washing out a man's seed. She felt as if her insides would fall out from between her legs and found that she was clenching herself tightly. She fumbled in her reticule and dug out the money to pay Sally.

'Come on, you'll be missed,' Sally said, pocketing Molly's money. 'Let's get you home.'

Molly's legs shook as Sally guided her back to the quayside. When she looked back she could see tiny red spatters on the cobbles where she had walked. Sally looked at the dusky sky and grimaced.

'You'll never make the walk back alone, and I ain't going with you. A midwife and a miscarried woman don't look good together. We'll have to put you in a cab.'

They searched the dingy gloom of the quays until they had found a tatty black cab for hire. Sally raised a hand to the driver, who hopped down and opened the door for Molly. She stepped up into the cab, swaying in Sally's grasp.

'Don't let him drop you just outside your house,' the midwife whispered as the driver took up the reins again. 'Remember how much it matters that you get this right.' She closed the door and the cab lurched off over the slimy cobblestones.

Molly had the driver drop her on the Square, as far from sight of her home as she could manage. Her face was ashen as she stepped down from the cab. She teetered a little and the driver snatched her gloved hand to stop her from falling.

'Are you sure you want me to leave you here, miss?' he asked. 'You look like you need to be at home, begging your pardon for saying.'

Molly waved him away. 'I shall be perfectly well, but have an extra sixpence for your kindness.'

She turned and walked through the gate of the public gardens, waiting until she heard the cab move off before she threw herself against the trunk of a tree for support. She pressed her face into the bark and groaned softly. Her petticoats were sticking to the back of her legs and she could smell the coppery blood. She looked at the sky; it was getting dark.

She had to get home to William. Molly shivered, the world went foggy at the edges, and she remembered nothing.

When Molly became aware of the frosty grass underneath her face, she lifted her head slowly. It was dark, the sky was an inky blue. She felt so very cold. Everything seemed far away, and it took her a few moments to hear the voice calling her name.

'Molly? Molly!'

William. Molly lifted her head and croaked a wordless reply. Her neck hurt; she must have twisted it when she fell. She could see the greenish light of lanterns on the pathway.

'William?' she called weakly. Oh, the relief she felt as his footsteps came closer. Her head lolled into a flowerbed, and she felt his arms around her.

'Oh, God, Molly!' William scooped her up into his arms and crushed her to his chest. 'I've found her!' he yelled back over his shoulder.

He wiped the smears of soil from her cheeks. 'Oh, Molly,' he kept whispering. 'Oh, God!'

Katy appeared at William's side. 'Oh, ma'am,' she gabbled. 'What happened to her?'

'We must get her home. Run ahead and get the bed ready for her, and get a message to Dr Hartley. Go now!'

Molly felt William's lips on her forehead. She rested her head on the fresh-smelling linen of his shirt, and drew closer to the warmth of his body as he pulled his black wool overcoat around her. Again and again came the cramping pain deep inside her, and Molly shrank further into her husband's arms.

*

William carried Molly back into the house and took her upstairs to their bedroom. Katy had turned the bed down and put warming pans under the covers in an attempt to revive Molly a little. William laid her down on the bed and pulled at her bootlaces.

'I'll do that, Mr Hamilton.' Molly heard Katy's voice. 'You go and get yourself a drink; you look ever so shocked.'

'I don't need a drink, and I can manage to get Mrs Hamilton into bed without your help. Go and fetch the physician, girl.'

Katy scurried from the room, and Molly's eyes fluttered open to look at William. His face was strained and heavy with shadow in the dim gaslight of their bedchamber. Deftly he stripped off Molly's boots and walking dress, unlaced her corset and pulled off her chemise and her bloodstained petticoats and stockings. He ran a careful hand across Molly's brow and looked down at her bare legs, which were smeared with her blood. He tugged her drawers off and cast them on to the floor with the rest of the bloody mess of clothes. Molly trembled, cold and naked on the bed. William would have to know now that she was no longer carrying his son.

'Oh, Molly,' her husband sighed. 'Poor little thing.' He held her shivering body to him, his warm hands smoothing away the gooseflesh.

'I have no water to wash you,' he said, as he drew her warmest nightdress over her head. 'Katy will clean you up as soon as she gets back with the physician.' He drew the covers over her and sat on the bed beside her.

'I should have gone with you,' he whispered. 'This is all my fault.'

Molly shook her head weakly and reached out a hand to him. William kicked off his boots and lay on top of the covers. His face was as close to hers as when they lay together, and the scent of his warm breath soothed her. She looked into his brown eyes – burning now, not with the mischievous desire she was so used to, but with another emotion she couldn't quite place. She felt exhausted. William rested a hand on her forehead, and Molly closed her eyes.

17

The low rumble of male voices stirred her and she felt firm fingers on her neck, feeling for her pulse. She heard the clipped tones of Dr Hartley, and a chill came over her as she realized that she was lying in Florrie's old room, with Florrie's old physician hanging over her. A little cry of fright escaped her lips, and she recoiled from the physician's hands. Instantly, she felt William's familiar touch on her shoulders.

'Don't be frightened, Molly. Dr Hartley is here to help you.'

'And so you believe she has lost the child?' Molly heard the physician ask William.

'I am sure of it. She was covered in blood . . .'

'I shall have to examine her to be certain. Would you step outside, Mr Hamilton?'

'No.' William's voice was firm, and Molly's sleep-addled mind filled with a sense of dread as she tried to fathom how Dr Hartley could examine her to confirm a miscarriage. She wondered why the physician would want William out of the room, before the realization hit her and she recoiled in disgust.

Dr Hartley was not paying attention to her. 'I understand that this is a great disappointment, Mr Hamilton, but if you allow me to examine your wife I am sure that I can help in some way.'

'I never said you could not examine her, but I shall stay here. I know my own wife's body, and I am not leaving her alone to be touched by a man she hardly knows. She's had enough of a fright.'

'Very well,' Dr Hartley said. 'I shall begin.' William sat on the bed at Molly's head, taking hold of her hands and twisting his fingers around hers while she tried to find the energy to shrink away from the man peering at her.

Dr Hartley's hands were cool and professional on Molly's body. He pulled back the sheets and lifted her nightgown, pressing a palm down on her belly. He examined the bloodstains on her thighs. Snatching a glance at William, he pushed Molly's legs apart with a practised hand and slid a couple of fingers into her. The pain was still fresh, and Molly hated the touch of this cold man in such a warm part of her body. Tears welled in her eyes and she stifled a sob, pushing her face into William's shirt. Through her hair, she felt William kiss her head.

'You are correct, Mr Hamilton,' Dr Hartley said, pulling his fingers out of Molly and wiping his hands. 'She has lost the child. Might I ask, Mrs Hamilton,' he added, turning to face Molly for the first time since he had arrived, 'where this happened?'

Molly, her nightgown still pulled up around her waist, wriggled in a vain attempt to get herself back under the sheets and cover her nakedness. William pulled her nightgown down and drew the bedclothes over her.

'It . . . it was in the gardens on the Square,' she said, trying to speak slowly. 'I think it was where I fainted.' She thought back to the room on the quayside, and the wrenching pain in her guts. 'I felt a pain, low down.' She started to gesture towards her body, before remembering Dr Hartley's hands on her and stopping. 'And then I felt something falling . . .' She hoped she would not have to describe the experience of fluids running down her legs. Humiliated, she began to sob. Dr Hartley nodded, and returned his gaze to William.

'It is only to be expected,' he was saying. 'A woman of her age, especially, is unlikely to understand exactly what is going on.' He lowered his voice. 'You may wish to send a servant to check in the gardens, where you found her, but do not be surprised if they can find no sign of the miscarriage. Animals frequently remove such things.'

'Yes.' William's voice shook slightly, and Dr Hartley changed the subject.

'Only time will tell if she can conceive again. I can feel no internal damage, but some women cannot bear another after a miscarriage. After she has recovered from this you should be safe to . . . ah . . . try again. In the meantime, keep her warm and quiet. Feed her normally. She needs to sleep; I shall leave some chloral.'

'No!' Molly cried, startling the men. 'Don't make me sleep!' She thought of her dreams after Florrie's death, and of the pale creature in the pot, with the boot-button eyes. She imagined what she might say in her sleep; how she might incriminate herself.

'Now, Mrs Hamilton,' Dr Hartley said as he rifled through his bag. 'You need your rest. I know this has been very trying for you, but—'

‘No!’ Hot tears coursed down Molly’s face, and she turned her gaze from the physician’s impassive face to her husband, with frantic, pleading eyes.

‘No! William, please . . .’

‘Don’t drug her,’ William said. ‘She can rest without it. Don’t distress her any further.’

Dr Hartley snapped his bag closed. ‘As you wish, Mr Hamilton. Send for me if she has any further complications.’ He strode from the room and moments later Molly heard the front door closing behind him.

Molly spent the rest of the evening falling in and out of a light doze. Sometimes she would be shaken awake by a cramp or the dampness of more blood, but generally she floated in a blissfully dreamless sleep. Once or twice she peered out from under heavy eyelids and took comfort in the familiar bedchamber, its edges hazy in the gaslight. Whenever she stirred, she sensed William’s presence: even with her eyes closed she could smell the musky scent of him and hear his sonorous breath. When, at some late hour of the night, she opened her eyes, William was curled up on top of the bed, barefoot and asleep in his shirt and breeches. Molly reached out and laid a handful of blankets over him, and he stirred.

‘Molly? How are you feeling?’

‘Well enough. You looked cold.’

William smiled apologetically. ‘I did not realize it was so late.’ He burrowed deeper under the blankets and gently smoothed Molly’s cheek.

‘I’m sorry about Dr Hartley touching you, Molly. It was for your health.’

Molly cringed at the memory and shook her head. 'As long as he doesn't come back,' she whispered. 'I don't like him being around me. He treated my aunt, before . . .' William nodded. 'As you wish. I had no idea.' He exhaled heavily. 'I just wish I could have done something.'

So this was what Sally Marsden had warned her about. As Molly lay on her side, face-to-face with her husband, watching his dark eyes in the candlelight, she understood. The truth stuck in the back of her throat, choking her, and she fought down a sob.

'Don't worry yourself, Molly,' William whispered. 'Go to sleep.' He turned away, huddling himself into a ball around a knot of the blankets. Molly lay staring at the ceiling, listening to the rattle of his restless breath. She knew he was not sleeping.

When Molly awoke the following morning, she was quite alone. Her husband had always been a late riser, leaving it as long as possible before dressing and going downstairs for breakfast. Gingerly, Molly reached down and pressed a hand to her belly. She felt a little bruised but the cramps had gone, and when she drew back the bedclothes there was no fresh blood staining her nightgown. She reached for the little bell on her bedside table and rang for Katy. She couldn't lie in bed and play the part of the invalid all day – she would go quite mad. Besides, she was very concerned as to her husband's whereabouts.

Katy dressed her in a comfortable house dress, all the while fussing over her and worrying that she should not be out of bed just yet.

'I'm sure you shouldn't be laced so tightly, ma'am,' the maid fretted. 'You had such a nasty turn yesterday.'

Molly hid a smile at Katy's tentative turn of phrase: *a nasty turn*. If only William would see it that way and stop agonizing over it. God only knew how upset he'd be if he knew the truth. *Remember how much it matters that you get this right.* Molly remembered Sally's words and sighed.

'Oh really, Katy. I'm not laced too tightly at all. You've barely closed the back of my corset. Any looser and I shall look quite indecent. Now, where is my husband?'

'Mr Hamilton's gone out, ma'am. He told me to let you sleep; he won't like it if you're up when he comes back. I'm supposed to be looking after you.'

'He's gone out – at this time?' Molly felt a cold rolling in her stomach, and she bristled slightly with a vague sense of discomfort.

'He said he had something to attend to. He left you in my care, Mrs Hamilton, and I'm sure that . . .'

'Well, *I*'m sure that if Mr Hamilton knew how much better I'm feeling this morning, it would be a different matter entirely. Don't you think he will be pleased when he comes back and sees that I'm looking so much better, Katy?'

The maid nodded, a look of alarm on her face. 'Whatever you think best, ma'am. I'll fetch your breakfast.'

After breakfast Molly sat in the parlour, slitting open her letters with a silver opener borrowed from William's study. She flicked through a few of the spiritualist periodicals, idly browsing articles on levitation and automatic writing. Florrie had never taken to the idea of automatic writing: 'I can't see our regulars paying to watch me scrawl on a piece of paper,' she had said. 'Where's the artistry in it?'

Molly closed her eyes and tried to remember her aunt's face. Her memory was hazy and she wasn't confident that she was accurately remembering the grey-peppered shade of brown of Florrie's hair, or the hazel of her eyes.

She reminded herself that it was Wednesday, and grimaced at the thought of being at home to callers. If William had put out word that she was unwell, they wouldn't trouble her but tomorrow was a séance night. When she heard Katy's footsteps in the hall, she called for her.

'Yes, Mrs Hamilton?' Katy was in the parlour in a moment, a feather duster clutched in one hand.

'What has been done about the séance schedule?' Molly asked. 'Has Mr Hamilton arranged for tomorrow's circle to be cancelled?'

'Yes, ma'am. He thought it best that you rest for at least a week.'

Molly shook her head. 'Tomorrow night will be fine. Go now and get a message boy to send word to the regulars.'

Katy paled, and Molly knew that she would be anticipating Mr Hamilton's rage when he returned home and found his wife out of bed and back at work. 'You really shouldn't tax yourself, ma'am,' the maid was saying.

'I shall not take any calls this afternoon,' Molly cut in. 'I am not overturning my husband's wishes; I am simply adapting them to the improvement in my health this morning. Now, go and fetch a boy to send those messages.'

*

When William finally came home, Molly was sitting in the parlour. She had been trying to focus on the book in her hands – Mrs Browning's *Sonnets from the Portuguese* – but, unable to settle, she flicked through the pages, reading a verse here or there, but without finishing a full poem. At the sound of the front door, it was all she could do not to fly at William. He looked across at her, but despite her efforts she could detect no anger in his gaze. He almost seemed relieved. When Katy left the room, he sat beside Molly on the sofa and took her hands.

'Where have you been?' she asked. 'I was worried about you!'

William didn't seem to hear her question. 'I did not expect to see you looking so well,' he confessed. His hands trembled, and his grip tightened on Molly's fingers. 'You were bleeding,' he murmured, 'and when I found you, you were so cold . . .'

'I'm stronger than I look,' Molly replied with a forced smile. 'I am only a little sore, and that will be gone by tomorrow night, I am sure.'

William frowned. 'Tomorrow night? I cancelled your Thursday séance.'

'Oh yes, of course. But I thought that as I am recovering so well it would benefit me to start getting back to normal.'

'Is that really what you want?' William's eyes on hers were alarmingly intent, and panic suddenly flared in Molly's chest: what if he thought she was a little too nonchalant about the loss of her baby? Was he testing her? Had she been seen going to meet Sally, or arriving in the Square with blood on her skirts?

'I was brought up to keep on going when life became

hard,' she replied. 'I cannot just sit and think about what happened.' Molly dipped her head and stared at Florrie's rosebud brooch, pinned to the front of her dress. Tears burned her eyes, and the husky tone in her voice was quite unforced.

'I want to make the best of what I have now,' she said. She looked up at William and was startled to see his brown eyes glassy and wet as he fought back tears.

'William?' She had never seen him this way. Was he steeling himself to hand over his new wife for the murder of their first child? Molly felt faint. 'William, what is the matter?' she asked, trying to keep the hysteria from her voice. He couldn't send her to the rope, please God. If only she had done the sensible thing and asked Jenny how to prevent pregnancy in the first place; if only she hadn't let herself fall into his arms; if only she'd finished him off with her hand instead; if only she hadn't craved the feel of him deep in her body . . .

Molly's lips were trembling and the tears coursed freely down her face.

'William! Please!'

'I'm sorry, Molly.' He set her hands down and got to his feet. 'I shouldn't upset you so. If you'll excuse me, I'll probably be of more use in the study just now.'

He turned and left and Molly cursed herself and her craving for male flesh with his every step. She pitched herself face down on the sofa and sobbed as a dizzying frenzy of heartbreak and terror boiled in her chest.

When she'd cried herself hoarse, Molly lifted her head from the cushions and drew a deep, shuddering breath. Her face felt tight and cold with dried tears, and her skin tingled with fear. She cleared her throat and sat up, brushing the creases from her skirts. She stepped slowly out into the hallway and started up the stairs. On the landing, Katy was polishing the glass of a picture frame.

'Is Mr Hamilton in his study?' Molly asked.

'Yes, ma'am,' Katy said with studied indifference. Molly tried to glimpse her reflection in the framed glass, wondering if her face was still red from crying. Katy had become preoccupied with folding the grubby parts of the cloth in on themselves.

'Very good,' Molly said, and whisked down the landing towards William's study.

She tapped on the door, but did not wait to be invited in. William was sitting at his desk, defacing a sheet of paper with scribbles and blots of ink. He looked up and faced Molly with a smile of casual greeting, as if she were an acquaintance from one of his clubs.

'Hello, Molly. What brings you here?'

Molly was temporarily struck dumb by the inanity of his question, as if they had not both been near to weeping in the parlour downstairs barely an hour ago. She cleared her throat, which still felt sore and swollen.

'Just to talk. We have scarcely had chance to talk lately, with . . . with everything that has happened.'

William looked baffled. Theirs had never been a relationship built on talk, and here she was trying to pretend that her dropping into William's study for a quick chat was the most normal thing in the world.

'Very well,' he said, drumming his fingers on the desk.

'So,' Molly began, 'how are things at the mills?' It was the best she could think of.

'Same as ever, I believe. I haven't been to any of them myself for a week or so, but I'm sure my managers have everything well in hand.'

If William had not been out that morning dealing with his mills then what had he been doing? Still he could hardly meet her eye. Molly's throat knotted with panic, and she concentrated on spreading her impassive medium's expression across her face.

'I saw your former manservant today. The insolent one.'

Molly jumped, startled by William's sudden outburst and the tone of his voice. But Eddie knew nothing about her visit to Sally Marsden. Even if he knew Sally, she would not have told him. It would be her neck too, after all.

'Eddie?' Molly's mind was whirling. 'Where did you see him?'

'Actually, he approached me. Honestly, I've met the boy twice and both times he accosts me in the street. Still, he told me some news that I thought I should pass on. The girl who was living here—'

'Jenny,' Molly said automatically. She felt her shoulders dropping a little, the aching muscles loosening.

'Yes, that's the one. The lad said that she was living in rented rooms.'

Rented *room*, Molly silently corrected him. Why and indeed how would Jenny pay out for more than one room?

'He said to tell you that she and the baby are well, although they both have coughs.' William bristled and Molly found herself relieved to see even a little of his old haughtiness. 'He said that I should pass the news on to you, if I felt you would still care.' Scrunching up the ink-splattered sheet of paper into a tight ball, he hurled it into the fire and added, 'I wonder that you tolerated him for as long as you did, Molly. The ingrate obviously feels that he has some right to pass judgement on your conduct; it's beyond belief. I think I should be the one to take on any future servants.'

Molly, far too relieved at the tiniest hint of a future with William, as opposed to the hangman, had no desire to argue.

'Yes, William. If you think it best.' She paused. Truth be told, she had hardly thought about Jenny since her visit to Sally. Now she found herself trying to see Jenny's face in her mind but, like Florrie's, it felt wrong somehow, as if some fault in Molly's recollection had distorted her old friend's features.

'Then Jenny is earning?' she asked William.

'Hmm?'

'Jenny must be earning. If she's renting, she must have money to pay the landlord.'

'Of course she's earning. She's back at the mill; I told the foreman to expect her.'

Molly closed her eyes for a moment and drew a sigh of relief. 'Thank you,' she whispered. Jenny was no worse off than she had been before. Peter wouldn't be off the breast for some time and as long as Jenny had food enough for herself, they would both manage.

'After her display of ingratitude towards you and her complete disregard of our hospitality, I was inclined to turn her away,' William continued. 'But I knew that would only upset you further.'

‘Thank you,’ Molly repeated, smiling weakly.

William shrugged. ‘It’s quite all right. I meant to tell you sooner, but . . .’ They both sat in silence.

William hauled himself up out of his chair and Molly saw his eyes flash to the door. She had outstayed her welcome.

‘I think I shall have a bath before I retire,’ she said. William nodded in a distracted manner.

‘I’ll stay here a while longer,’ he said, walking her to the door and out on to the landing. ‘I need some time to think. This has been a difficult time and I have some decisions to make.’

The door closed behind her and Molly was left staring at the paintwork. Fresh dread curdled in her stomach as she wondered what William might mean.

18

The following afternoon, Molly sat at the table in the séance room, clipping the stems of the bunch of irises she had bought that morning. Until lunchtime she had roamed the streets with Katy in tow, casting furtive glances down side streets for any sign of William. She had a vague, sleep-addled recollection of him coming to bed very late the previous night, but he had gone when she woke, and now she couldn't be sure if he had truly been there at all or if she had dreamed it.

Now she sat slotting the irises – the messenger flower – into a thin-stemmed porcelain vase, trying not to think about where William was and what he was doing. Whenever she heard the rattle of a carriage or the sound of voices from the street outside she tensed in anticipation of a knock at the door or, worse, her husband walking in flanked by a couple of peelers.

The vase filled, Molly slid it to the centre of the table and reached into her sewing basket for a skein of fine thread. Time to try another of Florrie's favourite tricks. She tied one end of the thread in a loop around the slim foot of the vase, and sucked on the other end until she could get it through the eye of a needle. She probed through the tablecloth with the tip of the needle, looking for the tiny hole in the top of the séance table, and slipped the needle through so that it swung from the table's underside. Molly caught it and unthreaded the needle from the line and gently looped the loose end of the thread on to the tiny hook that would hold it safe until she was ready. Brushing the tablecloth down, she gathered up her sewing basket. It was almost six o'clock. Time she dressed for the séance.

The sitters that evening were an assortment of regulars and newcomers: a portly, red-faced man with a Midlands accent and his pointy-featured wife; a young solicitor who 'had to see it for himself' and thrust his card into Molly's hands, telling her that if her husband should ever need legal representation he would be only too delighted; and a small, middle-aged woman who strode into the séance room ahead of all the others and took a seat opposite Molly. Molly glared at her, but was ignored. She looked at the shabby roan of the woman's limp locks, the colour of William's carriage horse, and concluded that it must have been red before the grey started snaking through it. Her clothes had once been good ones too – Molly could see that much – but now they were threadbare through constant wear.

The woman smoothed the crêpe-like skin under her eyes, and Molly felt a small stab of jealousy to see that she didn't seem to suffer the redhead's curse of freckles. Still, this shabbily dressed hag had to be fifty if she was a day. *Please don't ever let me look so undignified*, Molly thought to herself, as she gestured to the other sitters to take their places.

Closing the door, Molly took up her place. In the faint candlelight, she could see the shadows of the new woman's lined face staring her down. She was probably one of those who thought they could tell how it was done once they saw it, Molly decided. Her expression impassive, she instructed the ladies to remove their gloves, before blowing the candles out.

For a woman with a missing husband, an estranged childhood friend and a constant dread of impending arrest – all while recovering from a miscarriage – Molly thought she handled the séance beautifully. Once the two young women at either side of her had blindly grasped each other's hands in the dark, Molly was free to let the 'spirit messengers' announce their arrival in the room. She unwound the thread hidden under the table and tugged at it so that the vase teetered on its thin stem and toppled over on to the table, scattering flowers and sending up shrieks of fright from the women sitters. The brittle chinking sound as the vase hit the tabletop suggested that it had cracked, but it was worth the loss of the vase to hear the thrilled whispers of the sitters as they blinked and blinked against the dark of the room, trying to see the spilled flowers.

Instructing them to lay their palms down on the table, Molly tried to ignore the awful memory of her quickening. Drawing a deep breath to steady herself, she informed the sitters that the presence of spirits often caused things to move, and that the spirit world's power was such that even heavy furniture was not exempt.

'If you should feel movement under your hands,' she told

them casually, 'do not fight it. Simply allow yourselves to become conduits for the other side.'

Within seconds, the table began to shift under the palms of the sitters, its rounded feet scraping ever so slightly against the floorboards.

'Stand, if the table should move any further,' Molly advised, 'and move with it.'

As they got to their feet, somebody must have leaned slightly on the table's edge, for it lurched gently, startling the sitters. Molly shifted her weight slightly to encourage the table to move away from her – for surely there was no better indicator of genuine spirit activity than a medium's willingness to relinquish control of the séance to her friends on the other side – and the sitters moved with it.

By the time she had opened the circle and relit the candles, Molly was glowing despite herself. The regulars congratulated her on one of her best circles yet, and the ebullient solicitor frothed at the amazing power of the spirit world he had witnessed that night. Smiling modestly, Molly ushered them to the door, where Katy would meet them and escort them downstairs for their hats and coats. As she thanked Pansy Hart for coming, Molly could see, out of the corner of her eye, that the faded redhead was still standing beside the table. Turning to the woman, she asked if she would be so good as to follow the maid, who would show her out.

The woman looked at Molly, her face serene. With her gloves still bunched together in one hand, she ran a finger over the cracked vase as it lay on the table. Then she smiled sweetly at Molly and strode out on to the landing with the other sitters.

Molly ate supper alone that night, telling Katy that William's work would keep him out late.

'If he has had to travel, he will of course spend the night at a guesthouse,' she said, as Katy brought a solitary plate through to the dining room. Sitting by herself at the dinner table with the good linen and candles, Molly wished she had thought to tell Katy to serve supper in the parlour.

'If we're lucky, he may still manage to come home tonight,' she continued. *That's the truest thing you've said all day, Mol*, she thought to herself.

Even after the house was dark and Katy had headed up the creaking attic stairs to bed, Molly could not sleep. The bed-covers felt heavy on top of her, as if they were holding her down. After wriggling about for twenty minutes, she threw the blankets back and padded barefoot over to the window, where she sat on the ledge seat, looking out at the silent street below. She shivered lightly and walked over to the wardrobe for a shawl. She lit a candle and felt her way to her dressing table. She set the candle down on the table and dropped on to the stool in front of it. The golden-yellow light of the flame choked its way further and further down the candle. Molly watched the pale spectre of her face in the mirror, flickering in the failing light. The silence of the house taunted her. *I won't see him again*, she thought. *The next time I'll see William's face is in the crowd, just before they drop that bag down over my eyes.*

Sometime later – she had no idea how long – the candle burned out, sending up a little sliver of smoke and plunging her into darkness once again.

Stirring from an exhausted sleep, Molly lifted her head from the dressing table and winced as a cramping pain shot through her neck. She rubbed the sleep from her eyes and looked back towards the bed. It was still empty. A chink in the curtains revealed a bluish light stealing across the sky: morning, and William was still not home. In that moment Molly knew, with utter conviction, that he had spoken to the police; that he was avoiding her so that his resolve would not soften when she looked up at him with round, wet eyes. She was not safe. She was not safe. In desperation, she flung the doors of her wardrobe open. She had a few warm, plain outfits she could take, and if she left now she would be gone before William and the peelers came for her. She tossed her thickest shawl on to the bed and started to search for her largest reticule. Damn it! She had no money, and she'd not get far on foot. Her mind boiling over, she mentally combed the house, trying to imagine where she might find some cash.

William's study. The secret compartment in his desk. For a moment she swallowed down guilt at the thought of robbing her husband before leaving him, but then she remembered why she was being forced to run away from her home and her business. She could be in and out of the study in under a minute. She had to do it.

Easing the bedchamber door open, Molly held her breath and prayed that the hinge would not creak. She padded barefoot down the landing, picking her way over the floorboards that looked least likely to creak. She turned the cold brass doorknob of William's study and slid inside.

The study was dark, save for the dull embers in the grate. Squinting, Molly cast her eyes around the room and pushed the study door closed behind her.

'Molly?'

Swallowing down a scream, she clapped a hand to her mouth and span around. How had she missed him? There, slumped in an armchair by the dying fire, sat a drowsy William. The intoxicating whiff of port drifted over from his stained, rumpled shirt, and the shrivelled ends of cigars littered the hearth. She looked at him, slouching in his chair with a boot up on the fender, just as he had been when she had first laid eyes on him at the Meadowcrofts'.

'William? Why are you still awake?'

Fighting the conviction that he would snatch her up and drag her down to the jail, Molly stepped over the scattered newspapers and empty bottles littering the floor and knelt at her husband's feet. Looking up into his bloodshot eyes, she found the courage to reach up and stroke his ruffled hair. She ran the backs of her fingers down the stubble that was starting to grow on his chin and felt a hot rush of relief as William rested a hand on the small of her back.

'William,' she said again. 'William, I've been worried sick. Where were you?'

'I'm sorry,' he muttered. 'I've been out at my club, and I lost all sense of time. I've had more drink inside me in the past few hours than I have in the rest of my life, I think. When they locked the club doors it was getting light.'

'Why did you not come to bed?' Molly asked.

'I was going to. But when I stood outside our room, I felt . . .'

Molly watched as he fought with the words at the back of his throat.

'Felt what, William?'

William shook his head. 'It was the drink. It would have been wrong for me to do it. I thought it safer if I were to sleep in here and leave you in bed.'

'I wasn't in bed!' Molly cried. 'I sat up at my dressing table until I collapsed, waiting for you. How could you think that I would rest easier without you?' Her voice shook, and she took a deep breath to steady her nerves. 'You have avoided me for days, William. Why? What have I done that angers you so?'

For Molly, the next few seconds passed like days. She swallowed against the knot of tension in her throat as William hung his head and closed his eyes. When he opened them again, they were burning into her own with all his old fire.

'You thought that I am angry with you? That I blame you?'

'Why else would you not touch me; not speak to me; not share a bed with me? I am not the first woman to miscarry her husband's child and I won't be the last. Am I really such a disappointment to you?'

William dropped out of the chair, kneeling on the floor beside Molly. He dragged his overcoat down off the back of the chair and placed it over her shoulders. She had not realized that she was shivering.

'You are no disappointment to me,' William said into her hair. 'You are the only thing in my life that I chose for myself.'

Molly stared at him, trying to understand. 'What? Then why have you avoided me?'

William's voice was barely a whisper. 'Because I did not trust myself.' He drew Molly's red curls up out of the collar of the coat, spread them upon her shoulders, and sighed deeply.

'I'm so sorry, Molly. It's all my fault, and I did everything to prevent . . .' He broke off and slid closer to Molly, pressing his face into her neck. Molly could feel his shuddering breaths against her skin.

'What is it, William?' she said, suddenly alert.

'I never wanted to repeat my father's mistakes.' William's voice was harsh with unshed tears. 'But then I found you collapsed in the gardens, all alone, and the child lost . . .'

He believes it was his doing? All this time, he thought he brought it upon me?

'It was not your fault!' she pleaded. 'Please, William. I beg you not to blame yourself. And your father is dead and of no concern to either of us. Why would you think these things? What mistakes are you talking about?'

William drew a long, heavy breath.

'My father inherited the Hamilton Cotton business when it was much smaller. The Preston mill was half the size, and we had yet to acquire the mill in Leeds. Hamilton Cotton had been successful but it was my father who made it what it is today. It was all he cared for. He would spend long hours at the office, and rarely ate at home with his family.

'He married my mother for the connections and her

dowry. There was never any warmth between them. I was not the first child my mother bore but I cannot remember those who went before me: they died young, as did those who came after me. My father was furious. He never spent a night with my mother with any aim other than to produce an heir, although I'm told his face was familiar to the local whores.'

Molly kept her face down and wrapped her arms around him.

'At least I was a son for him,' William continued, 'but he never showed any real pride in me. Every day was a lesson in how Hamilton Cotton should be run after his death. From the age of twelve, I was constantly told to marry well and protect the family line. He always wanted the Hamilton name to be more than just a prominent one in the cotton trade; he wanted us to be recognized in the very best social circles. "Marry a plain little society mare," he would tell me. "They're nothing to warm yourself against at night, but they'll give you your heirs well enough. There are plenty of girls around to satisfy any other needs, if you can spare two shillings."

'But I was never the heir he wanted. I was sent to school to get a good education to prepare me for handling the business, but I was a bit of a devil while I was there – just boys' tricks, but they certainly affected the reports that were sent back to my father.'

Despite himself, William grinned, and the corners of Molly's own mouth twisted irresistibly to see his smirk.

'What sort of tricks?' she asked.

'Children's silliness; nothing that matters now. It was flooding the desks that got me expelled, though. I filled each one with water, soaking all our books. I was sent home before I could complete my final year.'

'Couldn't your father have just taught you the trade himself? That was how my aunt handed things over to me.' Instantly Molly cursed herself, and guarded her tongue against speaking more of Florrie's lessons.

William did not seem to notice. 'He might have, had I been willing to learn. But I was happier playing cards with the men we met at his gentlemen's clubs than comparing prices with them. I liked to spend money at the tailor's and I spent plenty more than two shillings on girls. I'm sorry, Molly.'

Molly rolled her eyes. 'I was brought up with more understanding of the world than any of those "little society mares". So what's your miserable father got to do with us, then?'

'He would have hated you, Molly. He dragged me to so many dinner parties to meet potential daughters-in-law of whom he would approve. He'd bring my mother, too, if she was well enough: pregnancy and childbearing took a toll on her health. The number of times I sat on the stairs when I was a lad, listening to her screams . . .' William screwed up his eyes as if to banish the image from his mind.

'To the wealthy merchants and businessmen with unmarried daughters I was the eligible Hamilton Cotton heir. I must have sat next to at least thirty trembling, well-mannered waifs in my youth. When Father started to press the marriage issue, I seized the opportunity to take a jaunt to London with a few of the chaps I'd met in the clubs. I knew he wouldn't argue if he thought I was finally getting a head for business.

But I took a ship to France while I was there, and stayed in Paris until I couldn't eat another head of garlic.

'I came back to Preston, although I stayed well out of my father's way. I only went back to his house when I got word that my mother had died. I didn't even have a chance to go to her funeral. I went to ask Father why he had not sent for me and he told me that he had not thought to do so; that being granted such an unfit heir as me was a greater disappointment to him than losing my mother while she was trying to bring another into the world – another which would surely die anyway.'

'That's how my mother died,' Molly whispered. 'Giving birth to me.'

William nodded. 'You seemed so terrified when we discussed your condition . . . I wondered what had made you fear childbirth so.'

Molly wriggled at the mention of her pregnancy. If William had grown up hating his family business, he would never understand why she had wanted to protect hers. 'So,' she asked, 'how did you come to be the head of the business?'

William shrugged. 'Father and I never spoke again, and the first I knew of his death was a letter from his solicitor informing me of my inheritance. In his will, he wrote that his dying regret was having to entrust his life's work to his spendthrift hedonist of a son. He left a letter for me with the solicitor; I know the words by heart: "William, if I could find a way to remain at the helm of Hamilton Cotton from my grave, I would do so rather than leave it to you. As it is, I can only pray that any son you might father will be yours in blood only, and not in character, and that all I have worked for will survive you." I tell you, Molly, keeping that man's dream alive . . . it is repugnant to me. If it were not for the question of earning our living and keeping us well, I would not do it.'

'Then why do it?' Molly asked. 'You don't have to keep Hamilton Cotton to keep us. Why not look for a new business?'

'I have thought about it,' William said. 'When I met you, and I saw the fire in your belly and the spark in your eyes, I made a decision: to marry you, and not one of the bland women my father would have chosen. My friends would tell me how their new wives lay under them as if they were dead, and I couldn't bear the thought. I wanted to touch you the moment I laid eyes on you, and you looked back at me as if you were not afraid.'

Molly couldn't help but smile. The light had returned to William's tired eyes as he remembered their clandestine courtship, his fingers caressing her waist in tiny movements.

'There is no reason to fear the influence of your dead father,' she said, 'or to pickle yourself in drink. Why are you torturing yourself so?'

His grip on her waist trembled.

'I cannot risk killing you as my father killed my mother,' he whispered, pulling his fingers away from her waist and screwing up his eyes. 'You suffered so with the miscarriage, and even if I try to be careful you could conceive again, and I cannot put you through that, not so soon. I don't want you to bleed all your energy and vitality out in fruitless childbed. That was why I turned away from our bedchamber door last night; I was merry with drink, and I got hard just thinking about my little copper-headed wife lying in bed waiting for me. I would not have been able to control myself.'

'So you are going to become like your father, then?' Molly said. 'You will not touch me unless it's to get the heir you need.' She hung her head. Florrie could have told her well enough: there wasn't a man alive who wouldn't see her as a place to grow his seed in the end.

'I will not let you die like my mother did,' William said. 'We will get used to it in time. Now I think you should go back to bed and get some rest.'

Part Three

19

By Monday morning, Molly no longer feared for her life, but she ached to tell William the true cause of her miscarriage. Surely even Sally could not have anticipated that he would assume fault on his part. Molly's neck was saved, but every time she looked at William, she choked a little.

He had finally returned to their shared bed, but although he would hold Molly close to him and inhale the scents of her skin and hair, he would not allow himself to touch her below the waist. One night, she reached down to take him in her hand as she had done when they were betrothed, but with a groan of frustration and regret William pulled her hand away.

'I cannot promise that I will not get carried away, Molly,' he said. 'When you are stronger.'

With a heavy heart, Molly continued to run the spiritualism business, consoling herself by thinking of how William's lust would return in time.

The sitters at the Monday séance were all regulars apart from a wealthy merchant from out of town and the ageing, roan-haired woman from Thursday night. The woman looked Molly in the eye as she swept up the stairs with the other sitters and confidently tossed her tatty shawl to Katy as if she herself were the lady of the house. Molly decided that Pansy Hart and Marianne Meadowcroft would once again be the best people to sit beside her, but the roan-haired woman took up the seat to the left of Molly's chair before she could utter a word of protest.

Molly despaired of this woman's ageing hands passing for her own. They were small and neat like hers, but the skin was dry and crumpled. However, she could hardly insist that the woman move.

'Best not to make a scene if anything goes wrong,' Florrie always used to say. 'If you come over all nervy, you might as well show them the strings and the trapdoors yourself.'

Molly drew a deep breath to calm herself. Marianne sat to her right; better it be her on the other side of Molly, she was less quick-witted than Pansy. With a carefree smile, Molly gestured to the remaining clients to take their seats.

Once the candle flames had been extinguished, Molly worked quickly while the sitters were still completely blinded by the sudden plunge into darkness.

'Please join hands,' she ordered. As she prepared to slide back to allow Marianne and the faded redhead to join hands, Molly's left hand was snatched by the redhead's sinewy fingers. Molly caught her breath; her heart pounded. The redhead squeezed until Molly had to fight down a yelp of pain. Finally she released her and reached across for Marianne's outstretched hand. Molly span around to look at the hostile stranger, but all she could see in the black of the room were two tiny lights glittering in the woman's eyes. Molly ran the tip of her tongue across her dry lips. Her whole body shook.

'*Seven years picking apart old rope and sewing boat sails together*,' she could hear Florrie saying. She had to continue. Feeling the words wavering in her throat before she had even said them, Molly forced the familiar lines out of her trembling lips.

'They have come.'

She knew the woman would confront her when the séance was over. This was no ordinary disbeliever. As Molly prepared to close the circle and send the sitters home, her heart thudded and a rush of blood roared in her ears. It came as no surprise to Molly when the redhead did not move from her place while the other clients stood and walked out on to the landing to meet Katy. Pansy Hart's gaze flicked back into the room. The woman sat at the séance table with a serene smile on her face, and she turned to Molly with a look of distaste.

'Thursday and now today! Shocking how some outstay their welcome, isn't it?' Pansy said in an undertone.

Molly nodded and smiled sweetly. 'Oh, the more eccentric souls are part of my line of work,' she said gaily. 'I shall spare a few moments to speak with her. I'm sure she has no idea of the inappropriateness of her behaviour. I hope to see you again shortly, Mrs Hart.'

Molly closed the door and turned to face the stranger sitting at her table.

'What do you want from me?' she finally asked.

The greying redhead's eyes glittered and she smiled cruelly at Molly. There was something about the woman's face that needled some place buried deep in the back of Molly's mind.

'Have you ever wondered why you haven't seen me before?' the stranger asked.

'Why should I have seen you?' Molly hissed, listening to the murmur of voices as the sitters followed Katy downstairs. 'I have met you twice; of what consequence are you to me?'

'Three times,' the woman said, holding up three fingers in the flickering candlelight. 'Although I will forgive you for not recalling the first. Can you not see it, foolish girl? Or have you become so like me that you cannot imagine yourself growing old? Time ain't been kind to me, true, but with the life I've had that's hardly surprising.'

Molly stared at the stranger: her once red hair, her shining green eyes, her small hands. Dear God. It was not only her clients Florrie had lied to.

'You're my . . .'

The woman at the table smiled bitterly. 'The fleshed ghost of Lizzie Pinner herself. And just look what my girl has done with her life.'

Molly's childhood nightmares came flooding back to her and she felt a sharp flash of fury at Florrie, the loving aunt who had told her that her mother had died giving birth to her. She felt cold, and when she tried to speak her voice was thin and breathless. 'I thought you were . . . Florrie told me . . .'

'We all thought it best,' the woman named Lizzie Pinner said. 'No questions would be asked if I had died and my sister raised the baby. Nobody would have come looking for me.' Lizzie surveyed Molly critically. 'I suppose the subject of your father was never discussed? Do you even know if you're a bastard or not?'

'I assumed I was,' Molly admitted. 'So you did not intend to have me then?'

'Of course I didn't,' Lizzie spat. 'I was only fifteen. You were the result of one night – one bloody night! – behind the Black Bull with a travelling tea merchant. You have his nose, I think. I got chatting to him – made sure I did. Florrie gave me a lecture on what could happen with men. With our mother dead, she always did think I needed her advice. But I knew exactly what she had to tell me; I'd been finding out for over a year. Your aunt had ice between her legs, and it looks as if that never changed. I read her obituary in the paper; died an old maid, didn't she? She never could understand what I saw in strong male flesh.'

The back of Molly's neck prickled.

'I read the announcement of your engagement, too,' Lizzie continued. 'My girl, aren't you? I wouldn't be correct in guessing that your marriage was a hurried one, would I?'

'Do I look like I married in a hurry?' Molly smoothed her hand over her flat belly and stood sideways in the light of the candle to show Lizzie her virginal shape. The half-truth sat uneasily in the pit of her stomach, but she couldn't bear this woman's inscrutable gaze.

Lizzie let out a short, clipped laugh. 'No, but there are ways round that too, aren't there, Molly?'

Sally. Sally had known Lizzie Pinner.

'You tried to miscarry.'

Lizzie nodded. 'Sally Marsden had just started out with the birthing, and she'd been told a few ways to stop a baby.

I went to her when I couldn't hide you any more. Florrie hadn't even noticed my condition until then, if you can believe it; probably too busy with the spiritualism. She'd learned a few little tricks by that time, like the one you were trying to pull on me and that gormless little rich girl tonight. She was always saying that she could earn us a living one day, and I always thought she was touched in the head. How was I to know that fools would start flocking to a charlatan's house to be told there were spirits flying around their heads? Anyway, I didn't care. Sometimes I could get a penny or two myself if I took a fancy to a rich man.'

Molly stared levelly at the strange harridan who called herself her mother.

'Get that look off your face, you spoiled little brat. You know you're no better than me. I was no whore, or I'd have made my fortune far sooner than my self-righteous fraud of a sister.'

'Sally,' Molly reminded her, 'you were telling me about Sally Marsden.'

'I'm sorry, am I delaying you?' Lizzie mocked. 'Got a ball to be going to? Yes, I went to Sally's, and Florrie insisted on coming with me. She didn't trust these new methods of Sally's, and she thought I needed her protection, of course. Sally tried the herbal brew, and it didn't work. Stubborn little brat, you were. Then she tried putting something up me, while Florrie shrieked and flapped about, saying I'd die for sure. I didn't, as you can see,' Lizzie flinched, as if at some remembered pain, 'no matter what they told you. But Sally didn't know what she was doing, and she stuck me; high up, where they couldn't reach to stop the bleeding. That put an end to my fun with the lads, I can tell you. Never been the same since, but you still hung on, didn't you? Come to think of it, Florrie wasn't too far off the mark when she said you were the death of me. You damn nearly were.'

Molly flinched. Half a lie, Florrie had always said. Stick as close as you can to the truth.

Lizzie drew a deep breath. 'It was Florrie who came up with the idea. Ever the liar, my sister Florence was. She adored you from the start, and I think she quite liked the idea of me going away and being replaced by a baby she could raise to be a little version of herself.' Lizzie cackled. 'That worked a treat, didn't it? Anyway, I was happy enough to go. I couldn't stay in Preston. I went up to Newcastle in the end. Sally agreed to go along with the lie, and they gave you his name, Pinner – at least I think that's what he was called – and said they'd tell folk we'd married before he went off and got killed at sea. I'm Lizzie Tranter, really, like your aunt was, and just like you. Nobody would have thought to argue, and they certainly wouldn't have looked in the pit for me; it was a warm spring, the bloody thing reeked. I left the night after you were born, although I could barely sit down in the coach. You don't know what pain is if you haven't given birth after the kind of injury Sally gave me.' The woman's eyes glazed over and she looked blankly into the candle flame.

'And so here you are,' Molly said. 'You went through all that pain and trouble to keep our lives apart, only to show up in my house years later and announce that you've been alive all along. Why? It's not a sudden rush of maternal love, I can tell that much, so why not just go back to wherever you came from? Is your life in Newcastle so dull that you have to come here and play tricks on me?'

Lizzie glared at her. 'Like I say, I saw Florrie's obituary in the paper. It was the article about the death of a spirit medium down in Preston that got my attention; she got half a page, going on about what a sensational medium she'd been. And then there was you, of course. Heir to her business and her money, and blessed with your late aunt's talents – what a bloody surprise.'

'What did you expect?' Molly snapped. 'Yes, Florrie made me her heir; of course she did! If you hadn't run away to Newcastle, it probably would have been you. You must have managed somehow all these years, anyway.'

Lizzie nodded. 'I run a pub up there. It's nothing special, but it's honest work.' She smiled. 'Not like the work my little brat makes a small fortune from. Florrie didn't half do you a favour by dying. What an inheritance, eh?'

'Don't you dare talk about my aunt,' Molly hissed.

'I'll talk about *my sister* all I like,' Lizzie snarled. 'She was my sister well before she was your aunt, and I knew her well enough to recognize her false piety when I saw it. Don't try her poor-but-honest act with me; it don't suit you.'

'Very well.' Molly brushed her hands on her skirts. 'What do you want? Money? I can get about five pounds from my husband's study; then will you leave?'

'Five pounds!' Lizzie threw back her head and laughed. Molly could see the blackened teeth at the back of her mouth, and smell their sickly rot. 'Five pounds, after all you put me through? I might not have spent my life spinning elaborate lies about life and death, but I can read a face as well as you can – I bet you were a natural in this job, weren't you? It was me you got that from, dearie, not Florrie.'

'You did not teach me my skills,' Molly said, her voice low and threatening. 'You left me as soon as I'd dropped out. I have Florrie to thank for my talents; she was my mother in all but name, and I will not give you thanks for my life, my money or my marriage—'

A tap at the door made them both jump. Katy popped her head round the door, blinking in a bewildered manner to see the faded redhead still seated at the table with Molly glaring at her from the corner of the room.

'Mr Hamilton's home, ma'am. He just wanted to know where you were. Shall I tell him to come up?'

'Yes,' Molly said firmly. 'We are quite done here. You may fetch this lady's things.'

Katy looked blankly at Molly.

'The green shawl,' Lizzie snapped.

'Oh. Yes.' Katy dipped a curtsy and scuttled off downstairs.

'You want to get rid of that maid of yours,' Lizzie said, turning to Molly as if they were old friends. 'She gave my shawl a filthy look; rude little bitch.'

'She's not used to seeing moth holes in people's clothes,' Molly countered, with a sweet smile. 'But if you won't take money to buy some more . . .'

The séance room door creaked open and William strode in.

'Good grief, Molly, how do you see in this light? I just wanted to tell you—' Breaking off, he turned and regarded Lizzie with an expression of bewilderment. 'Hello?'

'Don't mind her, William,' Molly said, taking Lizzie's bony elbow and walking her to the door. 'She was just leaving.'

Katy came back upstairs with Lizzie's tatty old shawl, and laid it about her shoulders as if it were a crumbling papist relic. Lizzie shot a swift look at William and turned to Molly with a cold, tight smile.

'Yes, definitely my girl,' she whispered. 'I'll be in touch.' Ignoring Katy, she swept down the stairs.

'Who on earth was that?' William asked. Looking closer at Molly's face, he laid a hand on her shoulder. 'Molly, are you all right? You look as if you've seen a ghost, so to speak.'

Molly shook her head. 'She was nobody; forget about her. Let's have some supper.'

That night, as they wriggled under the blankets, Molly remembered that William had something to tell her when he came up to the séance room. 'Oh – was there something you wanted to tell me before?' she asked, feigning nonchalance.

'Oh yes,' William said. 'I was going to tell you that I took your advice.'

'I beg your pardon?'

'About the mills. I've been putting it around town that I'm considering selling Hamilton Cotton – for the right sum, of course. The news has caused quite a stir, and there's plenty of interest. It's a relief to be able to see my way to shaking off the last traces of my father.' He drew Molly into his arms. 'I want us to be free to enjoy ourselves. To enjoy our life together.'

He started nuzzling Molly's neck. She could feel his hesitant, self-remonstrating caresses becoming more confident, and she gasped as his lips closed on her neck. William's kisses became more insistent as he nipped her lightly with his teeth until she cried out in delight. His fingers traced down to the ribbon at the neck of her nightgown and he pulled it loose. His late-night stubble was rough on the soft skin of her breasts, and as William traced a line of kisses and bites over her curves, Molly stretched out and sighed happily. It seemed the prospect of selling the mills had freed him of his fear of losing her in childbirth. His mouth moved down to her belly, and she could feel his hot breath through her nightdress. She was growing damp in anticipation of William sliding inside her, and she writhed in excitement as she waited for him to pull up her nightgown.

With a groan, William pressed his face to her belly and she gasped. When he lifted his head up and faced her, his expression was one of tortured desire.

'Oh, Molly. You have no idea how much I wish . . .'

'Then do it!' she cried. 'William, I feel fine. I'm sure I will not conceive.' She reached down and ran her fingers along his back. 'We should celebrate your decision to sell, after all.'

William shook his head. 'You conceived after just one hurried embrace; standing up against a tree, no less. We are obviously fertile together; the risk is too great.'

'Then let me touch you, at least!' Molly begged. 'You do not need to be inside me. You must have learned a few tricks from the whores you had in your youth.' She smiled playfully. 'Especially the French ones.' She started to slide down under the blankets, not entirely sure what she was doing, but hoping for the best. William groaned as she nuzzled him through his nightshirt, and he tensed at the touch of Molly's face.

'No!' he gasped, pulling her up. 'Just kissing you was too tempting . . . if you were to . . . I know I would lose all control. Molly, I want this more than anything, but it's too soon. Tie up your nightdress and let's get some sleep.'

Defeated, Molly closed the neck of her nightgown and tied the ribbon closed. She curled up and closed her eyes, squeezing her legs together in an attempt to still the throbbing. She could smell the frustrated lust hanging in the air. William lay on his back, staring at the ceiling. Just as she was about to sink into sleep, Molly heard him breathing rapidly and felt the bedclothes rustling on top of them. With a strangled gasp, William lay still. Molly screwed up her eyes so that no tears would escape them.

20

William woke Molly with a kiss the following morning, and chattered brightly as if nothing had happened the previous night.

'I visited my tailor yesterday,' he was saying, 'to order some new clothes. He had some very stylish hats in, too, and I thought that since we shall be beginning afresh, a new wardrobe would be in order. Why don't you get Ashton to take you into town today?'

'You've only just bought my trousseau,' Molly yawned.

'Yes, but we can afford it. Why don't you pick up some nice things for the house, too? It's a little drab around here. It needs a woman's touch. How about some flowers? When Ashton and I were setting up my study, I noticed that you have quite a few books on flowers. They'd brighten the place up a little; what do you say?'

'They were my aunt's books. Yes, I'll go and see what I can find, if you like. Will you be going into town today too?'

'Yes, I've arranged to meet a man about a business I'm interested in. We can take the carriage into town together, and I'll leave it with you once Ashton's dropped me off at my club.'

Molly nodded. 'I'll ring for Katy. We can have breakfast

early.' There would be no point in staying in bed. That much she knew.

When Molly stepped outside the house on William's arm, Ashton was lounging against the side of the carriage, his gold-blond hair bright in the sharp morning light. William escorted Molly to the carriage and held her hand as she stepped up inside. Molly smiled at him. He looked so handsome, and in his finery he was deliciously formal. William got into the back of the carriage beside her and Ashton slammed the door closed. William held the tips of Molly's gloved fingers and her stomach twisted in sorrow as she remembered how things had been.

Ashton dropped William outside a tall, neat-looking brick building, and William pressed a chaste kiss on to Molly's glove before striding towards the white door of the club. Ashton tipped his hat to Molly and gave her his standard smile – one that never truly managed to seem deferential. Molly wondered what Ashton had been told of her courtship with William, or, indeed, whether he had simply deduced matters for himself. She had no reason to believe that William had enjoyed regaling his male companions with tales of their trysts, after all.

'Where to now, Mrs Hamilton?' Ashton asked.

'I shall go into town for a little shopping,' Molly replied. 'Houldsworth's the dressmaker's first, if you please.'

After Molly had selected the colours and cuts of her new gowns, and Gretchen had taken fresh measurements to ensure a perfect fit, Molly sat with the seamstress in the fitting room at the back of the shop, drinking the tea Gretchen insisted on pouring for her, saying that she had heard about Molly's recent illness and that she must keep her strength up.

'My illness?' Molly asked. 'What have you heard?'

'Oh, it was nothing much, dear,' Gretchen said. 'Mrs Meadowcroft was in, ordering a new hat, and she mentioned that you had been unwell, but that you recovered enough to get back to work.' She laughed. 'Just like your Aunt Florrie; can't bear to leave the spirit world for more than a week! Still,' she added, the mirth on her face wiped away by concern, 'you are quite well now, aren't you? You're a little less plump than you were when I fitted your wedding dress, if you don't mind me saying, and you look a little . . .' Gretchen trailed off, searching Molly's eyes, '. . . glum,' she finished.

Gretchen reached across the tea tray and squeezed Molly's hand. 'How's married life treating you, Molly? I'd never ask any of my other customers, but I've known you since you were a little girl, and you were so nervous on your wedding day. He is gentle with you, your young man, isn't he?'

Molly nodded vigorously, smoothing the dressmaker's hand. 'William is very good to me, Gretchen, don't worry.'

'Then he's not making too many demands on you? It takes time to get used to being married; it's so different from being courted, isn't it?'

Molly's laugh came out almost as a sob. 'A lot has changed since we married,' she admitted. 'But William is not too demanding, Gretchen, I promise you. In fact,' she said, dabbing at the corners of her eyes with her lace-edged handkerchief, 'do you have any new nightdresses? The ones you were talking about last time I came in, with the French lace?'

Gretchen nodded, and Molly felt a twinge in her heart at the concern being shown to her by her aunt's old friend.

'I'll fetch you some to look at,' the dressmaker said. 'You stay there, love.'

Molly left the shop with a selection of ribbons, a fierce embrace from Gretchen, and a parcel containing three of the most delicate nightdresses she could find in the dressmaker's stock. She had felt a little strange, handing such provocative garments over to this friend of Florrie's and asking for them to be wrapped, but she was willing to try almost anything to persuade William to hold her and have her once again, rather than pretending to be asleep while he released his frustrations right beside her.

'Moss the florist's next, please, Ashton,' she said, handing the driver her purchases to stow away in the box on the back of the carriage.

'Mrs Hamilton!' the girl behind the counter exclaimed as Molly walked in. 'What will it be today?'

Molly pondered a while, wondering which flowers would best achieve the brightness William wanted. As if something so simple could change their lives in a meaningful way.

'Sending a message to your husband?' the florist's girl was saying. 'It's unusual for courtship to continue after marriage; I'll say that.' She coloured a little. 'Quite f-f-forthright, your husband, ma'am, isn't he?'

Molly turned on the girl with a scowl. What did this little drab know about William? Surely he could not have shown any interest in such a dull creature, especially one who flushed and stammered so?

'Are you acquainted with my husband?' she asked icily.

'No, ma'am,' the girl gabbled, wringing her apron. 'Forgive me, I misunderstood . . .'

'Then just wrap me an assortment of bright flowers for the drawing room,' Molly snapped. 'And stop being so presumptuous.'

She left the floristry blinking hard. Hot tears of embarrassment threatened to spill over, and she thrust the gaily coloured bunch of blooms at Ashton. She stood by the carriage door and clenched her hands into fists. For William to lie with paid whores in his youth was one thing, but to reject her as she lay beside him in bed, while turning those wicked eyes on to every shabby little scrap in Preston was another entirely. Molly swallowed hard. She had promised to return with a carriage full of fancies for the house, and she would do just that. Irritably, she turned around to see why Ashton was taking so long to put flowers into the back box. As she blinked away tears she squeaked in alarm.

Lizzie stood in front of her, her face inches from Molly's own.

'Having a good morning?' she asked.

Molly's eyes darted left and right. The crowds milled around them and few people seemed even to notice the well-dressed young lady almost pinned against her carriage by this scruffy crone. Deciding that it was safer to treat Lizzie as a beggar, Molly looked down her nose and announced as loudly as she dared that she had no money and did not wish to be bothered.

'I can raise my voice too, lass,' Lizzie said in an undertone, looking around at the well-dressed people strolling past. 'But do you want me to, or will you spare a moment of the royal time to talk to me properly?'

Molly grimaced. She caught hold of Lizzie's arm and pulled her into an archway between two shops. Molly was not about to let Lizzie into William's carriage. The woman stank of fish, and Molly's nose wrinkled involuntarily.

'Been a while since you've eaten eel pie, then?' Lizzie said.

For all that she denied her mother's influence on her life, the woman's sharp observational skills unsettled Molly. *By God*, she thought, *she never misses a trick*.

'What do you want?' Molly asked in hushed tones. Out of the corner of her eye, she could see Ashton standing at the door of the carriage, looking curiously at Molly talking to this old harridan.

'I'll make this quick, since I get the feeling you don't want to stand here and argue,' Lizzie said, leaning in close to Molly. 'You're a fraud and a con artist; you and I both know that. The only ghost you've ever seen is me, and I'm as alive as they come, my girl. Once the truth about you gets out, it'll be off to the big house with you, and the next few years of your life'll be spent rattling your chains in your cell. That dapper man of yours'll sue for divorce. Oh yes he will; they all run for the safety of a frigid little miss when the spicier girls get too hot for them. And when you do eventually come out, you'll be as stooped and ugly as me, with no man and no living, and no looks to get men to give you a living. Not a pretty thought, is it?'

Molly glared at her. Lizzie nudged her shoulder and nodded in the direction of a passing peeler. The polished leather of his collar glinted in the light and his tall hat cast him a giant's shadow. A memory of hiding behind Florrie's skirts as a child came back to her; peelers had frightened her like goblins and ghouls frightened most other children.

'Oh, now look there!' Lizzie trilled in a sing-song voice. 'It would be so easy, wouldn't it?'

Molly watched, dry-mouthed, as the peeler strolled past. Ashton had taken a couple of steps closer. She forced herself to adopt a calm, relaxed expression, hoping that Ashton would not see fit to rescue his employer's wife just yet.

'Yes, yes,' she snapped. 'I know perfectly well; you don't have to try and frighten me. What is your point?'

'That I'm being remarkably generous,' Lizzie said, grinning madly at Molly. 'Here I am, knowing all about your shocking lies, and still I haven't turned you in. I do believe I'm not so bad at this mothering lark after all. Just think of the secrets I'm keeping to protect you. I won't even tell anyone that I'm your mother, since I know that would humiliate you.' She cackled raucously. 'It might raise your man's eyebrows and all,' she laughed, 'if he thought his wife might look like me in a few years. Not going to want to warm his hands against you on a cold night then, is he?'

Lizzie's mouth twisted into a pout. 'I wouldn't have looked like this myself but for the hell you put me through. I'm not as old as I look, you know.'

Molly waved an impatient hand. 'You've made your point – I didn't fool you and never will; well done. Now will you go?'

Lizzie gasped in feigned shock. 'You'd let your own mother go on her way, after all she's done for you, and not thank her for it? Dear, dear, what are they teaching these young ladies nowadays? Listen to me, girl. I'm not going to take a little payoff and let you go that easily. I'm offering to keep your secret – and it's a big one – for life; and you'll reward me for that. Sod your husband's five pounds; five pounds a month is more like it. You can send it up to Newcastle to me; I'll give you the address.'

'You know perfectly well that I cannot spare five pounds a month!' Molly squeaked. 'And what am I supposed to tell William? He's bound to notice if large sums of money disappear from his study every month.'

'Not my concern.' Lizzie shrugged.

'This is ridiculous,' Molly snapped, suddenly tired of the whole argument. 'So you know that my talents aren't genuine. But you did absolutely nothing to get me where I am today, other than leave me in the care of your sister, who was worth ten of you. You have no right to anything of mine, and I will not spend the rest of my life dancing to your tune.' She thrust a hand into her reticule, rummaged around, and pulled out a handful of money.

'Take that,' she hissed, thrusting the notes and coins into Lizzie's hands. 'And get out of my life.' She turned and flounced away, refusing to look back.

'Don't you stroll away from me like a princess born and bred, you little sow!' Lizzie's hard grip was on Molly's wrist in moments, pulling her back. Molly pulled away from her.

'Ashton!' she shrieked. He was at her side almost instantly, sticking the handle of his whip into Lizzie's chest and pushing her away from Molly.

'Get out of here, you disgusting old hag!' he shouted. 'Clear off, before I call the police!'

Grumbling, Lizzie knocked the whip away. With a loaded glance at Molly, she turned and walked away, leaving Molly to brush off Ashton's frantic questioning.

'I shall be perfectly fine, Ashton,' Molly said as the driver settled her back into the carriage. 'She just frightened me a little, that's all. Now please take me to Hammonds' before I meet my husband for lunch.'

When they stopped to pick William up from his club, Molly watched out of the carriage window as Ashton and her husband exchanged a few words. She knew that the driver would be telling him what had happened in town, and so she was not surprised when William climbed into the carriage beside her and declared that he fancied taking lunch at home, rather than in a tea room. As Ashton touched his whip to the horse and the carriage rattled off over the cobbles, William looked closely at Molly. She could feel the cold pallor that had spread over her face, and she knew it was pointless to pretend that everything was fine.

'What happened, Molly?' William asked.

Molly sighed. 'It's a long story. I'll tell you at home.'

William nodded and hooked an arm around her, bringing her head down to rest on his chest. Molly inhaled the smell of his clean linen and wished that her childhood nightmares had been true, that she was indeed an orphan.

'So who was the woman?' William asked once they were alone in the parlour. Molly took a gulp of tea. Her sandwich sat untouched on the side of her plate. 'Ashton told me that a dishevelled woman waylaid you and tried to attack you,'

William continued. He caught hold of Molly's chin, pulling her face up to look at him. 'You know who she is, don't you?' He paused, looking thoughtful.

'Ashton said she had red hair. Is she the same woman who was here last night? The one who remained after the séance?'

'Yes,' Molly murmured.

'Is she causing trouble for you? Does she have some complaint about your work? I'll have Ashton throw her off the doorstep next time she comes here; never fear, Molly.'

'It's not that simple,' Molly said, her voice small.

'Why not? What need have you to worry about the ramblings of a mad old woman? She's a nobody!'

Molly shook her head. 'She's my mother.'

William was silent for a moment.

'What? Your mother? But you told me that . . .'

'That's what I was told,' Molly said. 'But it seems I was lied to. My Aunt Florrie . . .' Molly shuddered, pressing her handkerchief to her mouth. 'My Aunt Florrie always told me that my mother died while she was giving birth to me. I only found out the truth on Monday. William, she wants to ruin me. She knows . . .' The words died in Molly's throat.

William nodded. 'Your business.'

Instantly defensive, Molly jumped as if startled. 'What do you mean?'

William laughed, holding out his arms to her. She went willingly into his embrace, allowing him to pull her on to his lap.

'Oh, come now,' he said. 'I told you when we first met that I didn't believe a word of all that spiritualism nonsense. I don't know how you do it, but if I actually thought that the spirits of the dead were wandering around our home I'd be somewhat concerned, and if I thought that you believed they were, I'd probably have you committed, my dear.'

'It's not so unbelievable,' Molly sulked, muttering into William's neck. 'The Meadowcrofts and the Harts take it in, anyway.'

'That may be so, but this has nothing to do with your prodigal mother. She knows you're a charlatan, then, and she's threatening you with the law?'

Molly, a little uncomfortable at hearing the word *charlatan* from William's lips, nodded reluctantly.

'She wants me to buy her off. She hates me; she says that she suffered a great injury when she . . . when I was born. She blames me for the state of her life, and she's furious that Florrie and I came into money. She wants five pounds a month or she'll have me thrown in jail.' Molly looked up into William's eyes. He had not yet looked away from her. 'I'd go down for at least seven years, I'm sure,' she whispered. 'Maybe your father was right about marrying a dull girl with a name.'

'Forget about him, Molly. You've said yourself that the advice of a dead man means nothing to us. But you cannot just throw a monthly stipend at this woman.'

Scalding tears trickled down Molly's face. 'Not even to save me from jail?'

'Because it *won't* save you from jail. Once she realizes that you are afraid enough to comply, it will be ten pounds a month, then twenty, until we are both thrown into debtors' prison anyway. We are respected in this town, Molly, and she is a scruffy old hag with a sharp tongue; if we have her taken up by the police, they will not believe her word against ours. We can beat her at her own vile little game. Do not worry.'

Molly did not look convinced. 'And if someone does recognize her?'

'You forget, Molly, you were born into a different class of people. Anybody who could recognize your mother is not somebody the police would see fit to interview. You're not a part of that world any more.' William frowned. 'Now I think of it, do you know how she found you?'

'I assumed that she asked around when she arrived in Preston; there are no other spirit mediums here.'

'Hmm,' William said. 'I ask because of something your old manservant said when I had the pleasure of bumping into him; back when you were still ill from . . .' William shifted in his seat, straightening his posture, '. . . from your miscarriage. What's the lad's name?'

'Eddie,' Molly said, before realizing that William meant his surname. 'Eddie Rathbone.'

'That's the one. He was quite drunk, so I didn't take him seriously at the time.' William shook his head. 'Wherever did you find him, Molly?'

'He was the son of a friend of my aunt's. She took him in when he lost his position at the butcher's.' Molly decided not to mention the pocketful of stolen meat.

'What did he say?' Suddenly, she was filled with dread at the thought of Eddie bragging about their fumblings in the materialization cabinet.

'It was when he was ranting about that Jenny girl. He said you would *have to come back to your roots soon enough*. I thought nothing of it then, but what if he had spoken to your mother? If he told her where to find you?' William was growing angrier. 'Damn it, if he endangered our entire household by leading her to our door . . .'

'Don't worry,' Molly soothed her husband, despite the frantic thudding of her own heart. 'It would be far easier for Lizzie to find me through my clients than for her to track down my old servants. Eddie just resents me, that's all. His pride won't allow him to accept being dismissed by a former equal. Don't listen to him, William,' she added. 'If he approaches you again, don't upset yourself by listening to his poisonous lies. I hate to see you so worried by someone who is of no consequence to us.'

William nodded. 'Then don't you worry about this Lizzie woman. Let me deal with her. I mean it, Molly,' he said, looking at her dubious expression. 'You haven't managed to get rid of her by yourself, have you? And I don't want my wife fretting over idle talk from irrelevant people.'

Molly bristled. 'Speaking of which,' she countered hotly, remembering her conversation in the florist's shop that morning, 'why does the florist's girl think you are a "forthright and confident" suitor? I don't even know the girl's name and I am hearing reports of my husband's courting practice from her!'

'What?' William looked perplexed. Then he threw back his head and laughed – the first wholehearted laugh Molly had heard from him in a long time. 'Molly, I cannot keep up with you. One moment you notice every detail of everything I do and say, and the next you don't seem to be aware of what's right under your nose. I was in the florist's shop, true, but it had nothing to do with the serving girl!' He slid Molly off his knee. 'Wait there.'

William strode out into the hall, returning with a bouquet wrapped in tissue paper. Pale, pinkish flowers nestled amid tiny yellow blossoms. Molly drew a deep breath of the sweet perfume.

'I was getting these for you, you silly girl. I know you think I don't want to touch you any longer, but . . .' William pulled Molly into his chest, pressing the flowers between their bodies. 'I wasn't slipping the florist's girl an extra couple of shillings, you know. You seemed so upset the other night . . . I thought these might comfort you.'

'They are lovely,' Molly conceded. 'But they're no replacement for . . .'

William tickled her waist, and Molly instinctively slid her body towards him. 'I read a little of one of your aunt's books,' William whispered in Molly's ear. 'Everlasting pea and linden blossom. Maybe you should reacquaint yourself with their meanings.'

William left shortly afterwards to meet a potential buyer for the mills. As soon as he had gone, Molly left Katy putting her flowers in a vase and dashed upstairs to the spare attic room where William had ordered Ashton to store Florrie's old things. The dingy room was packed with a jumble of furniture and boxes. The smell of Florrie's violet perfume, mingled with the dust, prickled at Molly's nose. Florrie's bed, pushed up against the far wall, was stripped of its linen, and the bare mattress looked hard and lumpy. Blinking in the darkness of the room, Molly spied a stack of books on Florrie's old dressing table. She stumbled across the clutter on the floor until she could reach across and snatch *The Language of Courtship* from the top of the pile. Flicking through the pages, she came first to the letter E, and traced a finger down the yellowed page until she found what she was looking for. *Everlasting Pea: Everlasting Pleasures.* Molly smiled. *Linden Blossom*, the book continued: *Conjugal Matters.*

21

Four days later, Molly had still not heard from Lizzie, and she was finally beginning to relax. Perhaps the old crone truly had been driven off by Ashton; perhaps she had given up and gone back to Newcastle. After all, Molly comforted herself, Lizzie might have had great plans to blackmail her newly wealthy daughter, but she had no idea of how moneyed society worked. Maybe she had not taken into account the fact that Molly now had a husband and two servants behind her and would be able to afford to instruct a solicitor to take issue with Lizzie's scheming.

William was beginning to return to his old self, although he and Molly had not yet been together in the truest sense, despite the flimsy nightdresses Molly had bought from Gretchen and the bunches of flowers that he sent to his wife while he was out negotiating the sale of Hamilton Cotton. The biting January cold kept the florist's stock pretty sparse and the flowers William sent could only have been grown in a glasshouse. Now that her husband was beginning to return her caresses, Molly revelled in the warm touch of his hands. But still William would not allow himself to risk a conception, and Molly knew she could not tell him she had the knowledge to prevent one.

One Friday morning, Molly asked Katy if Ashton and the carriage were available today.

'Yes, ma'am. Mr Hamilton left early, but he said he'd send the carriage back. He'll be out until lunchtime. Ashton's in the kitchen, ma'am, eating his breakfast.'

Molly nodded. 'Send him up when he's finished, would you? I want to pop into town for something.' Since her encounter with Lizzie, Molly had not felt like going into town with only Katy for protection.

Molly strolled into the florist's as if she had not a care in the world, and shot a dazzling smile at the serving girl, who had splashes of water down her apron from tending the flowers.

'How is your stock of hothouse flowers?' Molly asked.

The girl dipped her head. 'Well, Mrs Hamilton, the best in Preston; Mr Moss takes a lot of pride in his glasshouses.'

Molly nodded. 'Then would you be so good as to send an arrangement over to my house? My husband has been so generous lately that I wish to give him a gift in return.' Another sweet smile.

'Yes, Mrs Hamilton. Which flowers would you like?'

'Red columbine and peach blossom,' Molly said smoothly, hiding a smile at the girl's blushes. 'And do make sure they're nice and fresh.'

When William came home for lunch, Molly was setting out some of the new ornaments she had bought for the drawing room. William walked into the room so softly that Molly did not hear him until he was standing right behind her. Just as she heard the soft rustle of his breath, William's arms closed tightly around her before she could turn around, pinning her arms to her sides. Molly smiled and pushed her body back into his as he gently nipped her neck with his teeth.

'My captive, no less,' he whispered in her ear.

'An anxious and trembling one,' Molly reminded him. She blushed to a delicate pink, wriggling herself further into William's embrace. 'You found them, then.'

'Mmm.' William's face was buried in her hair. 'I can't wait to be able to take advantage of my prisoner properly.'

'Really? How very chivalrous of you.'

'Ah, it's only too fitting for my new position in life,' William said, pulling Molly's hips back until he could press his body along the curve of her buttocks. She bent slightly over the end table she had been draping with a doily, and William grunted under his breath. 'As of this morning,' he continued, his voice throaty and harsh with lust, 'I am no longer the respectable proprietor of Hamilton Cotton, and may it all go to hell. I regret to inform you, Mrs Hamilton, that you are now wed to a suitably villainous liquor peddler, and that such men can rarely be trusted for long.'

'You sold the mills?' A glowing flood of relief swept through Molly, and it occurred to her that perhaps this would finally mean the return of the man she had married.

'Yes, to another local cotton merchant. He was happy to acquire three more mills, and to eliminate a business rival, of course.' William kissed Molly's earlobe. 'And you may be pleased to hear that he intends to keep the current staff. Jenny's job is safe.'

Molly turned and kissed him. 'I am pleased to hear it; delighted, in fact. So, what is this liquor business?'

'I shall be importing spirits and selling to the clubs and public houses,' William replied. 'I struck up a conversation with Mr Warren, the former owner, when I was out at my club. Thank heaven we met while I was still relatively sober.' He paused, closing his eyes momentarily in a bid to banish the memory of his days of drunken sorrow, and Molly gently laced her fingers in his. Squeezing her hand, he continued, 'Anyway, after I spoke to you, I remembered that Mr Warren was thinking of selling his business. The deal's gone very smoothly, and now the liquor business is mine. I've never been one to discourage vice in men, as you know.'

'No indeed. So when are you planning to begin your life as a brigand?' Molly asked, turning her head to nuzzle her lips against William's. He dropped a hand to her belly and rested his palm there.

'Soon, I hope. Before God, Molly, I hope you are recovered soon.'

'I feel perfectly well, you know that,' Molly protested. Her buoyant mood dropped a little as she detected the awful hint of guilt that coloured William's voice whenever they discussed that delicate matter. 'I have had my course as normal; I am quite sure there is no damage.'

'That may be, but Mr Hartley is a physician; he does not specialize in matters such as this. It just seems too soon.'

'Then if my next course is uneventful shall we say that we are safe?' Molly reasoned. 'I will certainly have had time to heal by then.' William nodded, and Molly smiled with genuine delight and relief. 'Until next month, then.'

His hand slid down between her thighs, and he pressed her back against him through her skirts. Molly gasped at the firm pressure of his fingers, and William pushed against her until she could feel his hardness through their layers of clothes.

'This may be the longest month of my life,' he murmured in her ear, before softly biting her pearl earring.

Early that evening, over dinner, Molly and William shot burning gazes at each other across the dining table, and looking at her husband, so handsome and self-assured in the warm light of the candles, Molly could almost imagine that she was back at the Meadowcrofts' dinner party, hoping that the good-looking stranger would find an excuse to waylay her. Her lips curled up into a smile as she thought of William's hands running over her body for the first time, as they embraced in the rocking carriage. She felt the bittersweet sting of desire shoot up through her body as she looked at his long fingers grasping his cutlery and his lips pressing against his glass. The month ahead seemed like a lifetime. But at least now William was returning her flirtatious looks instead of hiding his face in shame. Molly found herself astonished at how relieved she was to have back something of the man she had married.

Only looking down her dress at the rosebud brooch quelled her feverish daydreams. Each time the little brooch caught her eye, Molly thought again of the woman who had been under no obligation to be her mother but had been that for her and more; the woman whose estate she had handed over to William because of what happened that day in the public gardens.

'Molly?' William's voice jolted her from her thoughts.

'I'm sorry,' she said, smiling weakly. 'I was thinking of something else.'

'Well, whatever it was hasn't put much of a smile on your face. Come here for a while.'

Molly walked around to William's side of the table, and he pulled her on to his lap and held her tightly around her waist.

'William! Katy will be here any moment to clear the plates; you know that!'

'Then come upstairs with me. I thought you might like . . . shall we say . . . a few French lessons?'

William swept her up in his arms and strode out of the dining room, Molly laughing helplessly all the way at his scandalous behaviour. As his foot hit the bottom stair, a ring at the doorbell made him stop in his tracks, and they regarded each other, pop-eyed.

'For heaven's sake, William, get away from the door!' Molly whispered as he came to his senses and rushed halfway up the staircase.

But before he could carry Molly upstairs and out of sight, Katy scurried down the hall, wiping her hands on her apron. Molly and William froze, desperately trying to keep silent so the maid would not turn around and see them, and Molly forced herself to stare intently at the paper on the wall, knowing that if she looked at William, she would not be able to save herself from fits of laughter. She buried her face in the rough wool of his waistcoat, and as she heard Katy open the door, she prayed that whoever it was would just leave a card and go away.

But the muffled voice was one that Molly knew. Lifting her face from William's chest, she tried to place the voice's owner. Where had she heard those clipped, earthy tones before? Then Katy stepped back to let the visitor into the hall, and as she looked down the stairs Molly's blood ran cold.

Sally Marsden, shaking off her rain-drenched shawl, looked up and caught sight of William standing halfway up the stairs with Molly in his arms, but she didn't even flinch. When Katy followed the line of Sally's gaze and spotted them, she gasped in horror. Molly reached down and tucked her petticoats over her ankles, and William's grip on her wavered as if he were unsure whether to set her down or keep hold of her.

Katy had gone scarlet. 'Oh, sir! Ma'am! I am so sorry; I thought you were . . .'

It was Sally who took the situation in hand. 'It's quite all right; Lord knows I've seen worse. Molly, I need to speak with you.'

'Excuse me,' William began a little indignantly, 'but this is rather a bad time.'

Sally nodded, but her gaze did not falter. 'That's as may be, Mr Hamilton, but with all due respect, it's about to become a worse time. Molly, I need to speak to you now.'

Molly rested her palm against William's chest.

'It's fine, William. Sally here is the midwife who came to deliver Jenny.' She glared at Sally, who rolled her eyes. 'Would you like to step through into the parlour, Sally?' William put Molly down, and she looked at him with eyes that she hoped were warm, despite the icy dread in the pit of her stomach.

'I shan't be long, William.'

As she pushed the parlour door closed behind her, Molly span around to face Sally.

'What in God's name are you doing here? You yourself said that our being seen together would make my husband suspicious!'

'Shut up about your bloody husband and listen to me!' Sally snapped. 'It's about Jenny.'

Something in Sally's tone shot a bolt of terror into Molly's heart. Her legs quavered under her, and she dropped into a chair.

'W-what about Jenny?'

'Hasn't your husband heard?'

'No,' Molly managed to say. 'He sold the mills this morning; matters there are no longer his concern.'

Sally nodded. Her mouth was a tight, straight line. 'Jenny's son died today.'

Molly stared at Sally. 'What?'

'Well, since she'd got nobody to watch him, she'd been bringing him to work. She went to collect a bolt of cloth from the weavers so us downstairs could bleach it, and she took the baby with her. She carries him about in a basket – *carried* him, rather.

'It was Emily Harris who works on the mules that told me. Jenny went round the back of the machine where they were taking the cloth off, and she set little Peter's basket down on the floor. Emily said it all happened in the blink of an eye; no one had a chance to do anything.'

'What happened?!' Molly realized she was shouting, and she dropped her voice before William or Katy came in to see what was the matter.

'They rolled up the cloth and passed it over to Jenny,' Sally said. 'But they were careless. One end of the roll hit the basket, and it fell into the back of the mule.'

Molly gasped. 'Couldn't they get him out?'

Sally shook her head. 'It fell just as the carriage was moving back. It couldn't have been a worse time. The basket was smashed against the frame at the back; fell to pieces straight away.' She took a deep breath. 'The baby was crushed against the frame. Died right then and there. Didn't even cry, or if he did, nobody could hear it over the racket from the machines.'

'Dear God!' Molly whispered. 'Where's Jenny? How is she? I must go to her!'

Sally closed her eyes. 'Nobody's seen her since it happened. She lost her mind, Molly. She was totally crazed. Tried to jump into the machine and get the baby out; took three big lads to stop her, and you know what a little scrap she is. Probably littler since you last saw her too, what with nursing the baby. Emily ran for me; she thought I might be able to do something. 'Course I couldn't. They'd shut off the machines and they were just pulling him out when I got there. They didn't ask the foreman if they could shut the machines off; just did it. They're not a bad crowd, there.

'Jenny grabbed him straight away and shoved him into my arms.' Sally flinched at the memory and swallowed hard. 'I'm used to death; I've done enough laying out in my time. But I've got a family of my own, and the baby . . .' The midwife bit her lip. 'He looked like a broken doll. It was his head; it must've taken the brunt of the blow.

'But Jenny kept screaming at me, telling me to do something. She wouldn't listen to me when I told her it was too late. In the end, I had to grab her hand and lay it over his heart. There was nothing there, of course, and she just turned and ran. Nobody could stop her – there was a few that tried, and she just pushed them away from her. I took the baby home and cleaned him up. I don't know if she had a chance to get him baptized; if not, it'll be the edge of the cemetery, I'm afraid, on unblessed ground. But we have to find her, Molly. I can sort out the baby's burial if needs be, but I don't know where she is and I'm worried sick. That don't happen too often.'

Sally knelt beside Molly's chair and looked her in the eye.

'Molly, if we don't find her now, I think she'll wash up in the Ribble. She's lost everything.'

Molly screwed up her face as if she had taken a punch in the gut. She shook her head; it could not be true. 'No,' she whispered, 'she wouldn't . . .'

Sally grabbed hold of her shoulders and shook her, Molly's eyes flew open in surprise. 'If you waste time going to pieces now, she will die,' the midwife said. 'The only thing you can do for Jenny is to calm yourself and get out there.'

Molly gulped breathlessly and nodded. A lump formed in her throat as she remembered how she and Jenny would skip pebbles across the river when they were children, competing to see who could get their stone furthest across the water before it sank. Molly blinked back her tears.

'Get your shawl,' Sally said. 'You know her better than anyone – where would she be?'

William was still standing in the hallway when Molly flew out of the parlour, shouting for Katy to bring her walking boots and her shawl.

'Molly, where in God's name are you going?' William asked. 'What about—'

Molly turned to him with a hunted expression.

'Molly? Molly, whatever is the matter?'

'It's Jenny.' Molly's hands shook as she snatched her boots from Katy, and she bit her lip hard. 'Her baby was killed at the mill today, and she's gone.' Reaching up and grabbing hold of William's shirtfront, Molly looked up at him with imploring eyes. 'William, she's been my friend for as long as I can remember. If anything were to . . .'

William nodded, and gestured to Katy to bring his overcoat. 'I'll go with you; we can take the carriage.'

The three of them bundled into the back of William's carriage, and as Ashton set the horse trotting towards the industrial part of town, Molly and Sally stared out of the windows, keenly scanning the streets in the hope of seeing Jenny.

'You can't be the only person at the mill she was friendly with,' Molly said. 'What if someone there knows where she is?'

Sally frowned at the darkening sky. 'I ran out after her so quick, I never noticed the time.'

William dug his pocketwatch from his waistcoat. 'It's nearly five o'clock.'

'They'll still be there,' Sally said. 'It's worth a try.' William fumbled with the window and stuck his hatless head out into the night air.

'Ashton! The mill!'

The carriage rattled up to the mill, and Molly flung her door open and tried to jump out before Ashton had even pulled up the horse. William caught hold of her arm and dragged her back inside. Sally took her hand.

'No sense in breaking your neck, Molly,' she said, and Molly paled a little at her words. 'Come on,' Sally said. 'Let's see what the other bleachers know.'

When they walked in through the front door of the mill and into the cacophony of machine noise, Molly was struck by the silence from the workers, even in the midst of the bone-shaking racket from the weaving machinery. Sally strode down the shaky steps and between two banks of vast, clattering looms, and William tucked Molly's hand into his arm and followed. Glancing right and left, Molly saw surly faces turning from them or looking intently at their feet, or worse, into the flashing steel of the machines. Sally's eyes swept almost imperceptibly to the back of one of the machines, and as Molly looked across, a wiry lad with smudges on his face and a scrubbing brush in his hand ducked out of the way of the mule as it crashed back against the frame. He glared at Molly until the mule rolled away, bent very deliberately over a dark stain on the floor underneath the machine and resumed scrubbing.

As Sally led them to a small door, one of the weavers, a rather gormless-looking lad, spotted William and pulled his forelock. William nodded in reply, but a pair of workers were at the lad's side in an instant, elbowing him and throwing poisonous looks at the Hamiltons. Molly lowered her eyes and William marched her past them.

Downstairs in the bleaching room, Molly watched the women weaving their way around the huge, harsh-smelling vats. The air was choked with the odour of bleach, and Molly gagged as quietly as she could against the smell. The women workers barely seemed to notice it. Sally strode into the centre of the room and stood with hands on hips.

'They're here to help Jenny,' she said loudly. Her voice echoed around the room of silent women and softly sloshing vats. 'Whatever else you're thinking, the best any of you can do for Jenny now is to say if you know where she might be.'

The women stood still, looking at the Hamiltons from under dishevelled hair and limp caps. William cleared his throat.

'We have a carriage outside,' he announced. 'If any of you know where she might be, no matter how far away, we can find her and bring her home safely.'

A thickset blonde with strong-looking arms scoffed, 'Maybe she's gone to pay a visit to that friend of hers she was always talking about.'

'Bridget!' Sally shouted. 'This is not helping Jenny.'

The girl called Bridget was not listening. 'Oh yes, that friend who climbed out of the gutter like a rat up a drainpipe. The one who got herself up the aisle with the charming gentleman who used to pay us our pittance.'

William clenched his jaw and clutched Molly's hand a little harder. Bridget dropped her bundle of cloth on the floor, making sure to step on it as she walked over to stand before Molly.

'Bridget,' Sally warned.

'Still,' she sniffed, 'I'd rather be a dirt-poor bleacher in this hellhole than a treacherous little whore.'

'That's enough!' William cracked the girl across the jaw with the back of his gloved hand, and she reeled back. Molly caught hold of his hands, pulling him away, and Sally grabbed Bridget by the shoulders.

'Bridget, you know as well as I do that Mrs Hamilton didn't push Peter into that machine. I don't think Jenny would thank you for tearing strips off her friend, neither. Now, if you've finished picking fights, do you know where Jenny might be?'

The blonde spat blood on to the floor and stuck her tongue into her cheek, feeling for loose teeth. She shook her head.

Sally sighed. 'Do any of you know where Jenny might be?' The bleaching women all looked at their shoes, and fury burned Molly's throat like bile.

'Then I suppose I'm not the most useless friend Jenny has today,' she snapped. 'William, Sally, let's go. We'll get nowhere here.'

22

Darkness had fallen but even the cold January evening did not make Molly shiver as she stormed towards the carriage, with Sally and William in pursuit.

'Wait.' William caught up with Molly and put an arm out in front of her to stop her going any further. 'Look,' he said.

Ashton stood beside the carriage at the horse's head, holding a lantern. In the dim light, Molly could make out another man talking to him. Ashton was trying to push him away from the carriage but the stranger would not leave and he continued to thrust his face into Ashton's, talking insistently. When the driver looked across and saw that his employer had returned, he pushed the man away from him more forcefully, and reached into the pocket of his coat for his nightstick. Then the man turned his face towards the light of the lantern and Molly recognized Eddie Rathbone immediately.

'Ashton! Stop!' she cried out. Ashton, his stick poised a bare inch above Eddie's crown, froze, and Molly pushed William's arm down and ran towards Eddie.

'Molly!' William called out, running to catch up with her. He stood beside her as she faced Eddie, his hand on her shoulder.

She looked Eddie in the eye. 'I've no time for anything or anyone but Jenny right now, Eddie. Have you seen her?'

Eddie nodded. 'I was just telling your driver: she's in town, but she's in a bad way. I tried to get her to go with me but she was having none of it. I went to your house – I thought she might still listen to you – and Katy told me you'd gone to find her. I knew you'd try here first.' His breathing was ragged, as if he had spent a long time running, and he spat on to the cobbles. Molly could sense William's expression of distaste as he stood beside her.

'Take me with you,' Eddie panted, 'and I'll lead you to her.'

'So where are we going?' Molly asked abruptly.

'I told your driver: Cannon Street. He's taking us there.'

It was barely past seven o'clock when they arrived at Cannon Street, but already the pubs were humming with voices. There were no street lamps down these narrow side roads, and the glow from the pub windows lent the street its only light, making even the roughest establishments look warm and welcoming. Eddie knocked against the wall of the carriage to signal for Ashton to stop, and Molly cast her eyes around as she stepped down on to the road. She looked for any sign of Jenny, but all she could see were broken bottles and misshapen bundles discarded in doorways and corners. The air smelled of stale beer and tobacco smoke, with a musty hint of rat underneath. William pulled Molly closer to him as he reached into the carriage for a lantern and his cane.

'Molly, it isn't safe for you to be walking around here in

the dark. Get back in the carriage, you and Mrs Marsden. I'm sure we'll manage.'

'No,' Molly said. 'Jenny is my friend; I should be looking for her. I was brought up in streets like this one,' she added, neglecting to mention how conspicuous she was feeling now in her warm dress and shawl. 'Let's just find her and get out of here.'

'Very well.' William clasped Molly's hand and nodded to Ashton to watch the carriage, then set off down the street, following Eddie and Sally. Molly held her head high and scanned the narrow street from right to left for her friend, hoping that she looked more confident than she actually was. When a bundle of rags reached out of its doorway and grabbed at the hem of her skirt, Molly jumped and backed into William, but managed to suppress a scream. William lashed out at the bundle with his cane, and it retreated into the shadows.

A shout drifted from further down the street, and William held the lantern higher so that they could see. Eddie and Sally stood in the doorway of a pub, Eddie with his back to the door trying to drive a handful of men away, while Sally bent over a shapeless bundle that lay in the doorway behind him.

'Jenny!' Breaking away from William, Molly ran towards them, her boots slipping on the slimy stone. Behind her, the glow from the lantern bobbed frantically as William chased after her, until it melted away into the light that shone through the murky glass of the pub windows.

'Hello,' one of the men said as she skidded to a halt. 'This one's even better. Seems a shame to dress her up so nice, though, don't it?'

Molly ignored him, and pushed past to crouch beside Sally. A hand tugged at the back of her skirt, but an abrupt crack followed by a bellow of pain told her that William had brought his cane down on the drunkard's hand. While the men argued behind them, Molly pulled the tatty shawl away from the figure's face.

Jenny stared blankly at the grimy cobbles as if they were no more or less interesting than anything else around her. In the light of William's lantern, Molly could see that her friend's lips were cracked and bloodstained, and her eyes shot through with spidery veins and red-rimmed from weeping. But the dry trails that ran across her dirty face told Molly that her friend had stopped crying some time ago. Neither of them had been raised to go on fussing over things they couldn't change. Now Jenny just sat with an expression of utter disinterest, as if life could do what it would with her and it'd be all the same as far as she was concerned. Molly's throat tightened. Sally had been wrong: Jenny would not have drowned herself; even that required more energy than she had now. Another few hours here and Jenny would have been passed around a rabble of soused navvies – if not the ones behind them, then others – until her body was broken and bleeding and spent, and all the while she would have stared at the stars as if she were dead already.

'She hears us,' Sally said, laying a reassuring hand on Molly's shoulder. 'But I think she'll listen more to you.'

Molly tried to think of something to say. She reached out to her friend and stroked a tangle of hair away from her eyes, trying to ignore that terrible blank expression.

'Jenny? Jenny, it's Molly.' She leaned forward and rested

her forehead against her friend's. 'We both know there's nothing I can ever say to change what's happened,' she whispered in Jenny's ear. 'I'm not going to insult you by telling you everything will be all right. But you can't want to be here, Jenny.'

'I just want to be alone,' Jenny murmured. Her voice was as cracked as her lips.

'Then come home with me,' Molly said, taking hold of Jenny's filthy hand and squeezing it gently. 'You can be all alone for as long as you like, and nobody will bother you. When you want to speak to me again, I'll be there. You don't have to do anything you don't want to do.'

Behind her, William was bawling at the drunkards to get away from his wife before he had them all locked away. Molly closed her eyes momentarily as a wave of regret swept over her.

'I can't be there. Not in the room where he was born.'

Jenny's weak voice jolted Molly out of her hollow of misery.

'No, of course not,' she soothed. 'You can have Katy's room; it's as quiet as you could want, up there at the top of the house. Jenny, will you please come home?'

Jenny's nod could just as well have been a shrug, but Molly and Sally each took an arm and lifted the girl to her feet anyway. Putting her arms around their shoulders, they started to pick their way up the dirty street. Jenny was only a skinny girl, but she hung from Molly like a dead weight, and Molly found herself straining to stay upright.

'Ashton will carry her,' William said, beckoning to the driver. Running down to meet them, Ashton tossed his nightstick over to Eddie, who walked behind, fending off the drunk men.

'Come on, she looks like she could do with a meal inside her,' one of them was slurring. 'I'll do the honourable thing and pay her for any kindnesses she wants to show me.' His mates guffawed, and Molly span on her heel and shrieked.

'Piss off, the lot of you! Just leave her alone!' Her voice quavered and tears were brimming in her eyes. Eddie looked at her, his expression indecipherable. The ghost of a comforting smile was playing around the edge of his lips, but his eyes were distant and sad.

'Is everything all right?' The commotion had attracted a peeler. With his face hidden in the shadow of his hat, the constable reached into his cloak for his truncheon, and the rabble behind them backed away.

'It was them,' Molly panted, stepping forward despite herself and gesturing to the retreating drunks. 'My friend here is extremely distressed, and they were trying to take advantage of her vulnerable state.' A shudder of revulsion ran through her as the peeler lifted his lantern, surveying her with an imperious expression. Pursing his mouth, he turned to William.

'Is this true? You look like a moneyed man. Not one of your girls, is she?'

Realizing what he meant, Molly felt her hands hook into claws inside her gloves, but her old fear of peelers held her back. Jenny did not even lift her head.

'I beg your pardon?' William bristled. 'I am not some common pander; I am William Hamilton, formerly of Hamilton Cotton. I have my wife with me,' he nodded towards

Molly, 'and even if I were considering a sideline in whoring, I would not make it a family affair.'

'That's enough, sir,' the peeler said coolly. 'My apologies, Mr Hamilton. The girl looks drunk, and newcomers to the trade often are.'

'I suggest you stop insulting my friend,' Molly snapped, 'and go after *them*.' The drunks were now just shadowy dots on the horizon at the end of the dingy street, and the peeler exhaled heavily and shrugged.

'I'll never catch 'em now, and in any case, there's not much they'd be prosecuted for.' He tucked his truncheon back into his belt. 'Be on your way.'

Molly spluttered with rage, but a warning glance from William silenced her, and they stalked back to the carriage while the peeler sauntered off down the street.

Back at the house, Ashton hauled Jenny through the front door and Katy gasped with shock at her skinny wrists and dirty clothes. As the maid caught sight of Eddie standing outside, she stopped in her tracks and dithered, her hands clutching at her apron.

'She'll need some warm water and fresh bed linen,' Sally said, wiping her boots on the mat. 'If your girl can show me where they're kept, I'll help her fetch them.' Katy nodded and scurried off down the hall, with Sally in pursuit.

'I didn't invite you in.' William, poised on the stairs with Ashton, glared at Eddie, who stood in the doorway wiping his boots on the mat.

'William,' Molly pleaded, 'not now. At least let's offer him a drink – he did find Jenny.'

William nodded. 'In the kitchen, then. Once Katy is no longer required, she can draw him some cider or something.' He shot a loaded glance at Eddie. 'When you're done, you can leave.' Then he turned and followed Ashton, who had started to carry Jenny upstairs, with Molly's boots clattering on the steps as she followed them.

Katy was asked to make up her own bed with fresh linen and move her things into the next attic room, which she did in a matter of minutes. After the men had set Jenny down on the pallet bed, they headed downstairs for a drink, leaving Molly and Sally to strip off Jenny's filthy smock. Once Katy had washed her, Molly ran down to her wardrobe for her warmest nightgown (the one William had dressed her in after the miscarriage that had driven such a wedge between her and her friend) and they wrapped Jenny in thick blankets while Katy fetched a cup of hot tea.

When the maid had gone, Molly stood rigid, staring at the sad, faded figure in the bed, her closest friend for as long as she could remember.

'She wanted to be alone,' Sally reminded her gently, laying an arm around Molly's shoulders. 'She'll recover; she's just cold and weak. She needs time to herself now. I'll leave her some brandy; it'll calm her nerves.'

Molly reached for Jenny's hand and held it tightly. She drew a deep breath. Sally leaned in and whispered in her ear.

'I'll be here tomorrow to check on her. I'm going to have to ask about a burial, but I won't tonight. Just let her be for now.'

Molly stared mutely at the figure in the bed, and Sally set the heavy brown glass bottle of brandy down on the floorboards and walked towards the door. As Molly stood up to leave, Jenny's eyes fluttered open, and her fingers twitched against Molly's. Forcing a weak smile, Molly pressed her friend's hand once more before following Sally out of the servants' quarters and down the attic stairs. At the landing, Sally met Molly's eye and smiled sympathetically.

'Bridget's wrong, you do know that, don't you?' she said. 'Even when she was furious with you, Jenny never said you forced her to leave, and it was you who got her to come home tonight and saved her life, most likely.'

Molly looked away.

'None of this is your doing,' Sally insisted, shaking Molly's shoulder gently. She sighed. 'I'll be back tomorrow. Have something hot to eat and get some sleep. A night's rest'll do Jenny good, and it'll help you, too.'

Sally turned and walked downstairs, and Molly followed her as far as the landing, where she turned and went into the séance room, shutting the door behind her.

The darkness enveloped her, and Molly sat down at the table, resting her head on her arms. She listened attentively to the silence of the room and felt her muscles relax. As the tension left her back and neck, a flood of tears burned her cheeks and trickled down to pool on to the polished tabletop, and Molly drew a shuddering breath. She pulled her shawl from around her shoulders and draped it over her head, veiling herself in the warm wool, as if it would shield her from everything. Molly closed her eyes.

Through the shawl, the hiss of a striking match stirred her, and slowly, grudgingly, she lifted her head. She carefully pulled the shawl from her head and blinked in the yellow glow of a single candle flame.

William stood by her chair, shaking out the match. He took the shawl from her and shook it out before draping it back over her shoulders.

'I thought you might be in here,' he said. 'This is your place, after all. I've only been in here once. This is where you keep your secrets, isn't it?' He pulled out a chair and sat beside her.

The drying tears on her face suddenly felt very heavy, and Molly let her chin fall on to her chest.

'I wish things were different,' she whispered.

William touched a loose curl that hung limply down the side of her jaw.

'What things?'

Molly sighed. 'Me and Jenny fighting. Her leaving. The baby dying. Our marriage. I don't know.'

William sighed, crestfallen. 'You were young to be expecting a child, I suppose. Perhaps you were too young to be married, but I thought it would be for the best.'

Molly looked up at him. His brown eyes were dark and wide in the dim candlelight, and she glanced around at the flickering shadows cast by the furniture. It was the only room in the house that was exactly as Florrie had left it. Her heart ached as she thought of her aunt, but her stomach still tingled with desire each time she looked at William. She cleared her throat.

'I wish we had married under different circumstances,' she said, 'but I don't regret anything you and I have done.'

William felt for her hands and took them in his. 'It

will be better soon. I have the liquor business, and Jenny will recover. Maybe she'll stay here, if that's what you both want.'

'Chance'd be a fine thing,' Molly giggled wearily. 'She's as stubborn as I am.' William smiled. 'And you?' Molly asked, her face suddenly serious.

'Me?'

'Do you regret anything that has passed between us?'

William shook his head. 'No.'

Molly reached out to him and put her arms around his neck. William's dark eyes met Molly's; he laid his hands on her waist, pulling her towards him, and his mouth covered hers.

'Are you certain?' she asked, muffled by his lips. William's arms closed tighter around her waist in reply, and his tongue slipped into her mouth. Standing up, he backed Molly against the séance table and sat her down on the tabletop. Parting her shawl carefully, so as not to catch it in the candle flame, he pushed her down on to her back. He fumbled with the buttons at the front of her dress and opened the first few, just enough to bare the tops of her breasts and release the soft smell of her rose perfume into the room, before leaning over and covering her with a sigh, burying his face in her camisole. Molly wrapped her legs around his hips, and William reached down to the hem of her dress, pulling up her skirts and petticoats. From the top of her stocking, he traced a finger along her inner thigh, sliding it inside her drawers and making Molly gasp with delight as she felt his touch. He slithered his fingertip in a soft, slippery trail back and forth between her legs, and Molly reached for the buttons of his breeches.

William did not push her hand away, but leaned closer,

lying more heavily on her and allowing her to loosen his breeches and slide her hand inside. He was already rigid and ready to enter her, but Molly moved slowly as his fingers continued to send hot bolts of ecstasy through her. As she slid her hand towards his organ, she paused and rested her fingertips just above its base, gently brushing against the hot skin and combing the fine, curly hair. William groaned and ran his wet finger in a circle around and around, just outside the opening that was aching for him so badly that Molly could hardly bear it. She ran a finger up the length of his organ, and William pressed himself down on to her, pushing his finger into her and making her cry out in startled pleasure. Molly took William in her hand and gripped gently, looking up into his dark eyes. His other hand tugged at the ribbon of her drawers, and Molly wriggled and lifted her hips so that he could pull them off and cast them aside. Pushing her skirts around her waist, William freed himself from his breeches and let his full weight down on to Molly, pressing her between his flesh and the unyielding wood of the table. Feeling the touch of him against her, Molly pushed up and let her head fall back, her mouth open in a frenzy of relief and release. William thrust again and again, and she felt the underside of his organ against the most sensitive parts of her body. The sweet sting inside her throbbed more and more with his every movement, and as William reached down to feel his way, Molly lifted her legs higher and wrapped them more tightly around him, pressing his body down even harder against hers.

They both cried out as William pushed inside her and his thrusting became more insistent. Burying his face in her breasts, he pushed her back against the table again and again, and with each dull, bruising pain to her hips and the base of her spine, Molly moaned softly, revelling in the pressure of his body against hers, inside and out. As William's groans became deeper and his movements more frantic, she locked her legs tightly around him and arched her body into his. Her hips were driven into the table, and she trembled with desire as William pushed hard against her and let loose a strangled cry of spent passion.

They lay like that for some time, William still inside her, before he eventually stood up and took her hand to lead her to bed.

23

Molly awoke early the following morning and carefully slipped out of bed, leaving William sound asleep in a tangle of blankets. Picking up her nightgown and a shawl from the back of her dressing-table chair, she tiptoed out of the bed-chamber and headed for the attic stairs. The house was utterly silent and she deduced that even Katy was still in bed. Watching for splinters in her bare feet, Molly picked her way up the attic staircase, resting her hands against the bruises on her hips, which began to ache more strongly as she shook off the last traces of sleep. As she passed the door of Jenny's old room – now occupied by Katy – she heard the mouse-like patter of the maid's feet as she dressed and got ready to go down to light the fires and prepare the washing basins. Quickening her pace, Molly crept past the door and slid into Katy's old room, where they had left Jenny last night.

The small window cast a pale yellow light over the pallet bed where Jenny lay. Stretched out on her back, her features smoothed by sleep, she looked peaceful, free from the torrent of hellish emotions – agony, guilt, hopelessness – that had tormented her last night. Her chest rose and fell slowly, and

Molly watched in silence. Occasionally a flicker of feeling passed across her face, as if at some confused memory.

Eventually, looking out of the tiny window and seeing that the sun was shining higher and brighter in the sky, Molly reached a hand out to Jenny's, before reconsidering and pulling it away. She did not want to wake her from her painless sleep. Molly turned from the pallet and headed for the door. William would soon wake, and Katy would come to dress her for the day . . .

'Molly?' Jenny's voice made her jump.

'I thought I should leave you sleeping,' Molly said, crossing the room and kneeling beside the pallet bed. 'Did I disturb you?'

Jenny shook her head. 'The light.' She indicated the attic window. 'When I was little we were always up with the dawn.' Jenny blinked sleepily. 'That's when Ma and I would get the fire going – when Ma was still alive; when she died it was just me. Pa'd take his deliveries, and we'd be in school for eight, d'you remember?'

'Yes.' Molly nodded, smoothing out a tangle of Jenny's hair. 'You used to nick us something for breakfast if you could do it without getting caught. We'd eat on the way to school.'

The veil of grief was creeping back over Jenny's face as she became more alert, and Molly closed her eyes in sorrow at the sight of the delicate trembling of her friend's lips as she fought back a sob.

'It was because they were all I knew,' Jenny managed to say, her voice choked.

'Sorry?'

'His name, Peter Joseph. You asked why I'd called him that. His grandpa and his pa.' Jenny gulped. 'I know neither of them was worth much, but they were all I knew.' The tears rolled down her face, and she rested her head on Molly's shoulder. Molly pressed her cheek against Jenny's and their tears mingled.

'Jenny . . . Sally will be coming to see you today. To talk about . . .'

Jenny cut her off with a frantic nod and a wave of her hand. 'I'll be ready to see her then. I want to do the best for him, though it's not a patch on what he deserves. I hadn't a chance to get him baptized – they won't put him in consecrated ground.'

'Oh, Jenny . . .'

'I know what you're going to say. I know we all fall to dust just the same whether we're in a family tomb, a pauper's pit or common ground. But I could at least have done this one thing right for him. I need to make my peace and pray to God that Limbo's just nonsense, like that spirit fruit I used to chuck down the trapdoor for you.'

Molly looked yearningly into Jenny's face. 'I wish my gift were real, so I could help you,' she whispered.

Jenny smiled weakly, and the little pools of tears caught in the corners of her mouth glittered in the faint light coming from the window. With a gasp, Molly realized that the window was not covered, and she rushed towards it, pulling the sheet that served as a curtain over the glass.

'Jenny, I'm so sorry. We were all so worried about you last night that I—'

Jenny shook her head. 'Leave it,' she said, pointing to the

sheet. 'He ain't coming back – in the glass of the attic window or anywhere else. I just need time, Mol, that's all.'

Molly kissed Jenny's forehead and walked to the door.

'I should have known you'd find me,' Jenny said, lying down with her back to Molly and huddling into a ball. 'I love you, Mol.'

'I love you too, Jenny.'

William left later that morning to sign the last of the papers that would claim his new business, but as Molly stood in the hallway to see him off, he snatched her around her waist and pulled her to him for a forceful, passionate kiss, quite heedless of Katy, who stood by the door with his coat and hat.

'I promise I shall be back in time for dinner,' he assured Molly, while the maid behind him went scarlet and stared at her shoes. 'I don't want to have a late night tonight.'

Molly smiled as he went outside, where Ashton would be waiting with the carriage. Turning to Katy, she requested a pot of chocolate in the parlour, and told her to look in on Jenny to see if there was anything she needed.

'Do not stay unless she asks you to, however,' she added. 'And tell me at once if she wants me to go to her.'

Once she was settled in the parlour with her chocolate, Molly flicked idly through the post, most of which was for William. There were some dinner invitations addressed to both of them, and a couple of spiritualist periodicals for Molly. She tucked her papers under her arm and tossed the empty envelopes on to the table before settling down with her chocolate. The morning light shining into the parlour was bright – bright enough to illuminate the dancing dust particles that swirled in the air – and Molly closed her eyes.

The house was almost silent. Katy, far down in the kitchen, was barely making a sound, and Molly stretched out, savouring the peace and quiet. Yawning, she rested her head on the padded back of her armchair, and dozed off with her periodicals in her hand and delicious dreams of William in her head.

When she awoke, Molly licked her dry lips and swallowed. She felt parched. She touched the backs of her fingers to the pot beside her. Stone cold – she must have been asleep for a while. The clock on the wall told her that it was past lunchtime; Katy must not have wanted to wake her. Looking around for the bell to call the maid, Molly caught sight of the flower in her hand and dropped it with a shriek. It was a large white lily, perfect and undamaged. In an instant, Molly knew who had sent her this portent of death.

'Katy?' Molly's voice quavered. Reaching for the bell, she rang for the maid. 'Katy?' Louder this time, but still no reply. Slowly, Molly got out of her seat and kicked off her slippers. Reaching out to the post tray, she picked up the silver letter opener and tested the tip of its blade against the back of her hand. Her eyes scanned the parlour for any hiding places Lizzie might be using, and she edged her way to the door and out into the hall. Tiptoeing to the front door, she tried the handle. It was locked, and the keys were not in the china bowl where they normally sat. Her eyes darting from left to right, Molly crept down the hall and eased open the door at the top of the cellar stairs. With a last superstitious glance behind to assure herself that Lizzie was not there, she hurried down to the kitchen.

The room was empty, the tables and the stove clean and deserted. Where was Katy? Molly picked her way gingerly across the creaky floor to the back door, but it too was locked, and the key nowhere to be seen. She was locked in.

Jenny. The thought hit Molly like a shot in the chest; how could she have forgotten that Jenny was in the house? Holding up her skirts so they would not rustle, she ran as fast as she dared up the four flights of stairs to the servants' quarters.

Jenny was fast asleep with Sally's brandy bottle empty beside her. Molly shook her friend urgently, calling her name in frantic, hushed tones.

'Jenny? Jenny!' No response. Hooking an arm behind her friend's shoulders, Molly hauled until a splitting pain shot down her back. Still Jenny snored. Glancing again around the attic room, Molly touched a finger to her neck. Her pulse was strong, and she was breathing well. She pushed her on to her side so that she would not vomit and choke, and slipped out of the room, closing the door. She resisted the temptation to barricade the door with some of Florrie's old furniture from the spare attic room. It would only attract Lizzie's attention. Tightening her grip on the letter opener, Molly squared her shoulders and began to walk down the attic stairs to the séance room where she knew Lizzie would want to confront her.

As she reached the first landing, Molly paused. Looking across to the door of the bedchamber she shared with William, she felt in her pocket for a box of matches. She held the letter opener out in front of her and sidled across the landing, peeping over the banister for any sign of Lizzie as she silently opened the bedchamber door.

Looking out of the window, she could see the premature winter dusk stealing across the sky. It must be around four o'clock. Swiftly she closed the curtains and lit a single candle on her bedside table. In the hazy light, she could just make out the shape of the rug that lay on the floor between the bed and the chamber door, and she snatched it up and cast it aside. Molly lifted the trapdoor free of the hatch, then draped the rug back over the hole and slid the loose piece of wood under the bed. Carefully edging her way around the hole in the floor and creeping out of the bedchamber, leaving the door slightly ajar, she headed down to the séance room to await Lizzie. With any luck, the faint candlelight that shone from the bedchamber would spring the trap.

In the séance room, Molly paused in front of the materialization cabinet. Her knees trembled and her head span, and she battled her urge to climb behind the false back of the cabinet and hide. *No. You have to be able to hear her, especially if she does go upstairs to Jenny.* Steeling her nerves, Molly took her place behind the séance table, letter opener in hand, and waited. She pressed her back to the wall, recoiling from what felt like the gaze of a hundred invisible eyes. She had often sensed the subtle heat of the sitters in her circles as they sat around the table in darkness, and heard the silky hiss of their breath. She knew when she was not alone.

When she did finally hear a noise, Molly shuddered, as if her grave had been disturbed. Her palms were sweaty, and she fumbled with the letter opener and wiped her hand on her skirt so that the knife would not slip out of her hand. There was the sound of a door closing, followed by the dreaded footfall on the stairs. Molly's very breath seemed to scream out her whereabouts, and she drew deeper breaths in an attempt to silence the harsh, nervous rasp that betrayed her. Shifting sounds seemed to come from all around, and her eyes darted frantically around the blind darkness of the séance room. The footsteps on the stairs thudded up to the séance room door, passed it, and headed up the stairs. Molly swallowed hard and looked up to the ceiling where she knew the trapdoor would be lying open.

But Lizzie did not fall through the hatch and land, disarmed, on the séance table, and when Molly's ears picked up the sound of footsteps coming back towards her, she gulped and raised the blade.

It's too heavy. As Molly heard the steps coming ever closer, the realization hit her that these were not the steps of her small, scrawny mother; not even in clogs. This was a man's footfall, and as the door squeaked open and a figure walked into the room, Molly caught the scent of hair oil and barber's foam just in time to lower her blade and tuck it into her sleeve.

'Molly?' William pushed the door fully open, and the greenish light of the landing lamps seeped into the room, making it hazy and foggy. 'Molly, what in the name of God are you doing in here in the dark?'

'Sssh,' she hissed, pulling William into the room and slamming the door behind him, 'she's in the house.'

'Who's in the . . . what? Where?'

'I don't know, but this afternoon I fell asleep in the parlour and someone put a white lily in my hands. Katy's gone – I can't find her anywhere.'

'I wondered where she was; she wasn't here when I came home,' William whispered. 'What's that woman done with her?'

Molly felt her way towards William and clung to his waistcoat, forcing her hands not to tremble. 'I don't know. But I have to finish this; we have to get rid of her.'

William laid a hand on the back of Molly's head. 'She may be violent, Molly; we have to fetch the police. Ashton's down in the kitchen. I'll send him to fetch a constable.'

Molly thought of the blade in her sleeve and the trap that lay above them, and said nothing. William evidently did not understand exactly what she meant by 'getting rid' of Lizzie.

She bit her lip. 'Don't leave. Don't go looking for him; she's nearby; I know it.'

William laughed, but it was a hollow copy of his usual mischievous chuckle. 'You and your mystical instincts. Well, as long as you're not relying on your spirit guide to save us.'

A clatter of boots on the stairs made Molly spring, cat-like, to her feet.

'Wait – she's coming now.' Reaching out and feeling for William, she grabbed his sleeve and pulled him away from the table.

The boots were up the second staircase now, and she heard the bedchamber door swing violently open. In a flash Molly had it: surely an old-before-her-time nag like Lizzie could never run that fast; not up two flights of stairs. But the footsteps were too heavy for Katy, and Ashton never went upstairs unless specifically asked to. The heavy clump of work boots thudded across the ceiling above them, and Molly heard the dreadful hollowing of the footsteps as they came nearer and nearer to the open trapdoor and then were muffled by the rug.

'Wait!' she yelled, and the dark shadow of the rug dropped through the hole and past her eyes, followed by a sickening crack and the dull sound of something heavy rolling off the tabletop and hitting wooden floorboards.

'What the hell?' William flung open the door of the séance room, and the foggy light of the landing lamps swam into the room.

Crumpled in a heap on the floor, Eddie lay motionless, his head lolling.

'What happened?' William gasped, pushing the door further open. Looking up to the ceiling and seeing the gaping black square, he looked across at Molly.

'It was meant for her,' she whispered. Kneeling beside Eddie, she tentatively reached out towards him, but at the brush of her fingers he screamed in pain, making Molly pull away in fright and confusion. A shiny trail of spittle hung from his mouth and his lips twitched as if he were trying to speak, but the only sound he could make was a thick, wet croaking, as if his tongue had been pulled out.

'Molly, look.' Kneeling beside her, William pointed at the strange angle of Eddie's neck, still skewed from the impact of his head against the table, and Molly understood how he had come to lie in such a twisted position. Her eyes ached as if they would burst, but she shed no tears as she reached a shaking hand out to Eddie.

'Why, Eddie?' she whispered. 'It wasn't meant for you.'

'His neck is broken, Molly,' William said meaningfully. He laid a hand on her shoulder, and Eddie's eyes swivelled around, as if with great effort, to meet Molly's. She drew a deep, ragged breath.

'Can you do it quickly?'

Before she could even turn to him for a reply, William had grabbed one of the iron candlesticks from the table and brought it down with a nauseating crunch on the back of Eddie's head. With a throaty, bubbling sound and a frantic, wide-eyed gaze, Eddie curled like a drying leaf and lay still.

William dropped the candlestick and huddled close to Molly, whispering in her ear, 'You set it for her?'

Molly met his gaze. 'Yes.'

Behind them, the door of the materialization cabinet flew open, banging against the wall and making them both spin round. Lizzie stepped out from the cabinet and its false back swung out into the room. Her shadow, wild-haired and mad in the faint greenish light, followed her from her hiding place, and she turned and regarded Eddie's shattered body with a look of contempt.

'Stupid lad.'

At the sight of William, Lizzie faltered. In her hand she carried a heavy nightstick, and she gripped it a little tighter. Molly made a dive for the door, and Lizzie headed her off with little effort, bringing the nightstick down towards Molly's head, but William pulled her back.

'You hid in there all the time?' Molly gasped, rubbing the side of her face as if to ease the pain of a phantom blow. 'I should have seen it coming. Ever since you arrived you've wanted me to pay you off for giving birth to me, as if it were some favour I asked of you!' From the séance table beside her, Molly could hear the faint scraping of metal on wood as William's fingers closed around the candlestick.

Lizzie took a step forward, her nightstick raised, and William whipped around the other side of the circular table, putting his body between Molly's and Lizzie's. With a sharp blow, he struck Lizzie on the head, and she teetered dumbly before toppling over on to the floor, landing face first on the boards. Molly swallowed down bile at the sound of the candlestick striking Lizzie's skull. William edged closer to the collapsed body and plucked the nightstick from her hand.

'Molly?' Jenny stood in the doorway, dressed only in Molly's nightgown and still drowsy from her brandy-induced sleep. 'Molly, what happened?'

Molly's voice was a thread. 'My mother was alive,' she whispered. 'Alive all these years. And she just tried to kill me.'

William, standing over Lizzie with her nightstick in his hand, looked across at Molly. 'She's still breathing,' he warned. 'She'll wake soon.'

Molly nodded. Hopping over Lizzie's unconscious body, she snatched up the rug that had fallen through the trapdoor, and ran out on to the landing.

'Wait there,' she said. Racing upstairs, she pulled the loose trapdoor from under the bed, fitted it into place and threw the rug over it. Then she bounded down to the séance room, taking the steps two at a time, and skidded to a halt beside William. He nodded towards Jenny, who knelt at Eddie's side.

'She found him,' he said.

Jenny looked up into Molly's face, her anguished eyes making her horror clear.

'Why is Eddie . . .?' she whispered.

Molly shook her head. 'He fell through the trapdoor,' she replied. 'I don't know what he was doing here.'

'Mr Hamilton?' A shout from the hall downstairs.

'We're up here, Ashton!' William called back. His eyes flicked down to Eddie's body on the floor and across to Molly, who met his gaze with her dauntless medium's eyes.

'Wait,' she mouthed silently. Working quickly, she snatched up the candlestick William had used to put Eddie out of his misery, tossed it into the back of the cabinet and closed the door. As Ashton's footsteps approached, she took the nightstick from William and set it down on the floor, just out of Lizzie's reach.

When two burly peelers marched into the room, followed by Ashton and a trembling, weeping Katy, Molly caught her breath. One of them reached down and turned Eddie over by the shoulder, grimacing.

'They came in through the kitchen, Mr Hamilton,' Ashton said quietly. 'Katy brought them.'

'Who did this?' the other peeler asked. 'A murder has been committed here this evening; that much is clear. Who is the culprit?'

Molly stepped forward. 'She is,' she said, pointing to Lizzie's prone form on the floor. 'She tried to kill my husband and me, and my friend here tried to save us and lost his life.' A sob rose in her throat, and she choked it down, pressing her fingers to her lips in a ladylike manner. 'She's a madwoman!' she shouted as the peelers reached down to shackle

Lizzie before she could come to. 'She will hang for this, won't she?'

The peelers hauled Lizzie to her feet, and her head lolled against one of the constable's shoulders, a trickle of blood oozing from just above her eyebrow. Her face flickered as if she were dreaming. She would wake soon.

'I wouldn't worry about that, Mrs Hamilton,' one of the peelers said. 'There's not many murderers in these parts escape the rope.'

Molly watched as they dragged the faded redhead out on to the landing and down the stairs. Ashton followed, to let them out, but Katy remained in the corner of the séance room, crying helplessly and covering her eyes to block the sight of Eddie as he lay crumpled on the floor. Molly sank to her knees by his side and closed his eyes.

24

During the following week, all of Preston, from labourers and shop girls who had known Molly in her childhood to wealthy merchants and gentry who now attended her séances, hummed with the news of Lizzie's arrest.

In acknowledgement of William's standing in the town, and to spare the Hamiltons' reputation, Inspector Stafford interviewed Molly and William at home, rather than at the police station. At first Molly greeted each day with apprehension, fearing a statement from Lizzie that would condemn her, or suspicion from her clientele. But none came, and it seemed that both police and public were quite content with the tale of the half-mad mother who abandoned her child only to return once the girl had grown, willing to kill her own flesh and blood. Molly suspected that her fresh and innocent face helped almost as much as her money: next to William Hamilton's pale, petite young wife, Lizzie's scowling mouth and poison-laden glares made her look the part of the villainess.

There was, however, still the matter of Katy, who was interviewed in the servants' quarters after Lizzie had been hauled away to be held within the red-brick walls of Preston's jail. When Inspector Stafford walked back downstairs and into the drawing room where Molly and William were waiting, he shook his head.

'She's not committed any crime that we shall be prosecuting her for, but I suggest that you have words with your maid, Mr Hamilton,' he said. 'You may wish to reconsider her employment.'

William called Katy into his study as soon as the peelers left, but was unable to get any sense out of her. Exasperated, he called Molly in to talk with the girl, and once they were seated together by the fire, with William standing quietly in the corner behind them, Molly fixed her green eyes firmly on Katy and spoke slowly and clearly.

'Katy, did you let that woman into the house?'

A constant stream of tears dripped off the maid's nose and over her trembling lips. Silently, save for the jerky whooping of her panic-ridden breathing, she nodded.

'I – I never thought any harm would come to you or Mr Hamilton though, ma'am!' she wailed. 'I didn't know what she were planning!'

William huffed and stepped towards Katy, his hand held out for her keys, but Molly shot him a quick glance over her shoulder and he stopped still where he stood.

'Katy,' she said, her voice low, 'you know how serious a matter this is. What were you thinking of? Is this the first time that you have allowed strangers into our home?'

'I'd never have done it but for him telling me!' Katy cried. 'I ain't never done it before, but he told me he'd be sending an old friend round to see you, as a surprise, like, and that I should let her in. And . . . and I know it were stupid of me, but he said he'd take me out for a drink at the pub and that I wouldn't be missed here for a short while, and I couldn't help myself!'

'Who?' Molly asked.

Fresh tears coursed down Katy's face. 'Eddie. I hadn't seen him in so long, and I met him at the Bull after I let her in. But when he asked if she got there all right and I said yes, and that she'd brought you some white flowers, he came over all odd. When he found out they were lilies, he swore and dragged me out of there. We ran all the way back – we had no more money on us, see. Then he told me to go and find a peeler while he went in. And by the time we got back, and found Ashton . . .'

Molly nodded slowly. Eddie had betrayed her once again, although what he had expected of her meeting with Lizzie, if not her murder – which he clearly had not wished for – she had no clue. But he had not hated her as deeply as Lizzie had, and as Molly remembered the dark, rangy youth who had walked nervously into the parlour on the day Florrie had hired him, she felt her throat swell with sorrow. In the end, he had lost his life trying to protect her. Drawing a deep breath, she looked across at William, who strode over to stand in front of Katy, his face firm.

'I thank you for your honesty, Katy. Now, please return to your work; Mrs Hamilton and I need to discuss your employment further. Both of us might have died as a result of your poor judgement and conduct.'

With her face buried in her apron, Katy slowly got to her feet.

'B-b-but, Mrs Hamilton,' she stammered, turning pleading

eyes on Molly, 'the Resurrection Men'll come for Eddie. He had no money; he'll end up in the pit and they'll pull him out and chop him up.' She sobbed even harder, furiously wiping her tears on the hem of her apron. 'They'll take his heart out, so they say! They gut them like mad butchers!'

Molly shook her head, and swallowed down a gulp of foul-tasting bile. 'We shall be funding his burial,' she said firmly, glancing across at William's expressionless face. 'And Ashton will guard his grave. He will not be dissected, I promise you. Now, do as Mr Hamilton says and return to your work.'

As the study door swung closed behind Katy, Molly turned to William.

'He guarded my Aunt Florrie until the Resurrectionists would no longer want her,' she said. 'I have to do the same for him.'

Two days after Lizzie had been driven up to Lancaster to await her trial at the Lent Assizes, Eddie and baby Peter were to be buried in the new cemetery. Molly offered the drawing room for Sally Marsden to lay the bodies out, and Jenny spent the entire night before the funeral sitting in silence between the two coffins, her hand resting on the lid of the tiny casket that held Peter. Sally had discreetly taken Molly aside and advised her that Jenny should not look at her baby's body, and Jenny accepted their suggestions with what appeared to be blank indifference.

Her breasts had swollen with milk that her baby would never suckle, and when she was not leaking wet patches on to the front of her dresses, she complained of a hard, hot pain shooting through her chest. Sally suggested that Jenny bind her breasts until her milk stopped flowing, but Jenny often forgot to apply fresh wrappings in the morning, and Molly sometimes wondered if perhaps she was even prepared to hold on to the pain in her engorged breasts just to have some trace of Peter. Jenny had insisted on paying the gravedigger's fee, but accepted Molly's offer of a headstone – a simple piece, as much as was allowed for the burial of an unbaptized child.

'I want him to have a marker, but I should pay the digger, Mol,' she had said earlier that day. 'I meant what I said – I can't be beholden to my friend for everything. I can't work for you, and I can't have you buying everything for me. We grew up equal, and I hope that in some way we still are.'

'There's a fair few going to show for Eddie tomorrow,' Sally told Molly as they walked to the front door. Seeing Molly's pale, drawn face, she took a firm hold of her wrists and looked into her eyes. Sally's normally determined brown eyes faltered a little, and Molly realized that she had never seen the midwife looking anything less than resolute.

'There won't be any of the trouble you had at the mill,' she said. 'They know you didn't plan Eddie's death, and that you're the one who's stopping him from being thrown in the pit. None of us ever knows if we'll rot into a jumble of bones with a couple of dozen strangers or be pulled out and carved up, but at least that won't happen to him. They know you're not burying him as a disgraced manservant.'

Molly bit her lip, shaking her head. 'I never meant to bury him at all,' she said. 'In time, we might have made our peace.

I just wish I could ask the silly sod what he was doing with that old she-devil.' Her voice quavered, and Molly searched her pockets for a handkerchief. Glancing around the deserted hall, Sally drew closer to Molly and whispered in her ear.

'I told you that if you didn't see yourself as a mother it was best to be rid, didn't I? If I'd have known she was coming back for you, Mol, I swear to God I'd have told you the truth. I'm partly to blame for all this, I know. I botched the job and it probably pushed her over the edge; I made a shocking mess of it.'

'You can't know that,' Molly replied.

Sally sighed. 'I'll never know, true enough. But I'll never be sure that it weren't my meddling that made the difference between her being a bit of a wild girl and her trying to smother you when you were two hours old, neither.'

'What?' Molly realized that she had spoken too loudly, and she hushed her voice. 'She never said!'

Sally nodded, her face grim. 'Florrie and I found her – she'd pulled your swaddling clothes up over your face, and she was holding them tight. You were fighting her, even at that age. That was when we persuaded her to leave, before she managed to kill you. If I'd have made a proper job of helping her out in the first place, none of this would have happened.'

Molly smiled and took the midwife's hand in hers. 'No, it wouldn't. But I'm past regretting, and I don't regret this either.' She lowered her voice. 'I've been following your advice, you know, about how to avoid conceiving again. William's going to wonder why I haven't, soon enough, but I'm done with cursing myself for the way I am.'

The sound of footsteps made Molly jump, but Sally's face was as calm and composed as ever.

'Ah, Mr Hamilton,' she said, bobbing her half-hearted curtsy. 'We were just discussing a matter that I know will be of interest to you.'

'Oh yes?' William raised an eyebrow, and Molly forced herself to breathe slowly while trying not to glare at Sally. What the hell was she playing at now, and after all her talk of what her meddling had done?

'I came round for the laying-out, but Mrs Hamilton requested my advice on another matter.' She leaned closer to William and spoke in a quiet, confidential tone. 'It was regarding her ability to bear you another child after her miscarriage, sir. She asked for my advice, and after I examined her – and with all due respect to your Dr Hartley, sir, he don't know a woman's body like one who's got one of their own – I'm afraid that I have to tell you that it don't look so good, Mr Hamilton.'

William paled. 'In what way?'

'Sometimes the injuries a woman receives during a miscarriage prevent her from carrying again. It's not impossible and in time things may change, the damage might heal.' She shot Molly the swiftest of looks. 'But I wouldn't get your hopes up, Mr Hamilton.'

'I see.' William reached out towards Molly and his hands trembled slightly as they took hers. Turning back to Sally, he drew a deep breath. 'And this . . . damage – is it dangerous for Molly?'

'No,' Molly said firmly, before Sally could speak. She

squeezed William's fingers. 'Sally said I am in no danger, didn't you, Sally?'

'That's right,' the midwife said, nodding. 'It's just a matter of her fertility, sir.'

Molly frantically searched William's face for some form of reaction, but he appeared as calm as Sally. True, he was bound to start wondering about his wife's failure to conceive (Molly had not forgotten Sally's advice on avoiding such an eventuality), but the midwife had told him to accept that his heir was a distant dream. Still, Sally seemed unconcerned as she walked to the door and let herself out, promising to see them tomorrow at the church.

Immediately, Molly turned to William, her lips parted and her face pale with worry.

'William?'

'It's not so very unexpected,' he said. 'It isn't ideal, but perhaps Sally's right. Perhaps in time you will heal fully and be able to bear children.'

Molly resisted the urge to squirm under his intense gaze. 'And if I do not?'

'Then we are no worse off than all the other people in this country who, for whatever reason, are barren,' William said. 'I don't want to fall prey to the same demons as my father did, to be continually obsessing over an heir. And somewhere, there's a distant relative who will be pleasantly surprised when we die.'

Molly broke into a smile at the sight of William's grin, and felt the warm, tingling sensation of relief as he pulled her into his arms and she rested her head on his chest.

'Pity this is a house in mourning,' he said, gently swirling his fingers in spirals across her back, 'but even purveyors of intoxicants and richly dressed con artists must have their standards.'

After the funerals had taken place, William raised the subject of Katy's employment again. The matter had been avoided while preparations for the burials of Eddie and little Peter were still being made, but as Molly and William sat in the parlour one afternoon, he carefully broached the issue.

'We still have to make a decision about Katy,' he said. Setting down her spiritualist periodical, Molly could not help but notice that he had said 'we'. Since the day in William's study when Molly had been the only one able to get any sense out of the hysterical maid, he seemed to respect her skills when it came to dealing with and relating to the staff.

'Yes,' Molly said. She had been giving the matter some thought herself. The maid's quiet nervousness had given way to a state of near muteness since Lizzie's arrest. She spoke only when asked a question, and even then she did so so faintly that Molly and William had to strain to hear her.

'She's clearly fearing the worst,' Molly said finally. 'She fully expects to be dismissed.'

William sipped his coffee. 'I thought as much.'

'It would be a heavy blow,' Molly continued. She looked at William. 'Heavier than she deserves, perhaps. It was not she who concocted the scheme of letting my mother into the house, after all – she just went along with it because Eddie persuaded her to. She knew nothing of the danger the woman posed.'

William had remained silent, but now he was nodding

slightly. 'She seemed very attached to that manservant,' he said hesitantly.

'Yes. She's only young, and she wasn't thinking.' Molly paused. Perhaps she could see a connection between herself and Katy after all.

'Then you wish to keep her on?'

Molly licked her lips. 'Yes, if that is possible. We could give her a warning, although she's so petrified I hardly think she needs one.'

William drained his coffee cup and set it down on the table. 'Very well. She can have another chance to prove herself.'

Lizzie was found guilty of the murder of Edward Rathbone and the attempted murders of William and Molly Hamilton at the Assizes in Lancaster two months later. She was sentenced to death by hanging, in the open yard of the Castle court and jail.

On the Saturday she was condemned to die, Ashton rose early in order to have the carriage ready for the Hamiltons, having been relieved of his additional duty of guarding the graves of Eddie and Peter. They planned to leave before breakfast in order to ensure that they made good time in getting up to the Castle jail where Lizzie had been held for the last weeks of her life, and where she would finally die – as Molly believed she had almost eighteen years ago. William, striking and imperious in a brown suit, said he would collect money from his study for their breakfast on the road, and that he would see Molly downstairs.

‘Are you certain that you want to go?’ he asked. ‘We don’t have to.’

‘Yes,’ Molly replied. ‘I have to see the end of this.’

Molly was sitting in the parlour waiting for her husband when the doorbell rang. Checking the clock on the mantelpiece, she could see that it was barely half past six. Katy hurried past the parlour door as she went to answer it, and Molly sleepily wondered who would call at this hour.

‘Sally Marsden to see you, Mrs Hamilton,’ Katy announced. Since William had advised her of his and Molly’s decision, Katy had gone about her duties with great care, trying quite obsessively to be a good servant. ‘Should I bring her through?’

Molly nodded her assent, and Katy returned with Sally.

‘I know you’ll be off early,’ the midwife said. ‘I shan’t stay long, but I need to speak with Jenny.’

‘Jenny? But she’s still asleep.’

‘Aye, I thought she might be, but this can’t wait.’

Molly looked across to Katy. ‘Fetch Jenny, would you, Katy?’ As the maid hurried up to the attic, Molly looked at Sally.

‘What is it?’ she asked.

Sally held up her hand in a halting gesture. ‘All in good time.’

Jenny appeared shortly after, hastily clothed in a plain black house dress. Rubbing her eyes, she blinked in drowsy confusion at the sight of Sally and Molly together in the parlour.

‘Sally? What are you doing here?’

‘I came to bring you some news,’ Sally said. She looked at Jenny’s dark dress. ‘It’s probably not what you want to hear, but your pa was found dead last night. It were the drink that got him in the end, you'll probably not be surprised to know. King's ironmonger shop is yours.'

Jenny looked, open-mouthed in shock, from Sally to Molly and back again. Molly tried a weak smile. Jenny had suffered so much over the last few weeks that Molly doubted she was able to react any other way, and it had been some time since she'd seen her father. Sally came to the rescue.

'I know,' she said. 'You hardly know where you're up to now, do you, love? But if you've got the shop, at least you can plan for your future.'

Jenny dropped down into one of the parlour chairs. 'It's mine? But . . . but what do I do?'

'Well, I'm sure there are papers sitting in some solicitor's office waiting for your signature,' Sally said with a smile, 'but I think the first thing you should do is find out where the keys are, so you can collect them and open up. You can move your things back in above the shop tonight, if you like, I should think.'

Looking across at Molly, Jenny smiled, and something of the old light in her eyes made Molly's skin glow with pleasure. Jenny nodded.

'I think I should,' she said, 'but you know you're always welcome, don't you, Mol?'

Molly beamed. 'Of course,' she said. 'And the same goes for you.'

Molly and William made good time on their way up to Lancaster. Sheep and cattle grazed in the fields behind low walls of beige-brown rock, and on the horizon Molly could just about make out the faint outline of the city in the distance, climbing its way up a steep slope, with the Castle standing sentry over everything. William took his watch from his pocket as Ashton pulled off the road and drew up to a small inn to check the horse.

'We have time for breakfast before we go on to the Castle,' he said.

Sitting beside the tiny lead-paned window of the inn, they ate a simple meal of bread, cold beef and salty Lancashire cheese. Craning her neck, Molly looked out of the window and up towards the city. In the distance, she could hear the bells of the priory ringing out the hour. By evening, everything would have almost returned to the way it was: Jenny would not be squeezed into the attic room like a spare servant, Molly and William would be free to enjoy each other, and Molly's mother would be dead.

'Not long now,' William said. 'We'll get there just in time, I should think.'

As they drew into the city centre, Molly peered out of the window of the carriage at the crowds that choked the narrow, twisting streets. She had no idea how many people were due to hang that morning, but they would certainly have an audience. Traders with barrows sold cups of ale, hot pies and small squares of cake, and the bubbling noise of dozens of voices filled Molly's ears. She heard Ashton shouting at people to get out of the way, and inch by inch the Hamilton carriage edged its way uphill towards the Castle.

A narrow road brought them up to the top of the hill where Lancaster Castle stood: a vast fortress with great black double doors studded with iron. Ashton followed the road down the side of the building and around the corner.

A mass of people had gathered in the courtyard just outside a rounded turret with cream-painted French doors set into it a few feet off the ground. The gallows stood just outside the doors, the black-hooded hangman lazing against one of the vertical beams and the noose swinging gently in a light breeze. The looming face of the priory threw a shadow over the yard, blocking the weak sunlight of the early spring morning. Tucked away to the side against the wall, the surgeons waited with a cart covered in black cloth to claim the bodies for dissection. Drawing the carriage up just in front of the gallows and forcing grumbling townsfolk out of the way, Ashton halted the horse and William pushed the dirty window open.

The hubbub of excitement began when the hangman walked over to the rope to give it a last tug to test its strength. Molly and William exchanged a glance before looking back out towards the French doors as they were flung open to allow the first prisoner to be brought out. From the drop room in the turret behind the gallows came a pair of jailers, each holding Lizzie Pinner by the elbow. After two months in a cramped, dark cell, she squinted even in the dim light in the shadow of the priory, and she was more gaunt than Molly had remembered her. The fading red hair she had tried to adorn with clips and combs when Molly first met her was further drained of colour and tangled into knots after weeks of bedding down on stone and straw. Her wrists were bound with rope and she walked stiffly, but when she caught sight of the Hamiltons' carriage, her head snapped up and she glared at Molly through the open window.

The jailers marched Lizzie forward to stand under the noose. With the hangman beside her, she swept the crowd with a scathing glance as they waited for the killer's last words. Looking straight through them, she stood under the swaying rope, meeting her daughter's eyes. Molly caught her breath. The woman on the scaffold laughed – a short, bitter laugh – and spat on the wooden floor beneath her feet.

'Oh yes,' she said. 'Just like me.' Then she fell silent and looked up at the dark shapes of the crows that circled above the courtyard, impatiently awaiting the crowd's picnic lunches. The hangman looped a belt around Lizzie's chest, pinioning her arms, before whipping out the hood tucked in his belt and pulling it down over her eyes. The crowd grumbled at the criminal's short and dull speech. In the carriage, Molly watched silently as the hangman worked the loop of the noose down over Lizzie's bagged head and around her neck. He stepped off the wooden platform and laid a hand on the lever that would release the trapdoors, and Molly swallowed hard. With her fading hair covered, the small figure on the platform could almost have been Molly herself.

''Ats off!' the hangman shouted in a southerner's yelp. Some of the men in the crowd pulled off their caps. Molly heard the creak of the lever, and the floor of the gallows collapsed.

Lizzie danced like a mad puppet on the end of the short rope. The crowd cheered, but Molly barely noticed. Slowly, Lizzie's unnatural jerking settled down to little shivering spasms, and she swung in leisurely circles, while the tips of her toes still trembled as if she would run.

The townsfolk began to chatter among themselves until the next one was brought out. William stuck his head out of the window and nodded to Ashton, who turned the carriage around.

'It is done,' William said as they made their way downhill. He looked into Molly's eyes. 'Are you all right, Molly?'

'I wish it need not have happened,' she replied. 'But she was not prepared to live her life and leave me to live mine. There had to be an end, and at least now it has come.'

'And you are not shaken?' William asked, reaching out to her. 'Seeing death so close by . . .'

'I have been staring death in the face since I was born,' Molly said. 'Now I can call myself an orphan in truth, and she will never haunt me again.'

Outside the carriage windows, a hazel tree rustled in the spring breeze.

Acknowledgements

This novel could not have been written without encouragement and support from those close to me. I also need to thank those who helped me with the practical elements of research.

My thanks to my family and friends for their understanding and interest, and for tolerating my somewhat obsessive approach to brainstorming a storyline. In particular I thank my mum, Carolyn Davy, who (for the record) is *nothing* like Molly's mother, and whose ability to put up with me is almost superhuman.

Cheers m'dears to Deborah Lewis (The Good Twin), Fatma Osman and Jennifer McGregor, who proved themselves to be gracious and thoughtful proofreaders. Debbie, halo repairs are on me. Also to Claire Sutton, for listening to me waffle about where I'm up to and what I'm doing. Hugs to the menagerie (who can't read this, granted) for providing the only company I can cope with while writing!

Thank you to Kim Wilkins, whose incredible works of fiction never fail to inspire and entertain me. On a more personal level, embarrassingly profuse gushings of gratitude for all the advice you have given me, and all the times when you praised my work when my confidence levels needed it most.

I would certainly have come a cropper at some point without the fountains of knowledge who work at Lancaster Castle, so much appreciation there, too.

I couldn't possibly forget to thank Shelle Tinnell of The Dollings, who listened to my ramblings about green rhinestones and freckles and white roses, took that information and made the most wonderful little effigy of Molly to keep me company at my desk.

Thanks also go to the many online folks who helped me out with research, or just endured my emotional rollercoaster with grace and interest while this book was in production.

Finally, I'd like to express my immense gratitude to Will Atkins and all at Macmillan New Writing, without whom the book you are holding would not exist.